THE STANDARDIZATION OF DEMORALIZATION PROCEDURES

THE STANDARDIZATION OF DEMORALIZATION PROCEDURES

JENNIFER HOFMANN

A NOVEL

Little, Brown and Company
New York Boston London

Little, Brown and Company
Hachette Book Group
1290 Avenue of the Americas, New York, NY 10104
littlebrown.com

First Edition: August 2020

Little, Brown and Company is a division of Hachette Book Group, Inc. The Little, Brown name and logo are trademarks of Hachette Book Group, Inc.

The publisher is not responsible for websites (or their content) that are not owned by the publisher.

The Hachette Speakers Bureau provides a wide range of authors for speaking events. To find out more, go to hachettespeakersbureau.com or call (866) 376-6591.

ISBN 978-0-316-42645-9
LCCN 2020933473

10 9 8 7 6 5 4 3 2 1

LSC-C

Printed in the United States of America

Für Mama

THE STANDARDIZATION OF DEMORALIZATION PROCEDURES

1

1.1

Something must have happened. Bernd Zeiger had snored himself awake and did not know where he was. A wedge of light on the ceiling caught his eye. He followed its journey as it stretched and narrowed until the car from which it came disappeared down the road. Darkness returned to the bedroom like a calamity.

It was November, strong westerly winds and a drizzle. He strained his eyes into the shadows. A wooden dresser loomed next to his bed, dark and wide like the hull of a ship. A nightstand held up a clock and a tall glass of water. He looked at his things as if they were not his things, as if someone had entered and exchanged all his things for replicas of the things he should know. Lara, he remembered, was gone.

The wheezing nozzle of a cleaning vehicle approached along the cobblestone street. It hummed and rattled as it suctioned debris from the road. Loose newspaper pages, wet leaves, abandoned tin toys, umbrella skeletons, the bloated bodies of rats. Small-scale pandemonium. Zeiger pictured the driver as neckless and mustached, a sadist. Street cleaning arrived at 4:30, the loneliest hour. Beyond the receding noise of the vehicle the murmur of morning traffic echoed along Torstrasse. People driving to work, others returning from night shifts.

Zeiger's legs were caught in a complicated knot of sheets, his pajamas twisted almost entirely the wrong way around. A hand was clasping the edge of a pillow, his own. These were his things. Dresser, nightstand, pajama, pillow. The ancient, indisputable objects of his life.

The alarm clock pierced a hole in the darkness. He slapped at it like he would at a gnat. It was more than two hours earlier than his usual time, but anticipation had outraced his alarm. A thump in the apartment next door announced Schreibmüller, his neighbor, a blind man who refused government aid like walking sticks or guide dogs and navigated spaces by bumping through them instead. There was the choppy rhythm of another language, Ukrainian perhaps. Despite his disability, Schreibmüller seemed to be surrounded by a harem of women and preferred, as far as Zeiger had learned from stairwell encounters over the last decades, Eastern types with sharp cheekbones and porcine eyes. He had considered asking Schreibmüller how, logistically speaking, a blind man could determine a type, but the occasion for it had never materialized. The world threw mysteries at him in passing.

At sixty, moving into an upright position in the morning felt like an unconquerable task. There was an indentation in his mattress from many years of sleeping and it enveloped the loose meat of his body like the arms of a wife. *If you wake at this age without pain, you're dead,* an elderly woman had told someone in line at the Konsum. He had found that insightful. A lull in her voice suggested she longed for the latter state.

Management had assured him he would be finished at Hohen-schönhausen jail by eight o'clock. The time he would, on normal days, go for cheese toast and milk coffee at the corner café, to see Lara, the waitress. He would keep his regular routine despite an irregular start to the day. That was a comfort, even if Lara had vanished several weeks ago.

A roar like that of an ailing beast echoed from the street. He stretched out an arm and yanked the cord of his nightstand lamp. Light replaced darkness; after street cleaning came trash collection. There was an order to things. Above the sound of the truck, garbage men hollered to one another, shouting combatively. Zeiger rolled toward the nightstand, gaped into the dusty light. He dropped his legs off the side of the bed. His feet found his slippers, gravity popped his bones into position. He rested his forearms on his knees, letting the folds of his body expand. Then he plucked his bathrobe from the hook by the nightstand and draped it over his shoulders. It took a moment to absorb the heat of his body.

The coal oven was a moody piece of work and needed constant attention. There would be no use in firing it up this morning. It would take a good half hour and periodic poking of the embers even to warm the tiles, an hour before the bedroom was fully heated. He'd be in Hohenschönhausen by then. After Hohenschönhausen, the café, then an ordinary day at his desk, followed by another press conference in the evening he'd been ordered to observe. Thursday meant Ketwurst day at the Ministry cafeteria, something to look forward to.

The woman on the phone the night before, a low-level secretary no doubt, had all but screamed at him, sounding shrill and panic-stricken, like a woman in the habit of losing her child in strange places. Hysteria was trickling down the ranks. He was to report to Hohenschönhausen jail for the interrogation of someone or other, she said. *Bitteschön, Dankeschön, gute Nacht, Kamerad Zeiger.* It had been more than twenty years since he was last at the jail.

There was another thump next door, followed by a gargling of pipes, giggles, and splashing sounds, all of which suggested that Schreibmüller and his guest had moved their operation to the tub. Zeiger had the urge to pound the wall, but he resisted and rose from the bed. By the time he reached the window, dots were dancing before his eyes, things that were not there. Then Lara's face appeared, a prim and taunting smile, which caused the air to escape from his lungs with an awful hacking sound. He found the windowsill and steadied himself, peering into blackness. Outside, the hollow rhythm of heels on cobblestones, the unoiled wheel of a bicycle, traffic. Inside, the sound of his own heart furiously pumping blood to his brain by way of his ears.

Only a few windows in the building opposite glowed with light. He saw no movements in them. Through a gap in the buildings, the TV tower antenna blinked with the soothing rhythm of a digital clock. The night sky was shrouded in clouds. Not long ago, streetlamps had been outfitted with high-watt bulbs in emergency orange. A color so glaring it obliterated any trace of a star. Streetlamps in West Berlin had retained their soft yellow glow, but, as Zeiger had noticed during occasional visits, the night sky there was still as tremendous and black as their own. He did not register that he was smoking until he had opened the window and rested his elbows on the iced ledge outside.

The bakery below was closed—it was not yet five o'clock—but a line had already formed. Seven early risers stood in thick coats and raised collars, their faces and shoulders turned against the wind. The streetlamp threw a distressing light on the scene, adding to it an air of quiet catastrophe. By Zeiger's usual time, the line would have swollen and dispersed, and the bakery would have closed again, leaving a few latecomers to pace the corner like stray dogs. A woman in a towering *ushanka* arrived and placed herself at the end of the line, raising its count to eight. A man acknowledged her presence with a nod, then turned again to face the front of the line. Limited food and people trusting strangers with the naked planes of their backs. The pinnacle of human evolution. Zeiger smoked his cigarette down to the filter and tossed the butt out the window. After a brief flight it landed, spraying the ground with sparks, and died. No one looked up to seek out its origin.

The kitchen greeted him with a new shade of darkness and the bitter smell of cooked cabbage. He turned on the overhead light, then dropped an egg into a pot of water, stood over it as it boiled. He filled the coffee cooker, added a spoonful of coffee, put it on the stove, waited. This was not coffee. It was coffee, pea flour, and disgrace. This was Kaffee Mix and tasted like a nosebleed. One bad harvest in Brazil, a coffee shortage, and the largest revolts the Republic had seen since 1953. An entire nation with the jitters. Even well-stocked Intershops for foreigners and Party and Ministry officials had not sold real coffee in years. More than real coffee, Zeiger missed sweetbread loaves, which people now bought in bulk as exchange presents for relatives who sent real coffee from the West. There'd been talks of sweetbread-gifting prohibitions, which he had supported, but the Party had voted against it. He did not remember when he'd last seen a sweetbread loaf at the store. He'd have liked to buy one for Lara.

He retrieved an eggcup and placed it on the table. Shaped like a tiny rooster, complete with comb and wattle, it looked like child's pottery. Methodically, he began freeing the egg from its shell, staring into the space above the table, his mind clean and shapeless.

Then something changed. This was an episode. They came on suddenly, and lately more frequently, and dissipated as quickly as they'd come. Epileptic seizure, old age, a sudden loss of blood flow to the brain, all of the above. When it was finished Zeiger surveyed the kitchen. The pot stood where he had placed it, steaming soundlessly on the stove. The coffee cooker, the emptied pouch of Kaffee Mix, the tent of soft light slicing the table and parts of the floor. His hand and a spoonful of egg white hovered in the air.

He had theories about these episodes. One, his brain had reached capacity. At his age, he had seen, absorbed, and forgotten many significant and insignificant things. These things were bound to get mangled; the old with the new, the known with the unknown, the certain with the uncertain. Nothing to worry about, *alles in Ordnung.* Two, enlightenment. The physicist Johannes Held, his onetime friend, had once told him about hermit monks who emerged from their caves, tattered and emaciated, to see everything as changed. A tree was no longer a tree but a field of energy to which their minds attributed treeness, or so he'd said. Zeiger had not fully grasped that revelation, but in moments like these, he wondered. Three, Lara. Four, death. He was dying and these episodes were the harbingers of a vast emptiness to come.

He placed the spoon back in the rooster. The splashing and gurgling of pipes next door had ceased, and there were no more voices. But there was music; a faint hum, waxing and waning vibrations. He tiptoed to the bedroom. Above the nightstand, next to the hook for his bathrobe, there was a blank spot of wall. He pressed his ear to it and listened. Music. The nasal intonation of a radio set. Metallic keyboard sounds and guitars. The song had a catchy, cheerless aura. A male voice, low and monotonous, was singing words he barely recognized. English; his *own personal Jesus. Someone to hear your prayers. Someone,* the man sang, *who's there.* Zeiger detached his ear and stared at the wall. Schreibmüller had tuned in to a Western channel. At this volume, at this hour, right next to his own bed. How many times had Zeiger slept through these things? He pounded the wall, first hesitantly, then with conviction, until it rattled and the nightstand shuddered below. When he stopped, the sound had ceased. Not a whisper, not a floorboard creaking, definitely no music. He tightened his bathrobe, marched back to the kitchen. There he finished his breakfast, staring vacuously at the eggcup and its shameful childlike shape.

It was time. His closet greeted him with the smell of camphor and dust. His suits hung from their hangers like a queue of limp corpses. It was a subtle rainbow of browns and grays, with one black sports coat for functions of consequence such as banquets, funerals, the Youth Consecration ceremonies of the children of comrades he barely remembered.

Ties were an opportunity for self-expression. His collection was likewise a meticulous gradation of browns and grays. Buried underneath them was a tie with a pattern of small beer mugs, some in the process of tipping and spilling their foaming crowns. It was a vulgar tie, hedonistic, self-righteous, Bavarian, one that created in him the same level of discomfort he experienced viewing indecent films. It had been a birthday gift, an attempt at humor, by a secretary whose name he'd had trouble retaining. She had placed the tie on his desk, along with a card. In response, he filed a request to relieve her of her duties, making her the last in a long lineage of secretaries the Ministry had assigned to his one-man department.

He pulled out a dark blue tie with a subtle pattern of vertical stripes in white and wine red. A wide-collared sports coat and creased slacks in charcoal gray would take him from day to night.

There would be an interrogation at Hohenschönhausen, a quick stop at the corner café, where he still held out hope of seeing Lara, then Ketwurst day at the cafeteria. In the evening, Schabowski's press conference, where he was to blend in with the crowd, read the room, take its temperature. International journalists would be in attendance. Broad-shouldered Russians, Americans with sleek, pointed jaws and slim-fitted coats, West Germans in their white socks. A week prior, in his first act as Party spokesman, Schabowski had anesthetized an entire room of journalists with his old Berliner lilt. The conference room at the International Press Center was a hot, teak-walled box with an uncanny lack of air, and even Zeiger himself, positioned inconspicuously in the rear of the room, had caught his head once before it tipped back against the wall. Schabowski's monologue had rolled on at a glacial pace; many words were spoken, little was said. Hungary's leaky borders, riots and protests in the six-digit thousands, the possibility of travel reforms. The journalists' questions had been mild, no glances were exchanged, and Zeiger was left with little to report to the Ministry. Boredom, the great narcotic.

Zeiger had spent his early career creating a Ministry-wide reference work called the *Standardization of Demoralization Procedures. SDP Manual* for short. A spiffy title, with gravitas. His life's work, a substantial volume, the closest he'd come to fathering. It was a title and responsibility no circumstance or passage of time could take from him, even though the Manual had long taken on a life of its own—often, sadly, perversely so. He pictured Management turning up the heating, closing the windows, and using subchapter 1.1 on "Demoralization through Repetitive, Tedious Speech," instructing Schabowski to put an entire nation, a world, to sleep.

As he dressed, a crescendo of voices swelled outside. The line at the bakery was growing. The drizzle had stopped, and people were starting to converse. Next time, in the stairwell, if he found the right words, he could try to describe his episodes to Schreibmüller. As a blind man, someone more attuned to atmospheric shifts than people distracted by sight, he would understand. They would sit close, listen to each other, share awe and fear, examine answers to the most dangerous of questions, *Why*. He hoped he could catch Schreibmüller before he had to turn him in for that music at the Bureau for Suspicious Activity and Class Enemy Progress, on the Ministry compound. Depending on the urgency with which Zeiger furnished his report on what he'd heard through the wall, an officer could seek out Schreibmüller by the end of the day. Whom he really wanted to ask about his episodes was his old friend Held.

In the anteroom, he slipped into his leather shoes and trench coat, taking his time. A few years ago, he would have been asked to consult Management on the use of the *SDP Manual* for mass-demoralization purposes. It would have been he who took Schabowski into that soundproof room off the Zentralkomitee assembly hall and advised him to go slow at the press conference, strategically employ that fatherly bedtime tone. But this was not a few years ago and they had not asked him to consult. Instead, and there was no explanation as to why, they positioned him in the back of the room like a foot soldier, an infantryman, as if he were a common Unofficial Informant. The comrades in charge were, at heart, good people, the aging sons of plumbers and masons. Not dumb, just simple and easily frightened. Dangerous in that way. This interrogation at Hohenschönhausen—this was a good sign. This was hope. The Ministry had not forgotten him.

He found his reflection in the mirror and straightened his tie. His face looked back at him, flaccid and bloodless. Theory number four, he was dying. With the tip of a finger he pulled down the lower lid of one eye, revealing a sliver of tawny flesh. He felt around his jaw and the back of his neck for lymph nodes. His tongue was a mosaic of pale and gray faults. He closed his mouth and swallowed, wondering what Schreibmüller might know about death.

Zeiger unlocked the front door, peered up the stairwell. The windows in the stairwell had not been replaced since sector times. Their frames were porous and leaky and wind passed through them with bitter, grief-stricken moans. Hohenschönhausen, report Schreibmüller at the bureau, cheese toast and milk coffee at the café, see Lara—even though there was no reason to believe she would be there today, as she hadn't been there in weeks, ever since she put a hand on his shoulder, which gave him the courage to go to her apartment, speak to her there. Then Ketwurst at the cafeteria, an airless press conference in the evening, the end of his day, another to follow, nothing had changed, *alles in Ordnung.*

He grabbed his briefcase and stepped outside. Fresh, wet air and a sky made of glass. As he descended the two short steps onto the sidewalk, something hit his temple. A cracking sound, hollow and profound, and a lacerating pain. He touched his fingertips to the side of his head. A biscuit, perfectly oval, lay at his feet like a hoax hand grenade.

"I'll rip off your head and take a shit in your neck, you asshole," someone said.

There was a man on the sidewalk to Zeiger's right who had the build of a bullfrog. He wore a parka with a tear along one shoulder and clenched a biscuit in each fist. His face was purple with anger, hot and comical. He was looking not at Zeiger, but slightly beyond him, at the baker, who stood in mirroring warfare fashion off to Zeiger's left. Blood from the baker's marred lip speckled the pristine whiteness of his shirt and apron. With a detonation of deep, primal sounds, he hurled himself past Zeiger and at the man with the biscuits. Zeiger shielded his head with his briefcase as the men dropped to the ground in amateur entanglement, their faces so close they appeared to be going in for a kiss. A few paces off, a young man struggled in a choke hold, his teeth sunk deep into the bones of another man's wrist. Biscuits were everywhere. A mother was gathering her wailing child. Another woman sat on the curb, gaping through her fingers at a group of men shoving one another like boys on a playground. Zeiger clasped his briefcase against his chest, using it like armor. He spotted his Trabant across the street, mapped his route, and wove his way through the crowd, veering to circumvent clusters of people and avoid slipping on biscuits softening in patches of rain. In a puddle, frayed and wet like roadkill, slumped the towering *ushanka* that Zeiger had seen from his window.

He reached his car without incident. He could not conceive of what had caused the brawl. The amount of bread scattered across the ground suggested there was no shortage. This was not desperation. This was joy in chaos. It was then that he spotted Schreibmüller. His neighbor stood on the steps of their apartment building, one hand propped leisurely against the wall, the other wound tightly around the waist of a woman in slippers and a large men's coat. Her hand was cupped against his ear, shielding her whisper. His handsome face was tilted back and upward, away from the crowd, his blank eyes raised to the lightening sky. The king and his whore presiding.

Zeiger rolled onto Leninallee, followed it northeastward en route to Hohenschönhausen jail. Pairs of red taillights and windshields smeared with wet street dust and droplets of rain. The boulevard was flanked by rows of concrete slab buildings, symmetrically choreographed and angled as if in a giants' ballet. Elderly Berliners walked the sidewalks pulling caddies of food; people pedaled by on bicycles, their faces protected by shawls. A row of parked police cars stretched along the side of the road, their cherry lights ablaze. Zeiger craned his neck but could not locate the source of the commotion. Maybe a car wreck, a gas leak, or punks throwing rocks at passing cars.

Through his driver's-side window, broken and permanently cracked, wafted a smell like iron and lignite coal. Childhood memories, postwar smells. Zeiger held a tight grip on the wheel. The line at the bakery had exploded into pieces. Spontaneous, unregistered disarray. Protests in Leipzig a few weeks ago had been planned; the demonstrations last week at Alexanderplatz had been planned; Management's response to these planned happenings had been planned. Plans were made five years ahead of time. And now the baker's white apron was splattered with blood.

It had been a month since he'd last seen Lara. Lara, the blinding cherry lights ahead. Lara, the speckle of dried dirt on his windshield. Lara in the stratosphere, Lara in the ether. His whole life had reduced itself to her disappearance. He felt displeased with himself, positively disgusted with himself, as he tallied in his mind the usual routine of fruitless questions: *Where had she gone? What had he done? If, as Held had once told him, the weight of the world remains static, and not a molecule of matter is ever lost but is merely recycled, transmuted, into water, into earth, into the energy of thought, was there such a thing as disappearance?* And so on and so forth, until he wore himself out. This compulsion, this thinking, the *why*s and the *how*s, felt both rousing and banal, unhinged and pedestrian, but it had become a ritual, the twine holding together the softening box of his mind, and so he continued.

In rare pragmatic moments he considered inquiring with someone at the Ministry about Lara's whereabouts. He could think of some reason for his sudden interest in this innocuous waitress, perhaps turn up a lead, some direction. But it seemed shameful, blasphemous even, to speak her name within something as carnivorous as the Ministry compound, so he decided against it. Meanwhile he left keys in locks, misplaced cooking utensils he had just pulled from cupboards, forgot names, forgot dates, forgot the route to the Ministry lot, found himself smiling submissively at strangers, and had developed a death wish, passive but pronounced.

He glanced at the rearview mirror and into the bloated face of the driver behind him. The driver stared back like a man playing dead in a film. From his inner coat pocket, Zeiger retrieved his cigarettes, fumbled one into his mouth, lit it. The crack in the window sucked out the smoke. The world outside was a vacuum. He turned a dial on the dashboard and the radio sprang to life. A man was speaking, flat and throaty with a Dresden twinge that smacked of stupidity. *They all had on those white gloves, yes,* said the voice, *and those helmets and they all stood straight at attention, those soldiers. And the Comrades in the tank brigade, they had on red berets. And Honecker was there also, and Gorbi, but I couldn't see them, just heard their voices in the microphone. And there were many pretty banners, yes, the red ones.*

This was rerun coverage of the military parade along Karl-Marx-Allee one month ago, the celebration of the Republic's fortieth birthday. An event that bore strategic rehashing. Everyone had been there. Zeiger too. He would have skipped the parade, turned up at the Ministry, had he not been ordered to observe.

He'd arrived late, when the sidewalks were already crowded, and stood next to the bleachers. He'd purchased a small black-red-gold flag from a boy in blue youth organization garb, held it like a votive candle, stiffly and piously with both of his hands. Just as the Dresdner described on the radio, banners had loomed over the streets like bloodred archangels; one hue to the right and they'd have been brown. There were lashing winds and giddy children; the familiar, celebratory smell of burnt sausage and spilt beer; a thousand smiling mouths and peaks of shrill laughter. From his position at the edge of the crowd, Zeiger wasn't able to see Honecker or Gorbi. Just beyond the banister, the formation of soldiers stood at attention, the whites of their eyes blazing as they searched the crowd for familiar faces. They were smooth-faced, unnaturally tanned, with shoulders much too slim for the sharp angles of their uniforms. The safety and fate of nations were entrusted to children.

The brass band chugged out the national anthem and led the soldiers down the vacant boulevard. It was a newish composition, not the one he had known as a child. Germany, as it were, was no longer *über alles*. It had now risen from the ruins, a unified fatherland. These were aspirational lyrics; *verboten,* as of recently, to avoid mass embarrassment. In their most recent cross-Wall mudsling, West Germany had accused the German Democratic Republic of copying this anthem melody from Kreuder's *Water for Canitoga* movie score. A commission determined that the songs did indeed share their first eight chords, and that both were in turn similar to Beethoven's *Bagatelle op. 119 No. 11,* which had settled the dispute.

At the parade Zeiger did as he was told—took the temperature, read the crowd. He saw nothing but faces agape with stupid joy. This he later included in his report. What he did not report was the pall that descended over the scene during brass-band interludes. Thousands of onlookers, hundreds of soldiers, tanks, yet a silence so thick it made its own sound. Protesters had accumulated along side streets and they began pitching rocks and shoes at the crowd. *Gorbi, Gorbi, Gorbi!* they chanted into the aching silence, until the brass band resumed and drowned out their screams.

Do you have any congratulating words? the reporter was asking the Dresdner on the radio.

I would like to say all the best and happy birthday to everyone? the man replied, phrasing it like a question, as a Dresdner would do.

Even though it had been a bore and an embarrassment on an unimaginable scale, Zeiger didn't remember the day of the parade for its festivities. He remembered that day for Lara, because it was the first day he hadn't seen her at the corner café.

He turned the radio dial at random and landed on a soft, inoffensive tune, something classical. Along the road concrete slabs were giving way to low buildings and skeletal trees. He passed houses with shingled roofs, meticulous hedges, groups of red-hatted garden gnomes with hatchets and frightening smiles. These were the houses of government officials and Ministry employees, people blind to the things absorbed by Hohenschönhausen jail. On maps, the area just ahead was a pattern of small black dots; no-man's-land, a hole in the earth. He stopped at the gate, shut down his engine, and peered at the latch in which a guard's face would shortly appear.

In the silence, the symphony reverberated in all its complexities and soon bled into its mournful end. Eager to catch the composer, he turned up the volume. Three gongs sounded, followed by a disc jockey's voice: *Klassik Radio of the Federal Republic of Germany, playing Schub*—Zeiger smacked the dial, shutting him up. He jerked around to check the rear window, all four sides of his car. Nothing and nobody and idyllic silence. By the time he turned back to face the wall, a guard was waiting. As he rolled through the gate, Zeiger stole a glance. The guard's face revealed nothing under the shadow of his cap.

Zeiger parked his Trabant and took his time crossing the compound courtyard. It was quiet and spacious, angular and beige. Thick clouds loomed, bringing with them frigid sideways winds. A lone tree in the middle of the roundabout swayed catatonically, throwing a complicated shadow on precast concrete. In the far corner, a maintenance worker was wheeling a cart of dead leaves into a warehouse, which many years ago, Zeiger recalled, had served as a main prison building. Before that, it had been a Soviet labor camp for Nazis with useful skills, and before that a Third Reich soup kitchen, its initial use. The prison cells had been so damp and cloistered that the warehouse's nickname, the U-Boot, had stuck to this day. When contracts were signed and Germans returned, Russian officers were said to have hidden strategically placed piles of shit around the complex, some of which were never found.

The prison complex, built many years ago to replace the U-Boot, was a massive multistory structure with functional charm. Paint had peeled from the facade, exposing patches of brickwork like gaping red wounds. Windowsills were overgrown with pragmatic families of weeds. He examined it for a moment; they were much the same age, he and this edifice. Somehow it had shrunken in size.

The first and last time Zeiger had been to Hohenschönhausen was in 1965, almost twenty-five years ago. The interrogation-preparation module at the Academy had predicted blood and shit. And blood and shit were what he had received. Through a scratched two-way mirror that day, he discerned the broad, immobile shoulders of the interrogator, Ledermann, the back of whose head glistened like black lead. The subject had been stripped naked and put in position at the end of the T. He was Zeiger's age, but the language of his body read as boyish. Hunched shoulders, head hung low, his ribs lifting with the quickness of a smaller-bodied animal. This was Johannes Held, a young physicist at Berlin's Technische Universität and recent returnee from a State-sponsored placement at an institute in the American desert.

Behind Held stood an officer, a flat-nosed man with hair on the backs of his hands; a creature of folklore and arboreal fairy tales, a Russian. The spirit in the room was light, like the vaguely recreational mood of men footnoting a game on TV. Held was rambling.

A group of American researchers, so he explained, had strapped dogs into harnesses and shocked their paws with high-voltage bolts. The dogs twisted and turned to escape the pain but realized soon enough there was nowhere to go. Defeated, they endured the shocks without struggle. The interesting part, Held pointed out, was when they unstrapped the dogs and they were free to go: Not one of them moved. The dogs continued to endure the pain, even when unharnessed, convinced, Held explained, of their powerlessness.

Perhaps it was the mention of Americans or some deep-seated feelings for dogs, but as soon as Held had finished, the Russian stepped into the light, caught a lump of his hair in his fist, and began boxing the side of the physicist's head. Under the thick shadow of his brow bones, the Russian appeared to have no eyes.

It was a ten-minute procedure. Sweat flying at high velocity and sounds like cracking eggshells. Then Ledermann, patient and unmoved, waited for Held to regain his composure, and the room settled back into quiet, and the Russian, having retreated again into his corner, seemed to be gazing with reptilian concentration straight through the mirrored glass, directly at Zeiger. It was a memorable look, predatory and sage, and reminded him of old Slavic fables; of tsars and their stepmothers, cannibal wives turned to geese, young men on endless travels through ice-crusted tundra with rock formations that were giants in disguise; the whole of the Soviet experience.

Zeiger bowed his head and focused on Held, the pearls of black blood dripping from his temple onto his chest. But he couldn't for long keep his eyes away from the Russian, because Germany was back and Stalin was more than a decade dead, and though their nation was still young, both of them knew that Zeiger's would be a system so sweeping and efficient nobody would have to get boxed in the head.

Before long the Russian was at it again. Held winced when the brute caught his nails in pliers, he cursed when his tormentor liberated molars from his mouth. But he did not confess. The physicist kept his physicist secrets to himself, which, even though the term had acquired an aftertaste, filled Zeiger with true Prussian pride.

Years down the line, Zeiger spotted the Russian behind a sausage stand at Alexanderplatz, conversing with a group of Vietnamese tourists in khaki pants and visors, inserting for each of them a Ketwurst into a bun.

The worker reemerged from the U-Boot, dragging his shovel with the earsplitting sound of metal on gravel. Their eyes met briefly. Two mortal beings among concrete and stone.

Zeiger was received at reception by a young officer with a gluttonous belly and bags under his eyes who greeted him eagerly, informing him that it was early for interrogations of this kind. *This kind* being the unscheduled kind. "What ever happened to foresight and planning?" he asked Zeiger as he led him down into the basement and toward the interrogation rooms.

Zeiger hummed in agreement.

The interrogation cellblock was a drafty, windowless tunnel painted floor to ceiling in antiseptic pistachio green, a color complementary to rust and blood. At around four o'clock that morning, they had plucked a soldier off his guard tower post on Bernauer Strasse. He'd been cooperative, the officer explained, had sat silently in the back of the van all the way to Hohenschönhausen jail. From his breast pocket the officer retrieved a stack of papers and a note of instructions for Zeiger. Read the mood, take the temperature, use the soldier to gauge the border guard outfit's risk for dissent.

Zeiger straightened his back, squared his shoulders. This, thankfully, was not the work of an Unofficial Informant.

It was a joke, a literal one, along with a letter confiscated from his private mail, that had brought this particular soldier to Management's attention. The envelope was torn, stamped, and pencil-marked in various places, giving the impression that it was by now well-traveled. There was strict protocol for handling confiscated correspondence, each item requiring repeated confirmation of suspicious content by countless people. Zeiger knew some officers in the hermeneutics department, an irritable collection of literary types in knitwear who treated their assignment with Talmudic precision.

He arrived with the portly officer at a cell at the end of the corridor.

"Sport frei," said the officer, who would serve as guard, before unlatching the door and following Zeiger inside.

The soldier sat at the far end of the interrogation table. He was in the process of probing his ear canal, after which he scrutinized his bounty with calm interest. He was a young one, with a Slavic flatness to the back of his head, early twenties. A little younger than Lara. In the piss-scented light of the desk lamp, the details of his face were vague and unreal. Dampness rose from the wool of his uniform, freighting the room with a smell of stale cigarette smoke and, to Zeiger's amazement, sweat without the bitter accent of fear.

The rooms hadn't changed. They were concrete boxes with a T-shaped table at the center. On the interrogator's side, the roof end of the *T,* stood a carafe of water and a telephone on psycho-suggestive display. A sign above the door read BUSY! in bright blood-orange type.

Zeiger took a seat at the other end of the table, avoided eye contact. He shifted his weight on the chair, arranging his buttocks between the screws protruding from the foam and fabric. Bolted to the floor to minimize the risk of being used as a weapon, these chairs had always been uncomfortable. He had urged Management to replace at least the cushions—subjects were most malleable when at ease—but apparently there had never been the budget. He began lining up his things. The letter, his notebook, a single mechanical pencil. Out of the corner of his eye he saw the soldier roll a wad of earwax between his fingers and flick it to the ground. The young man's hands were fine-tuned machinery, sturdy bones and skin as smooth as sea glass, things to outlive them all.

When Zeiger met the soldier's gaze, he found him smiling. A row of small teeth, sharp like a bat's. Razor teeth. It occurred to him that he had seen him before. Here, a long time ago. Or not so long ago, and perhaps somewhere else. He grasped the paperwork, leafed through the pages, searched for the soldier's name, found it on the back of the letter. He did not recognize it. He turned to the officer, who had taken a splay-kneed position on the chair behind him, hands folded in his lap and tucked under his belly as if he were cradling a child. It took Zeiger a moment to comprehend that he was sleeping. How much time had passed?

"What's wrong?" the soldier asked. His smile vanished.

The sound of his voice startled Zeiger. It was high-pitched and wide-awake, and it was not his turn to speak.

"Should we call someone?" the soldier asked. "You look white. No, you look red. You look gray, actually. We should call." He rose from his chair as if he had germinated, sprouted from it like the bulb of a flower.

"Stop," Zeiger said. "Sit down."

The soldier froze. He showed the palms of his hands, a gesture of capitulation, and sank back into his chair.

The guard was snoring now. Deep, slack-jawed sleep.

Zeiger placed his hands on the table. "Why are you here?" he asked.

"Because of a joke, I suppose."

"That joke," Zeiger said. "Tell it to me."

"Do you think I'm stupid?"

"That's neither here nor there." Zeiger considered picking up the notebook to scribble some perfunctory nonsense. Instead he retrieved a cigarette from his inside pocket. Efficiently, methodically, he began to smoke.

"If it was Dirk who told on me, I swear to God. May I have one of those?" said the soldier, eyeing the cigarette in Zeiger's hand.

"Maybe after."

"I really can't believe someone told on me because of this," the soldier said. "Was it Thomas? Forget it, I don't even want to know. So, the CIA, KGB, and Stasi get into this competition about finding the best spy across all agencies. The jury gives each of the three contestants an old skull and asks them to figure out when this person died, right? So, the CIA guy returns after an hour and says, 'This is a skull from the seventeenth century! I figured it out with a chemical procedure.' Right? After a while, four hours later or so, the KGB guy returns..."

There was no ashtray on the table. A tactical mistake. Zeiger dropped the cigarette onto the floor, extinguished it with a crunch of his sole.

"KGB guy says, 'This skull belonged to a forty-year-old, and I know because I compared it to all these other skulls.' Then the Stasi officer returns, right?"

"Right," Zeiger said.

"Right? So, Stasi officer returns after ten hours. He's sweating. Shirt's all dirty and torn. He's limping. Says, 'This man was forty-two years old, died in January 1648, was a baker, and had a bitch for a wife.' The jury says, 'We're impressed! That's correct. How did you figure this out from just looking at a skull?'"

The guard behind Zeiger grunted, awake again, and stifled a laugh, startling them both.

"That's enough," Zeiger told the soldier.

"But I'm not—"

"I get the gist of it," Zeiger said.

The soldier slumped in his chair, cocking his head to catch a glimpse of the paperwork Zeiger had arranged on his end of the table. Zeiger checked his watch. He pulled the letter from the table, read the address. A woman's name, somewhere in Magdeburg. He slid the letter across the T. With the tip of his finger, the soldier pulled it close, placed a hand on it as if for protection.

"Slowly and audibly," Zeiger said. He leaned back and closed his eyes, going for an off-the-record feel. His inner eye was a landscape of blazing specks, figures with morphing shapes, a coded message. Held came to mind again, and the murderous desert, and Lara, as they usually did at the start of an episode. He could hear the soldier retrieve the letter from its envelope. He heard him clear his throat.

Hi Puppe,

I didn't hear back from you after my letter last week. Maybe it got lost in the mail? I have a feeling Jakob really did make good on his threat and is "keeping you company." I swear to God, if he tries anything I will poke his one good eye out when I'm back on leave. I've seen how he looks at you at Youth Center parties. Can't evade service and then take advantage of my girlfriend, is what I think—

"Really, all of this?" the soldier said.

Zeiger supplied no response.

—You wrote last time that you want me to put more effort into my letters and talk about my feelings. I don't think I have a lot of feelings. Does Jakob talk to you about his feelings? How does it feel to be unfit for service and have all that spare time on his hands?

I can try to talk about my feelings more, but sometimes I don't know the difference between a feeling and a thought. And sometimes I wonder why everyone makes such a big fuss about feelings. But if it makes you happy, I can try.

"I can skip reading it, just tell you what's in it," the soldier said, staring stonily and attempting a faint smile.

"You'll go on now," Zeiger replied, causing the soldier to melt back into his chair.

—So, they moved me to Bernauer Strasse now. It's quite nice up there on the guard tower. I like the mornings on P4 tower best. There aren't too many side streets to watch from that angle. And some of the houses on the other side are close enough to make out people and their morning routines. Everyone seems to have a coffee machine.

On the one side, there is the Wedding District. Calm in the morning, but for the construction cranes on duty. Sometimes, when they're all up and running, it looks like they're performing a waltz. On this side, our side, is Mitte. No cranes or diggers there, just a lot of silence and blue morning light and those grassy plots where buildings used to stand. Right below me is the death strip, which is really just a strip of dust, all wasteland browns. Families of rabbits live down there. Snow-white ones on suicide runs between those spring guns. Sorry, I know that sounds awful.

A feeling I have sometimes, one that I can tell you about, is that I wonder if anyone ever figured out why they built it where they built it. How they mapped its course. How can there be so much of something where before there was nothing at all?

It gets boring up there. Not like people really try anything. There's nothing to do but think (I think a lot about you) and I smoke a lot, and pace; once looking West, once looking East. And I try not to stare down into the dustbowl of the strip, though the rabbits are fun to watch when they're out.

"That's it," the soldier said. He dropped the letter and crossed his arms in conclusion.

For a brief moment, as the soldier crossed his legs and assumed a posture he must have hoped looked at ease, Zeiger was stirred by a diffuse, vaguely painful sensation, a stab behind his chest, a quick, melting image of Held. He was almost tempted to leave it there with the soldier, but then he thought of his episodes, their grand plot to kill him. Whatever this new feeling was—compassion, maybe, it occurred to him—it was a symptom, and thus unacceptable. The soldier jerked his chin at the cigarettes on the table.

"You'll go on now," Zeiger said.

Tension seeped out of the soldier's body, crumbling his shoulder. He picked up the letter. Defiantly, and with incredible speed, he read:

—If I tell you about my feelings, is it okay if I ask you not to tell? The truth is, I'm not bored up there. Not because of the death strip or because I'm scared someone will try something bad. It's that, a few hundred meters off, there is another guard tower. And there's

another soldier up there, just like me, pacing and all those things. Sometimes it's a stranger, but most of the time I know the guy from mess hall or even as far back as training days or FDJ camp. So, while I'm pacing and checking the perimeter, every once in a while, I pick up my binoculars and try to spot the other guy on the tower. And when I find him, more often than not, I see that he's looking through his own binoculars directly at me. And then we look at each other. Sometimes for a very long time. And we forget about the death strip or about scanning the streets or jumpers that never do come. Because really all that scares you up there is that other soldier, and that perhaps they could shoot you and make a run for the Wall. I'd be lying if I said I haven't considered that myself, which I think—or maybe feel?—is the most frightening part of all.

The soldier fell silent. He placed the letter on the table, smoothed it with both hands.

Calls to the warden would have to be made, the soldier put under arrest—threatened dissent. The guard would take care of it, legitimizing his existence. A windless quiet expanded in Zeiger's mind, filling the room like gas.

The soldier tried another smile. A desperate, sorry smile. The kind dying people save for their kin. "What will happen now?" he asked.

"It depends," Zeiger said. "Do you confess?"

"To what? The letter, the joke? It seems I already have." The soldier slid the letter back over the T. In turn, Zeiger retrieved a cigarette and rolled it across the table.

"Cabinets," the soldier said, inspecting the cigarette like something rare. "Mutti says, *Humor means laughing despite everything.* Says, *Be more frightened of those who don't joke.*"

Zeiger lifted his hand, extended a forefinger, and nudged the pencil out of alignment. The soldier smiled on, ignoring the maneuver. He was immune to chaos.

Zeiger stepped out onto the landing and leaned against the banister. Billowing clouds scudded across the sky, breaking to occasional bursts of sunshine. There was a clarity in the air, an ozone lucidity. A rhythmic swooshing sound, like waves breaking on the shore, wafted from somewhere just below. The maintenance worker was sweeping gravel into a heap with long, agile strokes. The man had a thick neck and paddle-wide hands, the gnarled texture of life lived in open spaces. It was hard for Zeiger to imagine his existence beyond these compound walls. The worker stopped after a while, scanned the courtyard, turned up his head toward Zeiger, then dropped the broom abruptly and made his way back to the U-Boot.

It was near eight o'clock. Enough time to circle back to the corner café, cheese toast and milk coffee, perhaps Lara had returned, though that was unlikely. Then he would stop at the complaint office, report Schreibmüller, Ketwurst at the cafeteria, and get on with his day until the evening press conference. He was cogwheel and machine; the redundancy of it all. Fatigue attacked him like an animal.

The officer appeared on the landing and leaned next to him against the banister.

"I notified the warden," he told Zeiger, staring into the distance. "He told me there was a call for you." He produced a piece of paper and handed it to Zeiger.

Zeiger accepted it, following the man's gaze into the concrete courtyard. With the maintenance worker back in the U-Boot, it was entirely devoid of life. For a moment they looked out together, quietly, contemplatively, as if beholding a landscape, a blazing sunset, something profound and beautiful.

"I will die in this place," the officer said in a grave tone.

"What's worse is that this place will forget about you."

"Won't matter," the officer said. "When you're dead."

"It matters now."

"I read the Manual, the techniques. Everyone has. We all know who you are. We'll remember."

Zeiger retrieved a cigarette from his coat pocket but did not light it. Something to occupy his hands. "We should not strive to be remembered, comrade, for our small contributions to the cause."

"I have to ask. That joke—" the guard started, then stopped himself, rubbing his neck.

"We made the skull confess," Zeiger said.

"That's what I thought."

With a twitch of a salute, Zeiger turned and descended the stairs.

Once Zeiger had settled into his car, he glanced at the guard's note. Ledermann had called. Zeiger was ordered to find him at his office in the Science and Technology Unit. There was an urgent undertone. He stared at the piece of paper as if it had come alive in his hands. Pointlessly, he checked his watch, considered his options. Corner café, a stop at Ledermann's. He had not spoken to Ledermann in years. There had been no reason, with Johannes Held jailed.

Ledermann was a freakishly tall, vain, aggravatingly athletic man; and he had always been so, even at the Academy, when they were all still very young and most of them, including Zeiger, had barely squeezed a few hairs from their chins. In a way that he couldn't quite explain, this physical ease of Ledermann's had filled Zeiger with unnamable contempt and loathing for him. Ledermann had had a short stint playing football for BFC Dynamo before he tore his Achilles tendon and was recruited, as was the logical conclusion, into the Academy on a scientist's stipend. Ledermann had parents who'd supported him. He spoke fluid Vietnamese. He had a son. Ever since the day they'd met—during a dreadful, friendly intra-Academy football match, when Zeiger had feigned a sprained ankle and watched from the bench as Ledermann sprinted, no, frolicked across the field with the delicate velocity of an antelope—they'd shared a deep and structural suspicion of each other. The tolerant yet skeptical coexistence of two domestic animals; canine versus feline. Ledermann awakened in Zeiger latently murderous instincts.

Traffic was smooth as he drove back toward Mitte; the sidewalks nearly empty, people filed away at work. In the distance the TV tower was pointing its sharp antenna into nothing, harsh daylight reflecting from its ragged, globular tip in the shape of a near-perfect cross. The Pope's Revenge, some called this phenomenon, and today it gleamed like fire.

The corner café was a generic establishment. Utilitarian fixtures, thick curtains, a hum in the air like the sound of heavy machinery. Klaus, the neighborhood drunk, sat at his single's table, along with his dog, a well-behaved black setter with dispirited eyes. The counter was occupied by the usual row of elderly regulars. With their leathered heads balanced on protracted necks, their faces thrust forward into their newspapers, they reminded Zeiger of a row of aging vultures, feeding on the news, devouring data for the afterlife. Nobody acknowledged his entrance.

He took a seat at his table by the window, his back turned to the kitchen door, and waited for Lara. A flash of copper hair, skin so white it was blue. Cheese toast and milk coffee placed in front of him by agile fingers, long but still plump from childhood. Bright chipped polish on tiny nails. A corner-of-the-eye apparition, a flare as from the edge of an eclipse. Not to be looked at directly. That was on regular days.

A stack of old newspapers lay folded on the windowsill beside him. Glancing at the headlines, he read, GDR COUNCIL OF MINISTERS ABDICATES. And: TREPTOW MAN TUMBLES FROM THIRD-STORY WINDOW, SURVIVES, BUT KILLS CAT. Zeiger pictured this. Arms flailing, a gruff scream, a cat's life reduced to a split second of infinite possibility.

Klaus lifted his beer to his mouth and lowered it, lifted and lowered, sipping and swallowing. He was sitting like a mourner in church, rigid and straight-backed. It was a posture of numb resignation, but also of vigilance. As if death befell only the inattentive. Klaus performed his ritual until the glass was empty. His movements were slow and fluid, nimble like the arms of a deep-sea anemone. This was Klaus in a vacuum. Klaus underwater. Klaus moving at a pace untouched by sunlight and time. Klaus would live forever.

And then, cheese toast and milk coffee set on Zeiger's table. A hand, tanned and manly, and ammoniac vapors. He looked up. It was Inge. The minimizing of pleasantries was a goal they had always shared. He said nothing, waited until she retreated, then turned to scan the café. Lara did not emerge from the kitchen with trays of pastries, nor did she carry stacks of glass ashtrays from one side of the room to the other. She did not emerge this morning, nor had she emerged in nearly a month, since the day before the parade, when she had placed a hand on his shoulder, sent a chill through his body, and implanted something formless and crude. Where had she gone after they spoke at her apartment? What had he done? Was she on holiday? Implausible. Had she quit? That he'd know. The longer her absence, the more he dissolved.

The day was losing shape. It was bleeding at the edges, hemorrhaging purpose. Subchapter 1.4 of the *SDP Manual*: "Demoralization and Disintegration Procedures—Goals." His life's work: planting rumors of infidelities, rumors of sexual deviance, rumors of unknown origin. *Origin unknown*—that's how thankless the job had been. Forged photographs depicting the subject in a questionable embrace with children, a neighbor's wife, or a pet, strategically propped on a boss's desk. Same-sex personal ads placed in the papers under the subject's name. Unsolicited bulk deliveries of ornamental fish tanks to their homes. Pants stolen from closets and replaced with pants whose waistbands were two sizes too small. An artificially induced loss of love. All more efficient than getting boxed in the head. The self is a vessel that when turned upside down will empty itself of meaning. It will grasp, cling to itself, turn in on itself, witness itself, go insane in that way.

Zeiger let the coffee cool, reviewed the reality of the table in front of him. A porcelain plate webbed with gray fissures. Kaffee Mix in a functional, handle-less cup. Other things, solid and tangible, with shapes and agreed-upon names. But Lara would not appear. He ate, aware of the food drying in his mouth; the pathetic and mortal necessity of feeding himself. The sharp, dungeon-like smell of Hohenschönhausen jail clung to his clothes, engulfing him like the remnants of a nightmare.

1.2

The Ministry foyer was all echo, iron and polished teak. Over an island of bile-green lounge seating, an enormous Shield and Sword emblem hung from a single, self-conscious nail. Zeiger joined a small group of people waiting at the paternoster lift. They spoke in low voices about the new bill being drafted at the Interior Ministry, where, given the mass exodus of GDR citizens through Hungary, they had been forced to discuss the potential relaxation of cross-border travel restrictions.

"Perhaps they won't require people to have a permit at all," a man whispered, straightening his tie with a jittery hand. "Everyone could come and go as they please."

"Now that would be chaos," another one said.

"If it happens," a woman added with a competent smile, "which it won't, it will be weeks if not months until it's put into effect."

Someone else echoed the sentiment, adding that it was progress on the bill, not its resolution, that Schabowski had been ordered to discuss at tonight's press conference. The paternoster compartment arrived, crying with exhaustion. The group embarked into it and huddled together, a collection of bodies and briefcases. Silence coagulated as they ascended.

Ledermann's Science and Technology Unit was a multiroom operation toward the end of the hallway. Zeiger knew where to find him. Muffled conversations and the hollow clips of nails on typewriters echoed from open office doors. A faint hint of acetone hung in the air, and something more pungent, like burning cinder blocks. He passed a break room in which a few people had gathered holding coffee mugs and cake on plates. Silent, their forks suspended in the air, they had their eyes trained on a television set propped high on top of a refrigerator.

Zeiger paused at the door. The pale figure of a *Tagesschau* news anchor spoke calmly from the notes on his desk. A beam quivered down the screen in periodic intervals, sending ripples across the man's chest. Underneath his voice, or above it, or embedded in it, there was a layer of static, like an arctic squall blasting across frozen plains. This was last night's West German news. The anchor spoke with customary West German calm. Anchors were unearthly beings, inhabitants of a realm untouched by the pain of their words.

A video segment showed Schabowski at last week's press conference droning monotonously about the Party's open-minded inclusion of the opposition; about hopes for a more transparent voting system. However, nobody should expect, Schabowski explained, that the Party had agreed to these changes under the suicidal assumption that they would be outvoted.

The anchor reappeared and indifferently broadcast the collective resignation of the GDR's Council of Ministers and the election of a new Council of Ministers a few hours later. Then, hovering like an apparition next to the anchor's face, there appeared an image of Egon Krenz, the new General Secretary. There was footage of Krenz in front of the Zentralkomitee building speaking deftly to a crowd of protesters. He was promising economically functional, politically democratic, morally hygienic Socialism. Everyone cheered.

When the news cut to the Czech and Bavarian borders, a few people in the break room dropped their forks and began paying closer attention. Images of multicolored Trabis in line at checkpoints filled the screen. Traffic jams, people crossing on foot, waving into the camera. The enthusiasm of the herd, their faces enlightened with glee and purpose.

Forty-four thousand GDR refugees, the anchor pronounced with precision. He paused, letting the number flap in windy silence.

"Six hundred sixty of them are already back. Swore they just went over to shop," said a man at the table, who turned to Zeiger. The man studied him with a faraway look, finally offering him the contents of his plate. "Care for some? It's Gundula's birthday. She brought Schwarzwälder."

Zeiger gestured a no. The man averted his face. The planes of his cheeks slackened, and the wet orbs of his eyes glowed white against the glare of the screen.

Zeiger continued down the corridor and found Ledermann's door. Through a crack he heard the sound of paper shuffling, some footsteps. He straightened himself. There was no preparing for Ledermann. He pushed open the door. The office had a laboratory feel. White tiles on white walls, lit by a shivering halogen light. Surfaces were littered with stacks of paperwork, coils of wire, boxes of gizmos, contraptions of indeterminate genus. The air in the room was heavy, dense, electric. Conditions conducive to tinnitus and cancers.

Ledermann's head appeared from behind his desk. They regarded each other. A frown, dark and knotty, washed over Ledermann's face, then he motioned Zeiger inside. Whatever was filling the halls with the smell of burning had originated from this office. It stung Zeiger's eyes and he suppressed an urgent cough.

"By God, it worked," Ledermann said. He slowly erected his body, one massive limb at a time. "Close the door, will you? By God, it worked."

Zeiger closed the door. The floor was covered with paperwork and bits of manila files singed black at the edges.

"I closed my eyes and slowed my breath and thought of you. And here you are. Here you are." Ledermann appraised him with affection. "Can you believe it?"

Zeiger took a step back, careful not to slip on the piles of paper trash. Affection. It would have frightened him less had Ledermann summoned him to beat him to death with a club. Ledermann had gone gray at the temples, a surprising development. Yet he was otherwise somehow exempt from a base circumstance like hair loss and aging.

"You called Hohenschönhausen, left a message," Zeiger said.

"I did no such thing."

Ledermann rushed to the chair opposite his desk, cleared it of a stack of files, and pointed at it. Zeiger sat. Something was the matter with Ledermann. On the wall to Zeiger's right, General Secretary Erich Honecker squinted at him from a frame, a feeble smile locked on his lips for all eternity.

"That's out of date," Zeiger said.

Ledermann was crawling on all fours across the floor behind him, raking papers with broad strokes. There was a buzzing sound. By the time Zeiger understood which of the contraptions had come to life, Ledermann had already picked up the phone's receiver and smashed it back on its cradle. It jangled in protest. Ashes soared, pirouetted, and settled back onto the desk.

"You're back at Hohenschönhausen?" Ledermann said, dropping into his chair. A piece of black ash stuck to his forehead like the sacred marking. Zeiger chose not to mention it.

"A favor of sorts," Zeiger said.

"And press conferences, I heard, observing."

Ledermann was breathing heavily, diligently through his mouth. A look of dull absorption coated his eyes. Zeiger weighed the possibility that he could be drunk.

"DFB cup tonight, are you watching?" Ledermann asked. "Stuttgart, Bayern München."

"Press conference tonight."

"Right," said Ledermann, far away.

"Alles in Ordnung," Zeiger said. "Nothing will change."

As if kicked, Ledermann twisted in his chair and began patting his pants pockets. Finally, he produced his wallet and extracted something, a yellowed photograph, and handed it to Zeiger. "There's Nadine," he said.

Nadine, Ledermann's wife. Zeiger had known her since they were children. They had lived in the same neighborhood, gone to school together. She had always been nervous, thin and stringy and morally sound, which, on some latent, unspeakable level, had always terrified Zeiger. A State and peasant girl at heart, she had now, as far as he could discern from the picture, acquired the look of seasoned disillusionment: a set mouth and the stiff, asexual helmet of hair that so many women his age seemed to be confusing with agility and youth. The photograph showed her in a garden, perched under a canopy of roses, her hands wound around a bushel of weeds, face crosshatched with time. Behind her, their dacha. With difficulty Zeiger pictured Nadine in shorts and sandals, hands caked with dirt, luxuriating in lake-filtered air. Who knew they had a dacha?

"I know Nadine," Zeiger said.

"Nadine has cancer," Ledermann said, producing another photograph. "This here is my son, Rudi."

Rudi, much like his father, was a colossal boy with a colossal set of cheekbones and piscine eyes, features reminiscent of circus performers with pituitary problems.

"I didn't know you had a son," Zeiger said, handing the photograph over the desk.

"What are you, weak in the head? Of course you did," Ledermann said, snatching the picture from his fingers.

Zeiger allowed himself a precious moment of hope. Ledermann had straightened. His face was considerably more lucid; the Ledermann he knew. He asked how Rudi was getting on.

Ledermann rose and dragged his chair around the desk toward Zeiger. "Horribly," he said. "He's going to be a locksmith. Look at him."

"That's a respectable job," Zeiger said, attempting to move his chair.

"Who do you think we are, Zeiger? He wanted to go to university to become a doctor. Like his grandfather, my father, who was a surgeon before frostbite. But Rudi here wasn't admitted. Do you have children, Zeiger? You don't. I know that. They said they didn't admit Rudi because he's not from a worker's family. Keeping the admissions process equal—all that. But they know who I am."

Zeiger remained silent, unsure what reaction Ledermann needed.

"I did some digging, had a talk with the admissions supervisor, over at his house. It took a moment, but what do you know? The comrade finally admitted they blocked Rudi's admission because he refused to take part in his Youth Consecration ceremony when he was a child. That's an understandable reason to block him from attending university, of course. But it's all a misunderstanding, you see? I showed the supervisor the photo from his Consecration day.

Rudi in his suit and dress shoes, holding his copy of *The Purpose of Our Lives.* This picture here—"

Ledermann fumbled another photograph out of his wallet. He held it up for Zeiger. There was Rudi in his oversize suit, no older than fourteen, holding a scroll and a copy of *The Purpose of Our Lives.*

"So I showed this to the admissions supervisor. Clear proof he took part in the ceremony, as clear as can be. Know what he said?" Ledermann paused. "Said the picture was forged. Do you know why he said the picture was forged?"

"Why?" Zeiger said.

"Because it is. Look." Ledermann placed the photo on Zeiger's knee. Surrounding the edges and curves of Rudi's figure was an aura, a halo, resplendently white. His body had been cut and glued into another boy's picture.

"Now what kind of clown would want to do that? Rudi was there, why forge the picture? What is the meaning of this? Nadine and I, did I tell you she's dying of cancer? Terminal. Nadine and I were up all last night looking at this, this piece of rubbish, this Frankenstein of a picture. We were both there at the ceremony. It was some time ago, but we were there. Nadine is speaking of karma now. But that might just be the illness. She's gone soft. What do you say?"

Zeiger held the photograph against the light, studying it. "I say this is quite a bad forgery," he said.

There was a moment of stillness. Absolute, abysmal quiet.

"I am aware, Comrade Zeiger, that this is a terrible forgery," Ledermann said. "What I want to know is, does this sound familiar? Is this something you cooked up in that damned Manual all those years ago? Look at it."

It was the oldest of standard procedures, a grade school–level demoralization technique. Rumors, lies, and false accusations. The only thing worse than failure and disappointment was an aura of misunderstanding. A whole chapter had been dedicated to the strategy of creating it. Inexplicableness and a lack of resolution were imperative. With enough patience on the part of the unit assigned to the subject's case, this procedure ranked among the most effective in causing, if not psychotic breaks, an extreme sense of disorientation, which was followed by solid confession rates.

"How does she know, Nadine, that she's dying?" Zeiger asked.

"The doctors told her."

"But does she know, can she feel it?"

Ledermann seemed to consider this for a moment, his face devoid of expression. "The hell do I know. All I know is that Rudi's gone. He's disappeared. Took it hard, the university business. Blames me. It's been months and not one word. We've gone through every channel. I called in all my favors, but nothing. Nobody just disappears, Zeiger."

A secretary entered, a woman with bulging eyes and a pigeon-like gait. She placed two plates of cake in front of them, swiped some ashes from the desk into the cup of her hand. "It's Gundula's birthday," she explained and left.

The two men ate their cake in silence.

Ledermann's demoralization procedure, Zeiger surmised, was likely fallout from last year's one megabit–chip affair, when it had dawned on Management that there were neither the resources nor the know-how to develop one-megabit chips at the exportable scale they had promised. Zentralkomitee meetings were held, people were let go, and Ledermann and his Science and Technology Unit had gotten involved, leaving in their wake an incomprehensible entanglement of circumvented Western embargo agreements (for technical parts), infiltrated research labs across all continents (for intelligence), and smuggled prototypes from Japan (disguised as tiepins for the plane ride home), until finally the people were presented their very first one-megabit chip.

"Socialism and its rule," Honecker had said at the unveiling, "is stopped neither by oxen nor by mule," which revealed everything there was to know about the aging peasant ruler's state of mind.

A day later, an underground opposition paper revealed that the one-megabit chip not only was as large as a grown man's fist—a "walk-in microchip," the article had quipped—but also was a hollowed-out dummy from the West. It wasn't unthinkable that Ledermann had been suspected as the leak.

The two men had collaborated on the Manual and together had led a group on improving cross-unit bonding and morale, which birthed the widely appreciated inter-Ministry mini-golf tournament. Yet if Management was responsible for Ledermann's demoralization procedure, they hadn't asked Zeiger to consult on it.

"I think I'm dying," Zeiger said.

Ledermann stabbed at the cake on his plate, swift jabs in quick succession. "Differently than the rest of us?"

"I believe so."

"What makes your death so special?"

"That it's mine."

Ledermann dropped his fork and rose from his chair. "Come with me," he said.

Zeiger placed his plate on the desk. The complaint office was located on the opposite side of the compound and closed well before noon. He would not have time to report Schreibmüller's music today.

He followed Ledermann out the door, down the hallway, past the break room, which was empty now, and onto the paternoster. They stood side by side in silence as the compartment descended with a screech. Two men on a Möbius strip. They were delivered into another hallway, where Ledermann turned sharply and led him to a room lined with shelves and stacks of boxes, one of many archival units in the compound. The room was enormous and only partially lit. Beyond the first row of shelves, more shelves receded into vast darkness.

Ledermann ushered him onward, toward a work desk, then disappeared. It took Zeiger a moment to realize they were not alone. Between the shelves, a young man sat straddling a shredder into which he was feeding loose pieces of paper as they were ripped from a binder by another young man beside him. They briefly turned up their faces, acknowledging Zeiger's presence, then resumed their work. Shredding paper was no insignificant thing, and Zeiger felt the impulse to address these two men, question them.

Just then Ledermann reappeared clasping a hardback folder. He dropped it on the desk. This, he said, contained kids like his Rudi. Young ones whom Management hadn't been able to locate. They hadn't been caught trying to cross out of the country, or at foreign embassies waiting for asylum visas, or shot dead at the Wall, or slithering through underground tunnels, or strapped to hot-air balloons drifting up and over the Wall, or breathing through snorkels while floating downriver to the other side of the Spree. These were kids who hadn't been found holed up in someone's living room drawing political flyers, or stiff from alcohol poisoning in a basement of some abandoned church, or spiking their hair in public restrooms, their faces pierced with holes. Murder and dissent, as well as kidnappings and cults, had been ruled out, Ledermann said. Of course, there was a small chance they were dead somewhere, but for all appearances they had just vanished. Then he looked at Zeiger as if his old comrade should have something to say.

Zeiger managed an expression of surprise, arching his eyebrows empathetically. "Not many," he said, and pointed at the folder, which was rather thin.

They located everyone, sooner or later, Ledermann said. Runaways, people wandering in fugue states. Even those who had been escaping through Hungary lately were registered by name as fugitives. "But not these," Ledermann said, placing a hand over the folder and letting it linger as if taking its pulse. There had been one or two recent cases, he confided, including Rudi, but most went back twenty years. The police had gotten nowhere, border control had gotten nowhere, all levels of unofficial informants from America to the USSR had been questioned ad nauseam, nothing. He'd been handed the folder by Management years ago because of the telepathy-research subunit his group was building at the time.

Ledermann looked Zeiger squarely in the face now, the earnest look of a man too desperate to feel ashamed. The telepathy-research subunit, now defunct, he explained, had been a small circle of middle-aged Russian women, vetted for telepathic abilities and sent over as exchange personnel by the KGB. There were four of them, all overweight, motherly types in favor of short haircuts, long linen dresses, chunky jewelry, and glasses with funky frames. Terrifying women, Ledermann recalled.

The unit installed two-way mirrors and brought in equipment such as encephalograms, heart-rate monitors, chimpanzees, and laboratory rats. The goal was to optimize, perhaps even tailor, these women's telepathic talents to specific Ministry and Management objectives. Subliminal suggestion on American government officials; a leg up on opposition activities or intra-Ministry dissent; on a larger scale, noninvasive regulation of voting behavior, those kinds of things.

These women were treated like queens, and they demanded as much, each receiving her own one-bedroom apartment, limo service to and from the Ministry compound, regular trips back to Russia, and lavish Intershop allowances. By the time the lost kids' files landed on their desk, the subunit had been experiencing small successes with these women. After repeated and prolonged telepathic suggestion—a procedure that involved periods of staring, heavy breathing, and humming on the part of these women—a chimp named Lexi had fallen into a suicidal depression, which, given her ordinarily cheery disposition, had been deemed statistically significant.

"I volunteered as a subject," Ledermann said. "They put me in a separate room and gave me a deck of cards with pictures of things: a dog, a house with a lawn and fence, a little girl holding scissors. Seven out of ten times they knew what image I was looking at. Described it down to the last detail. But they couldn't have known even if I had described the pictures to them. None of them spoke German."

"Nor chimp," Zeiger said.

They exchanged a long, multilayered look during which Ledermann seemed to be staring not at but beyond Zeiger, into another, more nuanced plane of existence.

Initially, the women refused to participate in the lost kids' cases, Ledermann said. Some misunderstood, thinking they were being asked to communicate with dead children; suicides, lost souls. It took some convincing, via translators and an orthodox priest. Only after they extracted a promise of unlimited travel to the West did they agree to give it a try. "It's hard to describe what happened then," said Ledermann, who was in the process of removing individual files from the folder and fanning them out on the table.

As the women requested, they were set up in a hotel room at Alexanderplatz, a presidential suite, complete with a bathtub and complimentary shampoos. They had asked for twenty-four hours of absolute quiet during which they would sit in a circle and intuit their way into the minds of these lost kids. There were to be no phone calls or visits, save for hotel personnel should room service be required during their stay. Twenty-four hours passed, then forty, with no word from the women. After two days Ledermann contacted hotel reception to inquire about room-service logs. Four full dinners, lunch, breakfast, snacks, periodic orders of gherkins, one request for four extra bathrobes, and a call to the technician to repair the television. When Ledermann and his team finally entered the suite, it was in a shambles. Toppled furniture and damp towels draped over windows. The women were gone, but on the dining-room table, among drained bottles and brimming ashtrays, Ledermann found a note.

Again he produced his wallet and pulled out a worn piece of paper on which a message was written in Cyrillic. "I kept the note," he said.

With difficultly Zeiger deciphered the words on the paper. *These people are not where they were before. We could not connect telepathically, apologies.*

After that, Ledermann went on, funding was cut for the telepathy subunit. Many months later, the KGB finally confirmed that the women had merely returned to Moscow. There were apologies for their swift departure. The Russians were a melancholic people, the KGB explained, rattled by weltschmerz, homesick even when at home.

"So it was all for nothing," Zeiger said.

"That's not the point," Ledermann said. He inserted the paper back into his wallet and turned his attention to the files on the table. He opened one from the top to reveal a photo of Rudi. The two of them stared at the picture until Ledermann snapped the file shut. "My point," he said, "is you're unemployed at the moment."

"Not technically," Zeiger countered.

"Basically retired, with everyone just using the Manual as they please."

"A worrying habit."

"See what you can find out about my son." Ledermann took a step back and began inching toward the door in slow, crablike fashion.

Zeiger reached out reflexively, going for his elbow, like a child reaching splay-fingered for a mother's arm. "What are you doing?" he asked.

"I have to go," Ledermann said.

"Where?" Zeiger said. *Why?* he wanted to ask, but his old comrade had already slipped through the door.

The hum of the paper shredder ceased. The absence of its sound delivered a lifeless silence. When Zeiger turned to the man on the shredder and his companion, their sharp, impassive faces reminded him of conscious, city-dwelling birds: pigeons on lampposts, or groups of crows picking at trash cans, their black, lidless eyes seeing things he knew nothing about.

Through a trick of the overhead light, the files on the table gleamed hot white. A contaminated, infectious glow. Vanished people were worse than dead people. He could not blame the Russian seers for fleeing. A dozen or so files, a meager count. He approached the table, flipped open Rudi's file. There was a log of the boy's activities that appeared to go back a few years, photo evidence attached. The surveillance order had been initiated by Management and signed off by Ledermann, fatherly precautions. Rudi at football training, Rudi at FDJ camp, Rudi meeting friends at corner pubs, Rudi checking in at military service, checking out, checking in, checking out, going home. The most recent entry dated back months, in the summer, and placed him at

Weinbergspark, in Mitte, where he'd enjoyed a beer with a friend. There was nothing of concern to report. Then a list of addresses, friends' names, some, if not most, marked with a tiny cross indicating Unofficial Informant status. This was a standard surveillance package. Standard in its totality, its fine-meshed intricacy, not a surprising treatment for someone like Ledermann's son.

Zeiger was beginning to feel hungry. A missed chance at reporting Schreibmüller at the complaint office. Ketwurst day at the Ministry cafeteria. Then an airless, arid press conference to observe. He tucked Rudi's file under his arm and collected the rest, opened their covers to glance at their names. Ludwig. Sabine. Marion. Richard. Gottfried. Peter. Kornelia. Axel. Anna. Manfred. Lara.

He squeezed his eyes shut, saw blackness and colors he could not name. When he opened them, the letters scattered, hurrying like cockroaches across the page. Nausea rose from his gut, a cold and enormous sensation, and a shrill buzz filled his head, a high-frequency static. Lara had a file of her own.

1.3

When Zeiger was a boy, the old baker had been found in the back room of the local shop facedown in the tin barrel of a kneading machine, his head submerged in dough. He had suffered a stroke and subsequently drowned in his own livelihood. Or if the dough had been too thick to fill his lungs, he had instead suffocated in its density. Zeiger had wanted to see the body. It seemed important to witness the scene. But Mother wouldn't allow it. Instead he was left to imagine the incident in sketches, like one of the Struwwelpeter stories of moral urgency, with lessons to be learned, that Mother read to him. The baker rises before dawn, hangs his nightcap. Then a slip, a fall, perhaps a shout. A wooden spoon goes flying, biscuits in the air, and two legs, spindly and gnarled, stick like candles from the barrel of dough.

This he would remember when, in 1954, his father returned after nearly a decade of silence from a Soviet labor camp in the form of a pile of gray ashes housed in a shoebox-sized carton. Shortly afterward, her hope extinguished, Mother fell face forward into her Walther service gun. He was an orphan then. He had barely known his parents, who had always been preoccupied with loftier, more patriotic causes than him. It was the year of his twenty-fifth birthday, shortly before he graduated from the Potsdam Academy, the year Germany won its first postwar World Cup, over heavily favored Hungary, as broadcast by radio to the nation in the legendary febrile commentary of Herbert Zimmerman: *Goal! Goal! Goal! Goal!... Goal for Germany! 3–2 for Germany! Call me mad, call me crazy!... Over! Over! Over! Overrrrrr!... The game is over! Germany is world champion!* Cheers like war cries echoed from the streets. Firecrackers sounded like bombshells. Germany was back.

It was Ketwurst day, but he had long since lost his desire to eat. He turned onto Oderberger Strasse and parked his car. The street was empty, swept clean, the cobblestone a jagged stretch of crooked black teeth. The only sign of life, at the far end of the street, was a tidy row of anoraks, beige trenches, green parkas, and pink plastic baskets standing in line at the butcher's. Zeiger rolled down his window to let in some air, only to be hit with the scent of smog, *Schwarze Pumpe* coal dust, fine matter that turned handkerchiefs black like the plague. He extracted a cigarette and his lighter, but the wheel and flint had loosened and he did not succeed in bending them back. Across the street, blocking a row of parking spots, stood three large trash containers, fluorescent orange like high-visibility vests. When he had parked here last, a month ago, the containers had been empty. Now they were stuffed to capacity with billowing fabrics and things made of wood; banners, pennants, and other relics of last month's parade.

He didn't want to remember the parade. He wanted to recall whether, on the night before the parade, after Lara had placed her hand on his shoulder at the corner café and he'd come to talk to her here, he had told her the story of Knight Kahlbutz, and how, as a child, Mother had taken him to see his uncorrupted corpse in the catacombs of Kampehl. In 1690, a maid had refused the knight's right to a *jus primae noctis,* upon which he avenged his honor by taking the life of her new husband, a shepherd. *It was not I,* he'd sworn before the courts, *or else, when I die, my body will not decay.* Had Zeiger told Lara how startled, how repulsed he'd been by the sight of the knight's undecayed remains? By the black slits and holes of his face, taut and brown like baked chicken skin? By his long fingers, complete with pointed fingernails, folded on his abdomen in eternal repose?

That night in her apartment his wish had been to recall everything for Lara, to offer her coherence, linkages, the sequence of things. But now he couldn't remember what exactly he'd told her of Knight Kahlbutz, or of how he'd asked Mother if this knight or Saint John the Russian or Saint Seraphim of Sarov or any other unearthly being they'd found undead in their tombs had been blessed or cursed by immortality.

He had been his mother's only child. This he most certainly had told Lara. Because it was then that she had shifted from the edge of the bed to the wall, drawn up her legs, and cocked her head in a manner that small children do when great mysteries are about to be revealed. The change in her demeanor had stimulated him, caused him to speak hastily, divulge too much. Mother was perfection, he had tried to explain, she was complete. She wore high-collared dresses with long sleeves and loose waistlines, altered to fit her body, which was rapidly but beautifully dwindling from war. What existed for Mother were the booming reports of the Front that issued from the black mouth of the radio set, and Father, who appeared at random while on leave from the East in his lacquered boots and gold-button uniform, and that pin on his lapel, that bright grinning skull. When Father appeared, Mother cooked. Boiled cabbage that Father said smelled like home and soil, which made Mother flash her teeth in a rare, blinding smile. When Father was gone she did not boil cabbage. She boiled many pots of water with which she filled the tin basin they used for their baths. Zeiger recalled for Lara the surge in his gut, as if he were falling from great heights, the restless prickle in his bones, as he waited, naked, in the scorching water for Mother to join him in the tub.

Sitting with Lara that night, he'd found this memory intact, unwilted. The cadaver of his boyhood, preserved by his mind, his gift to Lara. But then Lara, in a gesture he could not place, had closed her eyes and placed the soft curve of her forehead on top of her knees, and he knew he had failed. It had been too much for one night.

A clap like gunfire was followed by a squad of maintenance trucks rushing down the cobblestone street. As they passed, coils of wire, metal rods, and tin lampshades as large as millstones all banged furiously on the beds of the trucks. This, Zeiger knew, was lighting material for the newly refurbished section of the Wall, over on Bernauer Strasse. The workers' sculpted arms, still tanned from the summer, hung from the trucks' open windows. Their youth was a relief to Zeiger. After building the Wall came maintaining the Wall; after the old came the new; there was an order to things.

He collected Lara's file, tucked the rest of the stack under the back seat, and stepped out of his car. He searched the empty sidewalks and, in the distance, the diminishing line of people at the butcher's to make sure he wasn't being watched, then crossed the street. The windows in the opposite building were closed and lightless.

Entering Lara's building would not be a problem. The main lock had been removed and replaced by steel wire that kept the door only haphazardly shut. The entryway opened to darkness and the smell of waterlogged brickwork, decades of unwashed wood and stone. There was no use in finding a light switch, the bulbs had been stolen and repurposed a long time ago. He would use the wall as a guide, shuffle his feet to find the stairs, count the landings.

When he stepped inside he spotted a figure, a contour in the shadows, positioned halfway up the stairs. It moved, shifted, its outline growing more distinct to reveal a boxlike head. The head cocked, a motion of acute focus, a creature's sensitivity to things beyond sight and sound. It was Schreibmüller.

Zeiger skidded sideways, bumped into the wall, retreated to the front door. "Here?" he said into the shadows.

"What?" the voice said, cracking, a shrill rise and fall, a hoarse young man's voice. So it was not Schreibmüller. "I can't see a thing."

With that the figure slowly descended the steps and emerged into the daylight cast by the window in the door, where Zeiger stood, gripping his file. The man was barely past his teens. He wore track pants, torn in various places, paint-splattered tennis shoes, and a black leather jacket that looked new. It was the ordinary disheveled appearance those youths had adopted, the punks the Ministry had been failing to remove from Zion's Church up the road. A patch with a red capital *A* was sewn onto his collar. He had a mild and pleasant face with northern angles and generic blue eyes. Dense white-blond stubble glistened like moisture on his cheeks. It wasn't hard to imagine that half a century ago this face might have crowned a uniform of similar severity, of similar embarrassment to white-blond sons down the line.

"Didn't mean to startle you," the punk said, propping himself against the wall. Squinting into the daylight, he found a cigarette in his coat pocket. His movements were nonchalant, territorial, easy.

"No matter," Zeiger said. "Fire?"

The punk handed him his lighter and looked him over. His lids were pink, sleek, slithering things. What did he see in Zeiger? His father, his grandfather, the harmless neighborhood geezer?

"Is this your building?" Zeiger asked.

"Just waiting for a friend," the punk said.

"Alone, in the dark?"

"I don't like to be outside. The light," the punk said, lifting his hand to simulate a visor. The sky through the door's window was lucid, sharp like a mirror. "They say it has a half-life of thirty years, the cloud that floated up all over the place after the meltdown in Chernobyl. I'm not good at counting, but it happened three years ago. We all know what that means. By now it's settled into our trees, our hair, our mushrooms. Especially our mushrooms. It does funny things with the light too. Everyone politicking, getting all brutal and murderous, but everyone still breathing this air. Just imagine, when the Americans finally throw that bomb—"

"Unlikely," Zeiger said, before he could stop himself. He had no interest in comforting this punk. He glanced again at the rips in his pants, the paint on his shoes, the bloodred emblem: A for *Angst*. It was just as well that he was wasting his life fearing things beyond his control. Let him spend the undeserved prize of youth in fistfuls.

The young man narrowed his eyes and asked Zeiger if they'd met before.

"I believe not," Zeiger said.

"It's the toxins, I swear. Happens to me all the time."

The punk wanted encouragement, more geriatric wisdom, which Zeiger declined to provide. He returned the lighter.

"Do you?" the punk asked. "Live here?"

"I'm visiting," Zeiger said. "An old family friend." And shuffle by shuffle he slipped back into the shade to make his ascent.

Perhaps the Ministry had made a mistake. It wasn't unthinkable that she hadn't actually disappeared, or that they'd tracked the wrong Lara. He walked up to the second floor, stood at her door, and sucked on his cigarette, unsure of how to proceed. A frosted window on the next landing filtered the light in a dim, inoffensive blue. Next to that window, in a corner of perpetual shade, had been his lookout. Before the flurry of press conferences, before the surge in miscellaneous requests from colleagues, before the chaos, he'd had time. And he'd spent it here, in that lightless corner, waiting for a glimpse of Lara after her shift at the corner café.

With time he had learned to recognize her footfall: metrical, recklessly loud, unbefitting a girl of her size. She lived alone. She kept her keys on a keychain that jangled like bells. All summer she had worn a dress made of white cotton, held up by two straps that tied into a bow at the nape of her neck. From his position in the blue light he had counted the moles in a pattern on her back, observed her shoulder blades, which pointed like two sacred arrows down the length of her spine. Always two locks, one on top, one on the bottom, and her keys chimed like music before she vanished through the doorway.

In the six decades of his life—subtracting the fifteen un-blemished years he considered to be his childhood—Zeiger had, on various occasions, engaged physically with a series of faceless, scentless women. They occurred to him like a collective theophany, periodically and mostly at night, a grotesque composite. A terrify-ing creature, wrathful like a Hindu goddess. Here a stack of spongy white arms, there a bulging thigh, the crater of a navel like a bloodless gunshot wound—all set against the bare stone walls of a store basement, where the light had grown moldy, the floor black with other men's passion, and no feeling of consequence ever was or would be born. Lara was the closest he had come to love.

He gripped the knob now and found the door unlocked. This he had not expected. He hesitated at the threshold, looked back into the stairwell, the abysmal darkness of the stories below, somehow expecting to see someone. Someone to consult, someone to witness the scene. Nobody was there. He dropped his cigarette, killed it with the ball of his foot, and stepped inside.

Vanilla sugar, of course, because Lara liked to bake, and dust, and insulation hay decaying beneath the floorboards. And the putrid smell of clogged, rusting pipes, rotten food, and remnants of department-store perfume, lilacs, synthetic aromas. And infused in the elemental matter of things, a scent that was distinctly, painfully human: Lara.

He stood in the anteroom, perfectly still. There were her things, the downy winter coats, the mittens, the thick knit hats, the disastrous pile of boots and heels and sneakers. To his right he could make out the dark nook of the toilet with its porcelain fixtures in seaweed green. Ahead, the tubelike kitchen. A few paces off, beyond the bathroom door, the single room where Lara lived, the space in which she slept.

He peered into the room. Daylight from an open window by the bed flooded the space. The room was in a shambles, the Ministry's work—they'd been looking for her. Her closet, a massive peasant wardrobe, stood ajar, its contents spilling onto the floor in heinous disarray. The room was unheated and a stream of cool air came in through the window, creating a draft. Below the window, in the street, police cars flew past like darts in rapid succession. No blazing lights and no sirens, just the *brat-a-tat* of tires on the cobblestones. Zeiger closed the window and turned to face the room. A fresh angle. There was no order to things. Every surface was littered with clothes and books and bright, colorful things, and he looked at these things with the same naked shame with which they looked back at him.

After Mother's death came the Ministry. A monstrous machinery with roots and branches as extensive as those of Yggdrasil, the great ash tree in the myths of the North that joins the Nine Worlds. Lara had never heard of it, or of the Twilight of the Gods, or of how Wotan had used its branches as kindling to set fire to their heavenly realm. Lara had much to learn. He had been patient with her. A month ago, after he'd last spoken to her here, he had made plans to bring her to his apartment and play for her all four cycles of Wagner's *Nibelungen*. That plan felt laughable now.

He had to sit. He was beginning to feel weak, from hunger and agitation, the chill in the room, and Lara's scattered things. He took a place on the edge of the bed. Aging was a gradual diffusion, a slow, viscous untethering, chaos where previously there had been certainty and sense.

He tried to remember the sequence of things. The evening before his night with Lara, two elders had begun pummeling each other at the far end of the Zentralkomitee hall. Slow-motion shoving and clasping of collars; tangled arms. From Zeiger's vantage they could have been attempting to dance. They had been separated and seated at opposite ends of the hall—order was restored—but it had been well past midnight by then, and so the next morning was a late morning for Zeiger at the corner café.

Upon entering the café, Zeiger had noticed an empty barstool, a missing regular. With a nebula of quiet dejection, the three remaining regulars turned their heads as he entered. He did not like to be among the regulars when their papers were finished. There was a lucidity about them, a peasant awareness. Lunar cycles, harvest cycles, as we work today we live tomorrow, the premonitory properties of frost. *Mit dem ist nicht gut Kirschen essen.* There was a chance they could turn their attention on him.

He found his table by the window. There was Klaus, beholding his empty glass, his mind long evacuated to unthinkable places. His setter was curled at his feet, its black paws twitching in sleep. Clanking sounds came from the kitchen, metal on porcelain, a faucet in use, someone at work. Lara at work.

"Order is familiar chaos," Father had said when he came home with that pin on his lapel, that bright grinning skull, and saw Mother polishing the Solingen silver for his return.

"Poor Manfred. It's a bad diagnosis," one of the regulars was saying. It was a somber tone, one reserved for irrevocable tragedies.

"A bad diagnosis," another said after a pause.

"You mean prognosis," added the third.

"The prognosis is also quite bad," said the first.

They lit their cigarettes and smoked in silence, pursuing their own private thoughts.

Then, Lara's footsteps. The click of her heels slashed through the silence and woke Klaus's setter with a yelping start. Zeiger glimpsed a flash of red hair as she set his cheese toast on the table in front of him. Out of the edge of his vision, the coffee cup came into view. It would have been only a second before it clanged on the table, and he waited for the clang, but then Lara started, teetered, and the coffee cup toppled, ejaculating its contents onto the table. Swiftly, firmly, her hand came down onto Zeiger's shoulder. A shriek, birdlike, erupted from her throat. It was an incredible sound. And from sheer confusion, and despite himself entirely, he looked up into her face and saw that she was smiling, not at him, but down at Klaus's setter, which had nuzzled its wet nose into the flesh of her thigh, causing her to startle.

The walls inside Lara's room were too bright. He needed to get up from the bed and pace. He wanted to look for something, bring some sense into this mission, but he didn't know where to start. There were many eyes. Above the bed hung the posters he remembered — of three young men with very neat eyebrows and ridiculous hair. Pop musicians, he'd figured then, of some bizarre sort. And there by the foot of the bed, on the low lime-green chair he had sat in all through that night, was her toy *Monchhichi*, sucking its thumb and staring back at him with sorrowful eyes. A stuffed animal, a bear of some sort, poked out beady-eyed from under the bed. Loneliness was this kind of silence and a room full of unseeing eyes.

In the bathroom he found her toothbrush, a frayed, yellowed thing, on the edge of the sink. He folded back the shower curtain. There, three pairs of perfectly pink slips hung from a clothesline over the tub. He stared, astonished, and let the curtain fall. At home he had a stack of lingerie brochures he rarely, if ever, viewed. But he had noted with some surprise the relative modesty of the models' underpants. Even wedding specials advertised low-cut legs and high-cut waistlines, thick elastic bands and girlish pastel floral patterns. None of the brochures had exhibited slips of this kind. Slips of this kind could not be purchased at any State-sanctioned store. Again he pulled back the curtain. Three pink, undoubtedly West German slips. She had hung them from the clothesline like slabs of meat at the store. He reached out and touched them. They were hard as a plank and dry.

Her toiletries, her toothbrush, the slips, the mountain of shoes in the hallway, and the tangle of clothes on her bedroom floor. She had left it all. He covered his nose and entered the kitchen. The smell of rotten food was overpowering. A congregation of fruit flies swarmed about, scheming little plans, feeding on a lone slice of apple browning in its own soup in a bowl on the table. The kitchen appeared to be in the middle of something, ready to go. An ashtray on the table was stuffed with cigarette butts, filtered, smeared with rings of dollish lipstick. Historical artifacts. He stood, holding his breath, trying to shield himself from bewilderment.

The staff at St. Hedwig's hospital, he knew, had been relocating a dozen mental patients from the psych ward to make space for an unusual number of high-ranking Ministry and Management officials curiously suffering from acute psychotic breaks. Comrades known for pragmatism and levelheadedness had been spotted wandering the streets in nothing but nightgowns, screaming for Socrates at the top of their lungs. Colleagues with no discernible symptoms had admitted themselves voluntarily. Voices in their heads, they said, West Germans telling crude Ossi jokes. He thought of Ledermann, he thought of the punk and the Chernobyl meltdown he feared had infiltrated their air. And he thought of Zentralkomitee meetings and those elderly comrades. The men who built this nation reduced to scuffles and impotent blows.

Why had he come here to Lara's apartment? He walked back to her bedroom, removed the *Monchhichi* from its chair, and sat. It was now long past noon. He pulled Lara's file onto his lap, then remembered Rudi and, with a twinge of guilt, Ledermann's bleary-eyed request to find a trace of the boy.

"Rudi, tomorrow," he said aloud, but his voice sounded out-landish among Lara's things.

"You can't remove the mountain and leave the echo," Mother had said when Father left and took with him his gold-button uniform and that pin on his lapel, that bright grinning skull, which was the last time Zeiger saw him before he returned years later in that shoebox-sized carton, the year the World Cup miracle occurred in Bern.

Lara's file was as light as down. Her paperwork was encased in a standard envelope in paper-bag brown, smooth and clean and uncreased, as if just recently retrieved from its own protective casing. If it contained anything of use, Ledermann's subunit would no doubt have already found her.

Zeiger extracted a cigarette from his pocket, searched the coffee table, found a box of matches, and struck one. A sound, a single creak, sighed outside the apartment door. He tensed and cocked his head, listening as the flame died. A few children shouted and screeched outside; playful combat noises, avian hysteria. When the screaming receded, the silence held a new sort of resonance. He opened the file: Lara's name, her date of birth, occupation, all of which he knew. He struck another match and lit his cigarette. A table of contents, lists of names, timetables, bullet points that peppered the pages like puncture wounds.

He was startled once more by sounds coming from beyond the door. Old wood and sharp clicks, the sound of clocks passing time. For a moment the apartment was alive, moving and breathing, then stillness returned and Zeiger cast his eyes again over Lara's file. It was difficult to absorb the words. Outside, more police cars, this time with sirens, and more children shouting; school had let out.

Activity logs placed Lara at the corner café at seven in the morn-ing sharp, every day, since the day he remembered first seeing her there, a long time ago. There was no schooling, no record of her FDJ placement, no sporting competitions, no housing records, mothers, fathers, siblings, or boyfriends mentioned in her dossier. For the Ministry, there was no beginning to things with her, no sequence to Lara; the primordial soup of her life was the corner café.

Or, he considered, the file had not been completed. Her last activity was logged a day before the parade, the night he approached her in the stairwell and handed her the gift he'd picked up that afternoon in Meissen. That was a month ago now.

Zeiger leaned back, removed another match, and smoked into the silence. He flipped back to the table of contents. There he found another activity log, this time pages of facsimiled handwriting, rows of coiled longhand with bulging slopes and bubbles for dots on the *is*. Lara's handwriting. *Cheese toast and coffee, coffee and cheese toast, appearances increasingly late in the morning, more coffee and more cheese toast, a marked lack of anything to report.*

Zeiger stared at the page. It was conscious, an infant or an exposed beating heart. The moment was basic.

He heard another scratching noise but could not locate its source. Then a thump and a click, and when he glimpsed movement in the anteroom, he thought somehow he was seeing sounds in his head. But then a figure emerged and stepped into the bedroom light. Zeiger recognized the soft face, the downy hair, the red *A* on the collar. The punk paused in the middle of the room, arms dangling by his sides, feet planted wide. It took a moment for him to notice Zeiger. His face registered no shock or surprise, only plain recognition; simple, cross-species acknowledgment.

It was important to let him speak first.

"I should have known," the punk said.

"Interesting," Zeiger said. "I was thinking the same."

1.4

A month earlier, the day before the parade, as she'd placed a hand on his shoulder, the setter had rolled onto its back, offering Lara the full breadth of its tousled chest. She let go of Zeiger's shoulder, wiped the spatter of coffee from his table, and bent to pet the dog. She had stood so close he could smell her. A line of white fuzz descended the length of her spine. Blue veins webbed the backs of her thighs.

"You scared me," she scolded the dog.

The hoarseness in her voice surprised him. It was too resonant for a girl her age.

"You're a good one," she said as the dog leaned up to lap her face. "Nothing bothers you, does it, you good one, you perfect one, yes, you," she said with laughter in her voice.

Zeiger could have touched the small of her back, but just then the missing regular entered the café, disturbing the delicate arrangement of things. The man paused at the entrance and scanned his surroundings with a stupid, disoriented frown.

"Manfred," Lara said, darting toward him. "I heard. We're so sorry. What a bad prognosis," she said as she guided him to the counter, where he was greeted by the regulars with silent claps on the back.

Zeiger turned and Klaus was gone. In the many years Zeiger had observed him at the corner café Klaus had not so much as moved a hand from his lap. Zeiger stared at the empty seat, the empty glass of beer on the otherwise empty table. The vacant spot was telling him something he could not comprehend. Zeiger searched the floor for the dog, but wherever Klaus had gone, the setter had gone too.

He extracted some coins from his wallet, dropped them onto the table, abandoned his cheese toast and coffee, and left the café. As he stood on the corner, two young women pushed past with two tiny panzer-like strollers, the faces of their occupants contorted with terrible joy. Behind them, a flock of schoolchildren of indiscernible age with Thälmann ribbons blazing like rings of fire around their necks. Air as dense as dough. He looked up into the linden trees. Their leaves quivered like hands. *Nothing bothers you,* Lara had said when she turned her back to pet the dog on the floor. Lara had put a hand on his shoulder, planted something there, and in turn he would tell her everything, including the story of Johannes Held and the boys who disappeared in the desert.

Zeiger had no recollection of his drive to the Ministry that day. Nor of his walk to the cafeteria building by way of the parking lot. It wasn't until he entered the foyer and confronted the full reality of the familiar surroundings, the white speckled stone tiles, the teak-paneled doorways, the emptiness of it all, that he understood where and why he had come. It was Friday and therefore Klöpse day at the cafeteria, but the lunchroom was mostly deserted. Only a few comrades flocked along the long rows of banquet-style tables. Those in pairs spoke softly, their voices joining into a hum that resonated along the concrete flooring and in the chlorinated air.

Zeiger approached the counter and spotted Horst Kummer sitting at an empty table at the far end of the hall. Kummer waved at him, like an eager child in the schoolyard. Zeiger directed his attention toward the tray before him, the lunch-counter attendant who constructed a small mountain of meatballs on his plate, the ladle with which she drowned the lumpy pyramid in sauce. Her toad-like mouth, the blue pouches under her eyes. There would be no way to avoid Kummer.

Kummer was committed to a kind of childlike humor that Zeiger found hard to stomach. He was a father of four highly motivated children and was married to a wife with political ambitions. The two men had known each other since their childhood in Mitte, where all the boys met after school to play War with fake, makeshift rifles and slingshots in the ruins and bombed-out lots. Kummer, a year older than the rest, had told the boys stories. He'd been to the Front, he said; had seen the Führer, whose skin glowed like something divine, and even shaken his hand; had watched him lift a grown man off the ground. It was Kummer to whom the boys turned for counsel when they found something valuable among the rubble, or something human, a hand or a charred tuft of hair. His father had died early in the fighting, and the day the war ended, his mother drowned his three siblings in Lake Wannsee, then hanged herself from the beams in the attic of their home. Death was preferable to living with the *Untermensch*. She had spared him, Kummer claimed, because he had touched the Führer's hand.

As Zeiger approached the table, Kummer polished his fork with the silken tip of his tie. Zeiger recalled Kummer once telling him that the key to lasting happiness was a terrible memory and a cold pint of beer, and it occurred to him that Kummer's personal universe was pillared by a structure of wisdom so facile that the question remained whether he was dim-witted or had understood something so simple its profundity was forever lost on others.

"Bernd," Kummer shouted as Zeiger set down his tray.

"Horst," Zeiger said. But he remained standing and kept his eyes on the table.

Kummer was using his fork to crush his pile of meatballs into the sauce. He did so with such force that he looked to be slaughtering something alive. "Where is everyone?" he said, again in a shout. "It's Klöpse day. Old bags like us should be storming the place."

Zeiger took a seat. "The parade tomorrow," he said. "Or maybe the revolts."

Kummer angled his head down and gazed at Zeiger over the top of his nose. A didactic expression, devoid of irony. "You can't call them revolts if Management's allowed them," he said. "What department are you in now, remind me."

Zeiger aligned his cutlery with the edge of the table, then nudged his plate forward so that it centered the tray. He had no appetite, he realized. The food in front of him was unfathomable. "Head of the SDP Manual Department," he said.

A pause as Kummer reflected. "I see. Demoralization still. Now, when was the last time this Manual of yours was updated, remind me."

"There's been no need."

"Great piece of work, that Manual, don't get me wrong," Kummer said. "But everyone has one, right?" He tipped his plate and began spooning the sauce into his mouth, a terrible mouth, a dark, lipless hole in his face. "So if everyone has a Manual and there's no need for a second edition, what is it you do all day, Bernd? If you don't mind me asking."

Cackling erupted at the other end of the hall as more comrades arrived.

He watched Kummer chew. The word *mastication* came to mind. "There's a lot of consulting," he said. "The recent press conferences, for example. They're live on TV."

"Rhetoric, tone of voice," Kummer said.

"Body language," Zeiger said. "The color of their ties."

"I've noticed, yes."

"They need advice," Zeiger said. "The Manual helps."

"Funny, there's a whole Manual on something our wives do to us every day."

Zeiger looked up, noticed the smile on Kummer's face, waited for it.

"We should have assembled a couple of wives in a room and had them write down their own demoralization techniques. That would have been a hellish Manual. Confession rates through the roof. Ever think of that? Could have saved you so much work." Kummer chortled. "Subchapter 6.5 of the SDP Manual: 'The Silent Treatment.'" His laugh expanded into a guttural sound with a terrifying pitch. He dropped his fork for added effect, pushed his chair back, slapped his knee.

Zeiger turned to scan the hall. Nobody was taking note of the scene. "There is such a thing as Silent Treatment in the Manual," he tried. "It's when —"

"Subchapter 10.4: 'Love Deprivation by Withholding of Beer,'" Kummer continued.

"In fact, Chapter 4 of the Manual outlines —"

"I know, Zeiger," Kummer said, his laughter dying. "I read the goddamn Manual." He went on to speak of the protests, the upheaval among the ranks. He had just recently been transferred to the border-control department after that fellow had gotten shot. Western media had caught wind, Management had begun denying the existence of a shoot-to-kill order at the Wall, and his predecessor, a comrade at the tail end of his seventies, had made a scene ridiculous enough to land him in Hohenschönhausen jail. Unfortunate for him, lucky for Kummer. It was the border guards they now needed to watch. Things would calm down soon, he explained, return to normal. He mentioned reform, leniency, and compromise, and how science proved that only adaptable organisms survived and thrived.

With difficulty Zeiger followed his argument. Somewhere beneath his ribs, a dull ache spread, encircling his back, his neck, the top of his head. A quick and mortal pain.

Kummer began scooping his dessert pudding with pathetic enthusiasm. Zeiger considered the trustful look on his face, *alles in Ordnung,* and how someday Kummer, of all people, would also cease to exist.

On his way out of the cafeteria, Zeiger encountered two more colleagues standing by the glass doors of the foyer. He recognized them immediately as Mürbe and Torf, two new additions to the umbrella department, both in possession of diffuse rank and titles he hadn't bothered to learn. There was a scholastic quality to their positioning by the door, the way Torf alternately stroked and cupped his chin, gently nodding in response to whatever Mürbe was saying. It occurred to Zeiger that he hadn't ever seen either of them alone.

"Name! Identification!" Mürbe said in a soldierly tone.

Zeiger ignored the remark. He didn't appreciate the ease with which some younger comrades handled senior officers; the malicious schadenfreude, like a thinly veiled pity usually reserved for the terminally ill. When Mürbe extended his hand, Zeiger grabbed it and shook it with vehemence, hoping to accomplish this interaction while simultaneously slipping through the door.

"Mahlzeit," Mürbe said, barring his path. "Empty today."

All three scanned the foyer, beholding the obvious. The pair had moved in so close to Zeiger that the tips of their shoes just about touched.

Mürbe placed a hand on Zeiger's shoulder and kept it there. "Nice to see you, Bernd," he said. "You look good, wouldn't you say, Torf?" He shot a look to his colleague, who in turn offered a dangerous grin. "Listen, about that parade tomorrow, we're short a couple of eyes to watch the crowds around the bleachers."

"I have mountains of paperwork," Zeiger said.

"Just a few hours," Mürbe continued, unfazed. "Any help we can get."

"We'll have Management get in touch," Torf said.

"Expect a call," Mürbe added.

Zeiger inched backward.

"It's just one morning," Torf called after him.

Zeiger went out the doors, then turned and waved through the glass. The two men exchanged a look—a concise telepathic conference—and Zeiger made his escape down into the lot. He needed time to think about Lara.

He sat in his car and smoked. Something needed to be done. He had an unbearable impulse to return to see Lara at the corner café. He could take a seat at the counter like a normal regular, make himself known, converse with her on benign matters like weather conditions and the state of affairs.

In the parking lot a large woman was lugging two clear trash bags toward her car. She dropped the bags, searched for her keys, then emptied the bags into the trunk. An avalanche of papers funneled out—loose papers, stapled papers, ring binders, stapled binders, pale manila folders, some of which looked singed. When she was finished, she closed the trunk and paused, scanned the parking lot as if she'd heard a sound, then hoisted herself into her car and drove off.

He knew he could not return to the corner café. The regulars were there, maybe Inge too now that it was about to hit noon. He needed space and he needed time, more time alone with Lara. But he couldn't appear at her apartment without a gift. That's what Mother would have said.

He drove in a state of quiet frenzy, keeping his eyes on the two-lane boulevard. Only a few people were out on the sidewalks. Retirees on bicycles, young mothers with young children, sane and sober people with time on their hands. He passed concrete-slab buildings and pastel facades, sprinklings of overgrown, derelict lots, and soon the boulevard narrowed and emerged into a landscape that was rural and flat.

He had been experiencing chills and degrees of aches lately, subtle variations of pressure on his chest. Sometimes his head pounded, sometimes it pulsed, sometimes there were spots in his vision that looked like clapping sounds. But this was the first time he felt he could faint while sitting down.

"Mutti," he said. *Mom.* The word spluttered from his mouth, a pressurized hiss from the back of his throat. *Mut-ti,* he did not know why.

He stopped on the side of the road, stepped out, walked around his car, and vomited into a patch of grass. He finished with two or three heaves, then straightened himself and faced the stretch of fields. Calm washed over him. It was a fleeting state of surrender he'd experienced only rarely: at the East Sea years earlier, witnessing a wave swell as large as a bus; once at the sight of lightning slicing across a brutal black sky; moments like these, when his body revealed itself to be a weak, defenseless beast.

He could recall only one incident after which he had vomited with similar spontaneity. After those American scientists had made those boys disappear in the Arizona desert and Johannes Held had been recalled to Berlin. The memory rose to the surface, lingered, and popped: the ammoniac smell of urine, the slick deposits of lime and grime on the walls of the room where that Russian had badgered Held. There was the finely bubbled plane of concrete under the portico landing of Hohenschönhausen jail onto which Zeiger had vomited briefly but violently after reporting to Management what Johannes Held had said.

The grassy strip on which he had stopped his car dipped and then sloped upward into a vast field of black, barren soil, where a tractor with extensions like wings was inching along the far end of the land, the clattering of its motor and the whistle of its many valves absorbed by the expanse. Depending on eolian conditions, depending on the time of year, this thick, noxious smell of manure sometimes carried as far as Mitte. Zeiger had not been out this way since he was a child. After the Red Army had advanced along this route and scorched the land, leaving them with nothing, Mother put on Father's canvas overalls, tied up her hair in a shawl, smeared her face with dirt, and took him on foot to the peasant houses that flanked the sides of this road. She left him to wait in stables, where he sat in the hay and built his own army out of damp sticks of straw or slept until daybreak or watched chickens peck blindly at the ground, until Mother finally emerged from the farmhouse with a can of milk and a sack of potatoes as rubbery and wrinkled as her own dirty hands.

Zeiger returned to his car and let the bile settle in his throat. He took a map from the glove compartment and laid it flat across the passenger's seat. He calculated the feasibility of his plan. Three hours to Meissen, a minimal amount of time to complete his purchase there, and a three-hour return journey would locate him back at Lara's building just in time for the end of her shift at the corner café. The insanity of his plan was evident. He envisioned a faceless jury, their sharp forefingers pointing at the sky. *But why?* they would wail.

He circumvented larger villages, kept to the rural roads. This was marshland, Brandenburg in its gray early-fall palsy. He entered the Spreewald area within an hour and was engulfed by cheerless woods and thickets, the place where gherkins grew. Occasionally he passed a series of houses strung like beads on a necklace alongside the road. There were clotheslines with clothes flapping like flags in the wind, cars parked in driveways with toys stashed in rear windshields, beer tents with glittering pennants. Symptoms of people, but no people to be seen. He switched on the radio, found only static, switched it off. He drove south toward Dresden, then angled west to the small town of Meissen, where Mother had bought her porcelain figurines. He would find one for Lara; a dog, a setter, preferably. There was always a sequence to things.

After Mother's death, he had inherited the porcelain and the Solingen silver, some jewelry, and Mother's Walther, all of which had been confiscated a short while later by a plainclothes officer, a Chekist of some sort, his Potsdam Academy recruiter. He remembered with clarity the wet-dog smell of the man's leather jacket, the horizontal ridges in his fingernails, how he leaned both elbows on the kitchen table to punctuate his soliloquy on responsibility and choice.

With a sense of orderly decorum, Zeiger had collected and packed up his mother's things. "The figurines too?" he'd asked.

"It all belongs to the State," the man had said, sweeping his arm out in a gesture that included Zeiger, who sat on the edge of the bed on the other side of the room.

That same year, during his graduation ceremony at the Academy, Zeiger spotted this same man in the back rows of the audience alongside a woman with immense hair and a gerbil-like face. The charm bracelet dangling from her wrist, he was certain, was Mother's.

1.5

There was history in Meissen, tourist attractions. The village center was well kept and clean; a winding network of steep alleyways, half-timber house fronts, cafés with decorative flower arrangements cascading from sills. The parking lot was teeming with buses and cars. Zeiger had to drive slowly, yielding to groups of schoolchildren, middle-aged women with haircuts like helmets who clutched umbrellas and attraction brochures.

He parked at the far end of the square and stretched his limbs. Clean air was a luxury his body found hard to digest. He lit a cigarette and squinted up the hill toward Albrechtsburg Castle, where for more than two hundred years, all day, every day, even throughout both wars, porcelain had been produced. Glass and porcelain, iron and steel, some comforts were not bound to change. He walked toward the city center, navigating the narrow walkways, passing families with daytrip backpacks who meandered at a somnambulist pace. In time he found the alley, found the houses still leaning into the road like rows of swaying drunks. He hesitated for a moment, dropped his cigarette, then entered the porcelain shop.

He saw his neighbor immediately upon entering. There among the vitrines and display cases, the floor-to-ceiling shelves lit from within, was Schreibmüller, staring empty-eyed at a row of glazed plates. His presence was at once amazing and yet somehow foreseeable, as absurd as the coincidence of anyone's existence. Schreibmüller slanted his head at the sound of Zeiger's entrance, then refocused his clouded eyes into the space between them. He wore his regular uniform of very tight jeans, a turtleneck with a collar so high it grazed the lobes of his ears, and a slouchy tweed blazer with which student revolutionaries expressed their hard mental labor. His face confessed his real age. Wrinkles traveled like fractured glass from the corners of his eyes, lending him the wise and informed expression of gypsy seers, theologians, people married for many years.

Zeiger made his way to the center of the room, acutely aware of his body: its dank, human smell, the flutelike sound his nose made in the saturated silence. They were alone, he and his neighbor. Schreibmüller followed his movements with the angle of his head and a swift gesture, a small, spasmodic twitch. If he had recognized Zeiger, by his scent or the sound of his footsteps, he didn't let on.

A female shop clerk emerged from a side room, followed by another woman in heels. A customer, Schreibmüller's companion. The woman in heels picked a plate from the shelf and handed it to Schreibmüller, and the two began conversing quietly.

"Onion pattern," she said with a sharp Eastern lilt.

"Onion pattern," Schreibmüller repeated, clasping the plate with both hands.

"This isn't a museum," the shop clerk said, thrusting her face, rosacea-red, in front of Zeiger's, causing him to recoil. "What's it going to be?"

"What do you have?" Zeiger said, his voice low.

"Porcelain," the clerk said with irritation. "Personal, a gift?"

"A gift," Zeiger said.

"Wedding anniversary, birthday?"

"None of that."

"Just a little something?" the clerk said, and gestured at a vitrine full of tiny porcelain objects: painted thimbles, minuscule horse carriages, dollhouse furniture.

Zeiger sensed Schreibmüller move behind him.

"Neighing horses," Schreibmüller's companion said, and again Schreibmüller repeated the words.

"For a woman?" the clerk asked.

Zeiger further scanned the vitrine: turtles with hats and monocles, miniature Bremen town musicians, all slick and white and smooth like freshly licked teeth.

"Kissing couple," Schreibmüller said.

"How old is she?" the clerk said, when Zeiger still hadn't answered.

"Early twenties," Zeiger said.

"Your daughter?"

Zeiger said nothing. Why was he here? He turned away from the showcase.

"I think any girl would just love this one."

It was Schreibmüller's companion. She had moved in close, and her face now hovered mere centimeters away from the vitrine. She was pointing at something—a baby in a cradle? a kitten caught in a ball of yarn? She had a strong, unfeminine scent, heavy like motor oil. Despite her heels, her painted nails, she gave off an air of dishevelment, the disappointed aura of a woman all too aware that she too had once been a girl.

Schreibmüller, who stood behind her wearing a curious expression, asked what it was.

"An angel," the woman said.

"A standard Meissen figurine, a classic," the clerk added. "Quite popular."

"I'll take it," Schreibmüller said without hesitation.

"But Dieter, you shouldn't," the woman said, catching the clerk's eye with a look of flattered surprise.

"Don't be stupid," Schreibmüller said. "It's not for you." He gestured in the direction of the figurine, a remarkably accurate estimate of its placement in the vitrine. "Pack it up for me?"

The clerk extracted a set of keys from her pocket and unlocked the vitrine. The woman in heels crossed her arms and retreated to browse a nearby shelf with mock interest. Schreibmüller, unfazed, remained where he was, staring emptily at a space somewhere above Zeiger's head.

"I want this one," Zeiger whispered to the clerk, and pointed into the open showcase.

"And what is it you're getting for your girl?" Schreibmüller asked as his eyes circled and closed in on Zeiger's face.

Two men in a shop; strangers sharing a pedestrian moment. For an instant Zeiger wondered if Schreibmüller was truly blind, but then the light caught the man's eyes and shimmered over his irises like wedding veils, milky white.

"It's a dog," said Schreibmüller's companion from behind. "He picked a goddamn setter."

Outside, the woman took hold of Schreibmüller's elbow and guided him down the winding alley toward the main street. For a brief, delirious moment he considered following them, but something else caught his attention, a sudden shift in the air.

At the end of the street, just where Schreibmüller and his companion had turned, a scene was unfolding in which a crowd of people, too large for a group of holiday tourists, was progressing at an unnaturally swift pace and emitting grunts and whistles and chants, punctuated by sudden, aggressive lulls in the noise. Large banners made of bed linens floated like clouds overhead. FREEDOM!!! said one, with three exclamation points in red. TRAVEL REFORM NOT MASS EXODUS. A man wearing a visor and blinding-white tennis shoes hopped like a dancer ahead of the crowd, taking photos. Those too slow to keep up stood on the sidewalks with their fists raised in the air; the elderly, the disabled, disoriented tourists carried away by the cheers.

A chant, shrill and monotonous like a mad religious mantra, issued fantastically from the mouth of a girl about six years old propped high on her father's shoulders. "Stasi swine out!" she screeched at the policemen who stood gaping indecisively from the side of the road.

Mother had taken him as a child to see the mass rallies and speeches. Collective euphoria had always moved her to tears. *Wretched Nation!* was her favorite saying. *Barely free and you split yourself in two. Was misery not content with its good fortune?* It was a quote by Goethe that had turned out to be prophetic.

He slipped into a side street to circumvent the route of the protest. The porcelain setter weighed in his pocket like lead. The clerk had carefully padded and packed the item, then proposed a bow, decorative wrapping, and a brochure to go along with the box, all of which he had declined. He would have no nerve for a ceremonious unpacking of this figurine, which could mean only a waste of precious minutes with Lara.

He reached his car and was rolling out of the lot just as the first protesters trickled into the square. From behind the windshield, their whistles and stomps sounded dull and unthreatening. He wheeled past the girl. She had dismounted from her father's shoulders and stood straight-backed at the side of the road, her cherub face flushed with exertion.

The trip back unfolded without incident. Certain he would make it to Lara in time, he drove evenly, trancelike, back the way he had come, encountering only a handful of oncoming cars, no people, and one flock of crows that drifted aquatically across the blinding sky.

Zeiger, who had lived alone in his dank apartment for most of his adult life, had been flanked by many neighbors over the years: a woman of enormous size who soon married a man from Rostock and moved away; a nubile university student whose rotation of suitors left trails of ripe cologne in the halls; a man and his elderly mother who quarreled loudly and passionately well into the night; and then, eventually, Schreibmüller, whom he'd rarely ever spoken to and who had lived in the apartment next door for more than twenty years. But before Schreibmüller, there had been Johannes Held, and that's who he would tell Lara about.

For a very brief period in the late '60s, after Held had been recalled to Berlin from that institute in the Arizona desert and after those weeks of frequent, fruitless beatings by Ledermann's unit and their Russian, but before he was finally convicted and put away in St. Hedwig's mental ward, Management had moved Held into the apartment next to Zeiger's, and the two had become something like friends. Held was compliant, considerate, and preternaturally patient. He had a prominent overbite, which often caused his breath to erupt from his mouth laterally, with a sharp high-frequency hiss. His Adam's apple was so large it bulged from his throat like the heel of a sock. Seeing Zeiger as nothing but a pleasant neighbor, Held conversed with him respectfully, listened politely, bobbed his head and smiled benevolently as if at a rambling child. His kindness and inquisitiveness were so indiscriminate that Zeiger was never certain if Held truly grasped where he was.

From his weekly briefings with Ledermann, Zeiger had learned a few things about Held. The child of an alcoholic Austrian father and unschooled Silesian mother—both interned and terminated in the early '40s for Communist ties—Held had grown up at a boarding school outside Leipzig, where faculty took note of him as an eerily gifted child. Ledermann presented Zeiger with copies of Held's primary-school essays, which outlined in crude, infantile penmanship not only his plans to become the first man to walk on the moon, but also possible solutions to one of space travel's most stubborn obstacles—retrieving a capsule without setting it on fire. But it was the essay's last paragraph that Ledermann pointed out. Held, only nine or ten at the time, had suggested that the Allies should choose wisely which German scientists to capture and employ once the war was over. It wasn't the engineers and physicists who held the key to space, he advised, but the mechanics who knew how to build the carriers.

A few years after the war, Held, by then a young research fellow at a physics institute in Leipzig, was relocated to East Berlin's Technische Universität, where he studied a field far more curious than space—entanglements. Zeiger had not the slightest idea what that meant, though he didn't admit as much to Ledermann, who proceeded to recount, with a puzzled expression, how Held seemed to have no concept of the charges against him. These charges had not, of course, been explained to him explicitly, but the mere sight of those echoless interrogation chambers was usually enough to frighten even the most incorrigible prisoners into confessing. But no threat or beating had the desired effect on Held. (Even the otherwise imperturbable Russian hired for their sessions had been seen pacing the concrete courtyard, smoking combatively, mumbling into his fists.) Instead, day after day, Held took his seat at the interrogation table, grinning—eventually toothlessly—as if he were welcoming his hostile interlocutors to his own kitchen table. Zeiger and his new Manual, Management felt, promised a break in the case.

Throughout his interrogations, Held had insisted he knew nothing about how his American colleagues at the institute in the desert had made those boys disappear—nor, for that matter, whether something like teleportation could ever be real. But one night as the two men sat imbibing Mampe, before Held's final arrest, when they were just neighbors, Held had confided to him that *physics is faith* and *not much of anything can be either confirmed or denied.*

By the time Zeiger returned from Meissen, the city was dark. Thin fog clung to the streetlamps, paling their glow. He had time to spare. Without forethought, he stopped at the Konsum. *We're shopping all alone for Mutti at Konsum,* was the slogan forever lodged in his mind. The phrase occurred to him so often, looped so relentlessly through the bowels of his memory, that he wondered if, in the delirium of his deathbed, it would be the last he would ever say.

The supermarket was drenched in sharp blue light, the antiseptic, all-seeing glare of surgeons and morticians. He browsed the aisles, idled at the meat counter—white sausage, blood sausage, Ketwurst, a pasty pig's head with daisies stuck in its eyes—until the butcher appeared and told him to order or go. Zeiger walked toward the back of the store. The sweets section was empty, save for a few boxes of *Kalter Hund* cookies. He hesitated, then chose one.

As Zeiger waited in line at the register, the woman worked it with extraordinary slowness, taking great pleasure in peering over her glasses, locating each item's name, then lodging the information in a notebook on her counter. *Give small people power,* went the saying, *and you will learn who they are.* When it was at last Zeiger's turn, she took a moment to inspect the box of cookies. She held it in front of her face, examining it like an artifact of great historical value.

"These are expired," she said, matter-of-fact.

"By how long?" Zeiger asked.

"Two months."

"Are they moldy?"

"If anything, they're stale." She looked at him through the blurred edge of her bifocals as if bearing witness to the great philosophical conundrum she had just posed.

"I'll take them," Zeiger said.

The woman tallied him up, smiling approvingly.

Back in his Trabant, he rolled onto Oderberger Strasse, parked, and scrutinized the street, where streetlamps dotted the sidewalks, slicing through the darkness with cones of hazy, coal-speckled light. Though he had been all the way to Meissen and back, it would still be another half hour before Lara was released from her shift, perhaps ten minutes or so for her walk from the corner café to her home. Zeiger exited his car, approached her building with the nonchalance of a resident, felt his way up the lightless stairwell, placed himself in the corner of the landing above her door, and waited.

There were many things he needed to explain to Lara, things she should know. Because she had put a hand on his shoulder, indisputable proof that she knew he was there, that she knew he existed, that they breathed the same air. He patted his pocket for the setter in its box, tucked the *Kalter Hund* cookies into his jacket, then exited the car. There were three large empty trash containers in front of her building that he hadn't noticed, preparation for the remains of tomorrow's parade. The festivities had not yet started, but their grave was already made.

She would be frightened at the sight of him. He wouldn't blame her. He would be patient and kind. He would give her the present to open and the cookies to eat, and then he would have to tell her everything. Completeness was key; one could not tell one thing without the other. Mother and Father, his Manual days, his involvement in the conviction of the physicist Johannes Held. He would tell her that there was always a sequence to sin; that when people speak of evil they speak of it as if of free will. Misery was never content with its victories, not because it was greedy, but because it had no memory.

He waited and smoked. And if she asked *how,* and if she asked *why,* and if every *why* produced another *why?* Then he would tell her what Held had told the Russian during his last interrogation before his departure for St. Hedwig's, that *one should never forget people's need to transcend who they are.*

At last she arrived. Up came the chime of keys and the cry of old wood under footsteps. Then a brimming silence, Lara hesitating at her door.

It was Lara who broke the darkness with the sound of her voice. "Bernd Zeiger," she said. "I know you're there."

1.6

Today, one month later, it was the punk boy who stood in the middle of her room. Zeiger sat in the chair with Lara's file spread on his lap. He took his time closing it, then folded his hands on top for conclusive effect.

"Why?" the punk asked—the obvious question. His posture had something of a wilding warrior. He had widened his stance and flared his arms, suggesting imminent physical violence.

Zeiger studied the details, the cold air clinging to his clothes, the complete softness of his jaw. He was slender, his legs wiry, not quite as imposing as his outfit was aiming for. Then Zeiger sensed movement, a disturbance in the air. A second person entered, a girl, quite positively not Lara, but similar in age. She paused, stared stupidly, first at Zeiger, then at the punk. She too wore a leather jacket, men's size, and leggings speckled with a mix of very bright colors. She had done something to her hair so that it puffed up, balloon-like, around her pale face; a mystifying static accomplishment.

"What you standing there for forever and three days, close the curtains," the punk told the girl. "You know me and the light."

She moved to the window and pulled the curtains shut. The room was darkened now, not disagreeably so.

"You're here for Lara," the punk said.

The thickness of his inner-city vernacular hadn't registered during their encounter downstairs. It was a familiar and cruel language, riddled with resentment and ill-disguised fear. Zeiger had taken great pains to eliminate it from his own intonation long ago. He placed Lara's file on the floor beside his chair. He could feel the punk watching. The veil had been lifted and they were no longer two strangers in a stairwell; they were now two people with things to discuss. He wondered what the boy saw.

"I'm a family friend," Zeiger said.

"Want me to polish your face, old man? Lara doesn't have any family friends, does she."

The girl, who stood behind the punk, shook her head and crossed her arms.

The punk nudged his head back at the girl. "Her and I are Lara's family, we're her friends, and you're no friend of ours."

"I'm Bernd," Zeiger said. He lifted himself from the chair into a low squat, reached out, and offered his hand.

This the punk had not expected. He took a small step back and glared at Zeiger's hand as if at a weapon. "Careful there, don't want you falling," the punk said.

Zeiger, who was teetering, sat back in the chair, a maneuver that left him dizzy and breathless. Multicolored dots and a jumble of images like flipbook pictures bloomed in his head.

"I came here looking for Lara," the punk said. "Been coming here every day since the parade, hoping she would turn up. Every day for a month, and no Lara. But today, here you are."

"This is an official matter," Zeiger said.

"Don't make me laugh. If you're an official I'll eat a broom sideways. Two weeks ago, whole crew of them was here hunting her. Took us and questioned us for hours. Apparently it's weird for people to just disappear. They might jump the Wall or crawl through tunnels or get fake visas, but they don't go *bamf!* and vanish around here. It's like suicides, you know? In this country they don't exist. Or radioactive fallout from meltdowns. It's all just Western propaganda, is what they want us to believe."

The girl stared at the side of the punk's face, breathing through her open mouth. "Fallout," she repeated faintly, then returned her focus to Zeiger.

"I'd know if you were a gnat," the punk said.

"A what?"

"You know, something that gets on your nerves? That's what we call government assholes. Gnats. Catch up, *Alter.* I can spot one at ten kilometers against strong headwinds, and you're not one of them."

"Oh," was the only thing Zeiger could say. Then, "Why not?"

The punk relaxed, slackened his arms. He was in his element. A chance to declaim. He finally found a seat on the edge of the bed, propped his elbows on his knees, and took a deep breath into his hands—a professorial and parental posture often assumed by people with many unverifiable things to say. The girl sat down cross-legged on the floor below him and cocked her head in anticipation. She seemed to know what lay ahead.

"For starters," the punk began, "downstairs you had no idea what I was talking about when I told you about the contamination. Dead giveaway. Like it's never crossed your mind that the government may be poisoning us—correct that, *sedating* us—all of us, by letting us eat radioactive mushrooms and breathe this air. Any real government official would know all that for a fact. Sometimes

I can feel my own brain happening. I know you can too. Tell me that's not a symptom of deliberate meddling."

Surprisingly, coincidentally, and on many levels, this was true.

"And then look at you. Suit and tie and leather shoes? They come in jeans nowadays, to look more like us." The punk explained that he and Lara had gone to the Depeche Mode concert a while back, and that half of the audience had been officials in *obvious* disguise. Sure, the Ministry had let the band play in East Berlin, to pacify the masses, but it had then packed the audience with officials in jeans. "Did they think we had tomatoes on our eyes?" the punk asked, incredulous. "Anyone could spot them. They were all stone-cold sober!"

Zeiger shifted uncomfortably, smoothing his pants over his thighs. He had never owned a pair of jeans.

But the clearest disqualifier, according to the punk, who pointed his fingers like a pistol, was that Zeiger was really much too old.

At the Academy in Potsdam decades ago, Zeiger had attended the Mass Transport Logistics seminar taught by a certain Professor Konrad Eckhard von Feilenstein, a scholar of south German origin and vague professional past who rolled his *r*'s like machine-gun fire when unpleasantly aroused. Instead of the suits that younger professors wore, Professor von Feilenstein arrived, shuffling his gait, making eye contact with no one, in a coordinated outfit of forest-green trousers, socks, and shoes, and a polished Edelweiss pin, sometimes on the right, sometimes on the left side of his equally green knitted vest.

Von Feilenstein would begin each lecture reading indifferently from the notes on his desk, until something—a word, someone's face, a memory too private to comprehend—sparked a diatribe of explosive proportions. There was a waddle-like pouch under his chin that quivered when he screamed, a pattern of liver spots on the top of his head that turned deep purple. Sometimes he found fault in his students' ignorance; sometimes he lamented his own long-gone youth. Most of the time it was the absurdity of teaching itself, and the delusion that collective lunacy could be on the decline, that enraged the professor so thoroughly that people in the outside hallway cupped their ears to muffle the echo of his screams.

The man was prehistoric, an artifact long fossilized by layers of fresh blood. The students, including Zeiger, had viewed him with equal parts pity, awe, and respect for his cause. Only recently had Zeiger learned that Professor von Feilenstein, like many others of his professional past, had not supplied his expertise in mass transportation to the Potsdam Academy out of free will, and it was not until this moment, as the punk blathered to Zeiger about the preposterousness of his age, that it occurred to him that Professor von Feilenstein had not been quite as old as he'd thought back in those days.

Daylight filtered through the curtains with a tranquil, oriental glow. A soothing effect offering in utero comfort. Zeiger had by now established that the punk was unarmed, and in her very bright leggings and the bulky leather jacket that now lay next to her on the floor, the girl also had no place to hide a weapon of any concern. It was possible the pair was capable of preventing his departure by brute force, but he felt tired and happy to be seated, and he had no interest in testing the hypothesis. Much more worrisome was the speed at which the punk was speaking about matters that Zeiger could not quite comprehend. More rock concerts, officials in jeans, air-pollution levels, the occasional mention of Lara, safety protocols for reactors in the Ukraine and beyond.

"But even if I wasn't an expert in picking out Ministry personnel," the punk said, "and even if your age wasn't a problem, and the Ministry was some kind of paleontology institution instead of a cutting-edge, brainwashing authoritarian super-machine, it still wouldn't make a lick of difference."

"Sure wouldn't," the girl agreed, staring gloomily at Zeiger from her spot on the floor.

"Because Lara has vanished," the punk said. "And she's not coming back."

2

2.1

There in the half-shade of the landing above Lara's door, as he fixed himself against the damp wall, clenching his breath in the impotent illusion of escaping the sound of Lara's voice addressing him, the image of a face rolled like a marble through his memory and landed with a *clack* against the edge of his mind. His Academy recruiter, and there, impossibly, another one, his first supervisor at the Ministry, both as clean and complete as if they had never been entombed.

After the Academy had come his first Ministry placement. He had been paid a reasonable entry salary to analyze and re-summarize citizen-behavior reports for an Information Group subunit whose convoluted objective he'd never managed to penetrate. His desk was one of twenty in a low-ceilinged basement office that reeked of furnace oils and polyester perspiration, a room in which a vent at the far end did not replenish the air but merely stirred it with pained, human sighs. Members of the subunit were anonymous, and Zeiger never cared to know their names. By the time he came to rely on the appearance of a particular man's backside, or to study the predictable scratch of a neck, the bald patch that shimmered like a polished knee under the overhead lights, a similarly particular yet entirely unfamiliar man would take his place. It was only in passing that Zeiger collected rumors of a cleansing among the ranks. Exiles, executions, internments, hurt feelings over the counterrevolutionary coup attempt a few years earlier.

But it wasn't long until he, too, was greeted by a yellow slip lodged in the teeth of his typewriter. He was to report to his subunit's supervisor at his earliest convenience. Zeiger sat at his desk for the rest of the morning, guiding his breath, swallowing his saliva, pondering the meaning of a word like *convenience* in relation to one's own, now imminent, demise. At noon he rose, turned, and stood for a moment facing the aisle, until the man next to him, first by a twitch of his head, then by a gradual straightening of his back, began sensing this irregularity and shot Zeiger a look of alarm.

In the supervisor quarters, Zeiger sat stiff and numb-faced in the waiting room while a secretary frowned scandalously at the pages of a dime novel. A minute before, after he'd announced himself, she had blinked at him with such confusion that Zeiger had nearly retrieved the yellow slip as proof he'd been ordered to report, but then she pointed at the chairs for him to sit. With envy he watched her careless absorption in the drama of her novel, the taut muscles of her calves as they bounced one over the other under her desk, the completeness of her painted, not entirely becoming face. He imagined her a woman with a taste for whole-grain seeds, perhaps pumpernickel; someone nourished by the thick, earthy love of a father with whom she walked barefoot in summer across family-owned fields. She chewed the edge of a fingernail, and for the first time in his life, just moments before all was to end, he felt the urge to lay his head in such a woman's lap.

His recollection of the encounter that followed was thick and stylized, rendered in primary colors, and possibly trustworthy only as a composite of many such conversations he'd had over the years. When he entered the office, his supervisor was hunched over something, his fat forearms propped on the desk, his shoulders lifted around his neck like the high collar of an ancient queen. Behind him, a man Zeiger faintly recognized sat piously on a wooden chair, his hands splayed on his knees. Without raising his head from whatever he was reading, the supervisor gestured at a chair across his desk. As Zeiger sat he realized the man behind the supervisor was his recruiter, whom he had last seen at his Academy graduation and who was now gazing at him with passive, bovine eyes. The same man who had taken Mother's effects after her death. On the floor next to him, propped against the wall and hidden in the shade of the desk, was a garish painting of Stalin lifting his chin as if greeting a bright morning sun. His eyes were set somewhere beyond the scope of the frame, cast toward the boundless future, which at this moment contained Zeiger's own trivial existence. It was then that Zeiger noticed the two objects at the center of his supervisor's desk, spaced neatly as if for dramatic effect: Mother's Walther and Father's pin, grinning brightly from the open mouth of its black velvet box.

The supervisor spoke first. "How is it, Comrade Zeiger, that I have never heard your name?"

The man, while not bald, was sparsely haired, with a crop of blond bristles sprouting bravely from his scalp. This, for whatever reason, made Zeiger acutely aware that beneath his hair his own skull was covered only by a sliver of skin.

"It's quite an accomplishment," the supervisor was saying, "to be situated in this department without so much as having your name cross my desk at least once." He leaned back in his chair. "I don't even recall signing off on your placement here. The devil knows how you did that. How did you do that, Zeiger?"

"I can't be sure," he said.

"He can't be sure," the supervisor announced as if to a jury. "Did you hear that? Comrade Zeiger cannot be sure. Dry as a fart, this one. Quite seriously, now. How?"

The only explanation he could think of, Zeiger said, was that there had been some mistake in the paperwork.

"A mistake in the paperwork," the supervisor said. "Humble, too. Now *that's* what I'm talking about!" He smacked a gummy hand on the desk, and both Zeiger and the recruiter twitched in their seats.

A moment passed. Zeiger produced a meek, hopeful smile.

"Comrade Bernd Zeiger, I brought you here for a reason," the supervisor continued. "Let me describe to you something like a theoretical scenario. Hear me out," he said, raising a hand as if Zeiger had expressed a wish to speak. "Imagine you're married. Are you married? No, you're not, I did eventually find your file. But imagine you're married for, say, twenty-three years. Theoretically, of course. Twenty-three years with the same woman, a woman you met when you were both children—out in the countryside, playing cowboys and Indians. You understand me so far? Now imagine this wife of yours, theoretical wife, after twenty-three years of incessant bickering about you going to pubs after work, or, say, not coming home from work at all now and then, imagine that wife of yours leaves you for your cousin, let's call him Peter. What do you, Comrade Bernd Zeiger, think of this scenario?"

This was important. The recruiter had closed his eyes and was covering them with the palm of one hand.

"I think, Herr Comrade, that would be a scenario of moral depravity our late Comrade Stalin wouldn't have approved of," Zeiger tried, pointing at the portrait on the floor.

The supervisor puckered his lips, coughed with urgency into his fist.

"Whom I denounce, of course," Zeiger added quickly, "in the name of the Republic, of course."

"Right, comrade, quite right," the supervisor said, leaning in, "though it's not like all of it was so bad." Then an emptiness settled over the supervisor's face.

The silence ticked on for so long that Zeiger grew certain the conversation had come to an end. That mention of cowboys and Indians—he had a vision of himself. A child among children, many years ago, during the last months of the war, when more stray dogs than grown men had roamed the streets and not much else had kept people occupied besides starvation and sleep. One afternoon, as the neighborhood children congregated in a nearby lot, Kummer, whose mother had not yet murdered herself and her children, had arrived to announce the invention of a game. Dog's Choice, it was called. They captured the stray dogs, placed them in a parcourse built of rubble, and let them choose between one of two paths: one that led nowhere and a second that led to Kummer and the boys, who waited with hammers and rocks to kill the dogs dead. It was Nadine—now Ledermann's wife, a dying woman—quiet, chap-kneed, and determined at the time, who had separated herself from the group of girls screeching from the side-lines, marched toward Zeiger, and told him she would never speak to him again.

"Be that as it may," the supervisor finally reemerged, "we need not look to Comrade Stalin to recognize the moral depravity of such a scenario. Say this wife of yours leaves, takes everything you have, but also happens to be, say, the daughter of a prominent Party district manager. What is it you'd propose to do to set such a woman straight?"

"Nothing," Zeiger said. His legs, though firmly planted on the ground, had started shaking uncontrollably. He placed his hands on his knees in an effort to steady them. "Nothing, I mean, to the wife," he tried again. "It's the cousin, Paul, who should be taken to task."

"Peter," the supervisor corrected. "Go on."

Zeiger obeyed, but he wasn't listening to himself. With nonchalance the supervisor had produced an orange from the pocket of his sport coat, then begun operating on the fruit, first by digging the sharp edges of his fingernails into its dermis, then by methodically denuding it. Zeiger observed the procedure, mesmerized as if by a magic trick, his own voice distant static. He hadn't seen an orange in years.

"Interesting," the supervisor said when Zeiger finished. "Quite cunning. Yes, Peter's reputation. I had a feeling about you, Zeiger," he said. Then, with a gesture so violent that Zeiger gasped a lungful of air and the recruiter, again, jumped in his seat, the supervisor tossed the ravaged orange into the garbage bin beside him and leaned forward to catch Zeiger's eye. "I know who you are," he said. "I know the likes of you." He directed the tip of his index finger first at Zeiger, then at the Walther. "This Walther, see the eagle inspection stamp here? Comrade, this was a *Schutzstaffel* gun. And this"—his finger now hovered above Father's pin—"is a *Schutzstaffel* pin, SS."

"No," Zeiger protested, reaching toward the pin. "Just a panzer division. Nothing like that."

The supervisor picked up the box and extracted the pin. He held it up between thumb and forefinger, squinted at it as though inspecting a gem. "This pin is made for a cap," he said.

"I have done nothing," Zeiger said.

"His *SS* division is stamped on its back, you see."

But Zeiger couldn't see. The scene before him seemed to come to a halt. The supervisor turned into the light to reveal a hectic, snakelike artery pulsating on his throat; the recruiter, behind him, beheld the pin with the impartial look of someone who had deeper, more intimate concerns; and Zeiger, as if outside the moment, felt himself a porous and extinguishable being. This, he understood, was a body preparing for pain.

"As you may have noticed," the supervisor said, inserting the pin back into its box and glancing toward the recruiter, "we have this comrade here with us today. We had a bit of a conference about you. Estimate your suitability for this position, those types of things. That's when this comrade here, your recruiter, produced these things, told us about your parents, their political leanings. He voted against this promotion."

The recruiter, hands lodged between his knees, gaped at the floor with the stoic look of a death-row inmate.

"And now he wants to apologize. Apologize," the supervisor said, addressing the recruiter without looking at him.

"Sorry I took your things," the recruiter said, dispassionately.

"I don't understand," Zeiger said.

Father's pin box snapped like a joint in the supervisor's fist. He laid it next to Mother's Walther. Then, fanning his fingers, he pushed the objects slowly toward Zeiger's side of the desk. "These are your things," he said. "They're valuable. You're moving up the ladder, so no more secrets between us. You should have them back." When Zeiger made no attempt to retrieve them, he added, "Go on, Zeiger, take them, and don't look at me like that. For all we care around here, Hitler was from the West."

And thus he was promoted.

He was moved to a citizen behavior–modification unit staffed mainly by KGB exchange employees with a terrible habit of spontaneous singing, until finally he was tasked with the conception and development of the *Manual for Demoralization and Disintegration Procedures,* during which time he worked mostly in comfortable solitude, save for consultations with a St. Hedwig's psychiatrist named Witzbold, who was often either in a haze of confusion or nowhere to be found.

There was a scraping sound on the landing below. Pebbles under Lara's heel. "Hallo?" she said again, irritation and confusion in her voice.

The truth was, he regretted having come here. He stepped out of the shadow in the corner and into the dim, frosted light above her door. He looked down at her and she looked up at him. And that was it for a while. A neutral moment, simple and clean, as if agreed upon a long time ago, until suddenly Lara launched into motion. Her body contracted backward, and she began fumbling through her keychain, glancing up at Zeiger. She stabbed at the door lock with her key.

All this happened at once.

"I won't do anything," he said, but the words echoed feebly in the stairwell. He grasped the banister and lowered himself onto the steps in a manner he hoped appeared benign. He asked how she'd known he was there—how she knew his name.

Lara's key met with success and she slipped her hand through the door and turned on a switch inside. A sheet of light poured through the crack and sliced across her face. She squinted up into the darkness, her coiled lip exposing a row of thin, disordered teeth. Bad teeth, preposterous but charming. "You're at the café every day," she said in a defiant, mid-conversational tone. "And I saw the cigarette butts up there on the landing. Nobody lives up there anymore, and besides, nobody but someone like you could afford to smoke Cabinets."

He descended another step, then another, neighborly, casually. His legs did not feel like his own. "What do you mean, *someone like me?*"

"Watch out," Lara yelled, lunging forward, her arms spread wide.

Zeiger leveled himself just in time to catch the edge of the step. He windmilled his hand toward the banister, grazed it with his fingertips, but slipped, spilling like something boneless to the bottom of the steps. He rolled sideways at once and propped himself upright. He apologized, then tried to move, avoiding meeting the eyes of Lara, who stood very close to him, bent at the waist, her arms extended as if still hoping to catch him mid-fall.

A grotesque, helpless creature he was. Or so he read in Lara's face. In the light her grim face, bloodless and pristinely freckled, evinced an earnestness. Nothing about her was quite as soft-boned as he'd thought at the café. A canine tooth was caught behind her lower lip, adding a layer of dense apathy to her face. The limp copper strands of her bangs hung low into her eyelids, and they twitched when she blinked, which was often. This was Lara—tiny, filthy, somewhat profane. He had prepared himself for her revulsion, her girlish disgust. Sympathy he had not expected. He did not know where to look.

"By *someone like you* I mean people with good jobs, from good families," she said, and inched back again toward her door. "You're bleeding," she said, pointing at his face.

Zeiger touched the end of his nose. He was bleeding, not profusely, but steadily, though he didn't recall having hit it.

"Who knew you people could bleed?" Lara said.

Zeiger gazed at his wet fingertips. It had been years since he'd seen his own blood. Somewhere at the base of his skull a weakness unfolded, cold and light.

"Don't faint now, okay?" Lara said. She wore an acid-washed jean jacket, a thick men's knit sweater over black leggings that were faded and sagging at the knees, and white high-top tennis shoes and white tennis socks that glowed like moons in the dark. "Shit," he heard her say.

A moment later he somehow found himself sitting, knock-kneed and perspiring, in the low-angled chair at the foot of her bed. He was alone now. The room was drafty. In the far corner, a one-legged lamp spouted a cone of inconsequential light at the wall. Garments lay coiled and twisted on the ground, alongside papers and knick-knacks, jars without lids, small things with large shadows, and, on the floor before him, a toy *Monchhichi,* stiff and jug-eared, staring up at him with a look of crestfallen surprise.

Out in the kitchen a faucet gargled and sputtered, followed by the clanking of glassware and porcelain, someone at work, Lara at work. Briefly, hysterically, Zeiger attempted to reconstruct his last steps. He felt for the box, the porcelain setter in his jacket pocket. Whatever he had come here to do was, like all profound stupidity, irreversible.

Lara reemerged holding a towel, a glass of water, and a plate. She handed him the dish. "Sugar," she said. It was something she'd baked.

She seemed unsure of what to do next, but there was a meticulousness in her movements, how she bent over carefully to set the water on the floor next to his chair; the way she strangled the towel in her hands. *Strangled,* Zeiger thought, eating the cake she'd brought, because the slim, sharp edges of her knuckles were white. She took a step back and sideways, the same unnatural maneuvering with which he'd seen people bypass gangs of crows on the street.

She offered him the towel for his nose, unfolding it as she handed it to him. "It's silly, I know, with those chickens on it," she said, using the word *Hähnchen,* "but it's the only one I have."

Zeiger paused mid-chew. "Those aren't *Hähnchen,*" he said. "They're *Hühner.*"

"What's the difference? Both mean 'chicken.'"

"You only call it a *Hähnchen* when you're going to eat it."

"Is that so?" Lara said, a reckless laugh escaping her throat. "Maybe I'll start calling you *Berndchen* instead?" She hesitated only briefly before bunching the towel into a ball and tossing it into his lap.

Through the window a faint spray of rain glimmered orange in the ray of a streetlamp. The earth below sounded wet and dark, and the rhythm of tires on cobblestones was amplified. They were here now, alone and together, exactly what he'd wanted.

Lara folded her arms, extended her right leg, and tapped her foot like a dancer, pretending to wipe away a stain with her foot. "What is it you're doing here?" she asked him.

"I'm here to talk."

"I talk with you people all the time. Who's this about now?"

"This is nothing like that," Zeiger said. He set the plate on the floor and leaned forward. "It's about you."

"What did I do?" Lara's eyes widened. "I swear I've done nothing." She wiped a strand of hair from her forehead and tucked her hand back under her armpit in an apparent effort to conceal that it was shaking.

"That's right," Zeiger assured her. "You've done nothing."

"I must have done something."

"I have something for you," he said. He took hold of the box and dislodged it from his pocket.

"What the fuck is that?" Lara said, squinting as if he were holding the sun in his hands.

"It's nothing. It's just—" He slid open the top of the box, extracted the lump of paper and padding, and began clawing at the adhesive tape. Out of the corner of his eye he noticed Lara retreat. She stood a few paces away, at the head of the bed, her back turned to the black window, arms crossed over her chest. Zeiger placed the setter on his flat hand, turned its vague, welcoming face toward Lara, and lifted it up for her to see.

Stages of bewilderment washed across her face; she craned her neck. "Now that's nice," she said. "What is it?"

"A setter like Klaus's at the café."

She moved to snatch the figurine from his palm and pulled back toward the head of the bed. She held the setter with both hands, drew it close against her chest. Then she rotated it between her fingers, her jaw loose and slightly protruding, her lower lip limp and pink. There was wonder on her face, implausibly young.

"That's nice," she said at last.

"Turn it around," Zeiger said, pointing. "See what it says on the bottom."

"Meissen," she said.

"It's where my mother bought all her figurines."

Lara lowered herself onto the bed and it moaned softly under her negligible weight. "This is your mother's?"

"No, I bought it for you. But she had one just like it a long time ago."

"I like dogs," Lara said. "One of the Omas at the orphanage used to ask us what animal we wanted to be reborn as. She always said she'd like to be a hawk. Fly up high, go anywhere, see everything. Every time I see one, I think of her."

"You've seen hawks?" Zeiger asked.

Lara shrugged her slim shoulders and began listing the names of Brandenburg lakes, all of which Zeiger had visited and none of which were inhabited by hawks. Her tone suggested a new kind of ease, a lackluster babble, though she sat in profile and directed her monologue not at Zeiger but at the setter, still rotating it in her hands.

"So you believe we'll be reborn?" Zeiger asked. He smiled encouragingly at the side of her face.

"I do. I think whoever we are in life will make a difference when we go."

"That's not very hopeful for most."

"It is, though. Because it's not like those priests say, that you're either good or evil. I heard one talk about that over at Zion's Church. Before they let us have our concerts they make us sit through their sermons, you know. But I don't believe that, heaven and hell"—Lara shook her head vehemently—"good or evil, that kind of stuff."

"When you're as old as I am," Zeiger said, "you'll be more inclined to believe there's something to it."

Lara lifted her head, frowned at him. How did they get here? She seemed to detect something on his face, some friendliness, and she gave a twitch of a smile in return, and finally and with great distress the likeness struck him. It was Mother, staring through him over the kitchen table, her eyes as wet and swollen as if stung by bees, her slim mouth contorted into a terrible grin, her whole cadaverous face sagging, as though dripping like wax, over the shoebox-sized carton that had just arrived, holding Father's ashes.

"If people do evil things—" Zeiger started.

"Why, we have to forgive them," Lara said. "They just didn't know any better." She shoved aside a collection of trinkets on the coffee table, creating a space for the figurine setter, which she set down gingerly and pivoted its tiny face until the dog sat just right.

"If you died now," Zeiger said, "what would you become?"

"One of these," she said, pointing at the setter.

Part relief, part cheerful insanity, Zeiger leaned back in his chair and laughed. "I had a friend once who thought he was a dog," he said.

It was time to begin. He wanted to tell her everything: what had happened and what he was. The perfect confession—beginning, middle, and end. If he was dying, what would be left of him? His legacy, his life, would be nothing, wasted, a puff of hot breath on a windowpane. What hope was there but to leave this for her?

He would start with the Manual.

2.2

His collaboration with Dr. Witzbold on the conception of the Manual had been Management's idea. It was a sadistic match, as rude and unreasonable as if made by God himself. The order came late one night in the shape of a phone call to Zeiger's office during which Management informed him in a drafty, extraterrestrial voice of a certain Dr. Witzbold of St. Hedwig's hospital, a psychiatrist with whom he was to consult. The next day Zeiger went to the hospital, where he waited in a conference room, his paperwork laid out before him, for a meeting that had been quickly scheduled, until a woman with a cap like a paper ship on her head informed him that Witzbold would not be able to attend.

New meetings were called, phone calls were made. For several weeks Zeiger walked daily through the hardwood corridors of St. Hedwig's, side-eyeing open doors for a sign of the man and becoming quite familiar with the ward's square, smoke-yellow conference lounge: the swishing cadence of its coffee machine, the grimy, angular outline above the door where a cross had once hung. Witzbold had always just departed, had never arrived, or was otherwise engaged, until Management grew weary and Zeiger frightened, and he resolved to hunt the doctor down.

One day before dawn Zeiger dragged a chair in front of the staircase, placed his briefcase on his knees as a makeshift table for his conference-lounge coffee and home-buttered bun, and waited. Around 6:00, a morning-dazed patient appeared, holding a transparent sack filled to capacity with gold-colored liquid and attached by a tube to somewhere inside his terry cloth robe. As if on a quest to find the sack's rightful recipient, the patient lifted it like a trophy high above his head and, with a chicken-like gait, began pacing the hall. Soon a nurse appeared and guided him back to his room. The sack sloshed between them as they vanished down the corridor. The hallway remained quiet for the rest of the morning, save for the staircase, which occasionally deposited hospital personnel, nuns, and morose-looking loved ones with sad bouquets. But Witzbold did not appear.

In the late afternoon Zeiger removed his briefcase from his lap and with some effort began dragging the chair back to where he'd found it. When he passed one of the many narrow corridors lining the main hall, a flitting figure darted at the edge of his vision in a flash of white. Zeiger left the chair and retraced his steps, peeked into the corridor, and there, his squirrel-like back hunched with exertion, his arms pumping, the gauzy white rim of his hair fluttering in the wind, was Witzbold, waddling away at a strenuous pace.

Zeiger broke into a slow jog. By the time he caught up, Witzbold was huddled in front of a door, mumbling in frustration at an elaborate set of keys in his hands as he made a series of frantic attempts to unbolt the door. Witzbold was small, but wide. His belly, controlled under his belt, drooped together with his crotch like a pouch of curd.

"I don't want to hear it," the doctor said. "Heard it all, know it all, they explained everything. Don't want to hear a word from you."

"I've been sent—" Zeiger tried, but the doctor slashed a hand through the air.

"You're here to see insanity," he continued, his voice thick with spit. "Everyone needs to know: *What is insanity? Am I insane? Could I, one day, become insane? Are people I know insane? Is insanity the cause or the result of all this?* But what difference does it make? Let me tell you, this is insanity: not being given a choice."

"Part of the Manual's conception," Zeiger said, "is defining successful demoralization. Quantify it. Know when the job's been done."

Witzbold stuck a key into the lock, rattled it forcefully, then found that the door had been open all along. "How does one quantify insanity, Herr—?" And he cocked his head at the floor.

"Zeiger."

"Zeiger. Who is the judge and jury?"

"Ideally," Zeiger tried, "a competent system?"

"And are you competent?"

"I don't know."

"Do you know the difference between a gun and a grapefruit?"

"I assume I do."

"Then you meet the definition of competency these days. Saltines?" Witzbold said, producing a cellophane packet of crackers from his pocket.

"I don't think I . . ."

Witzbold leaned against the door, which opened to a short passageway. "Go on, then," he said.

They stepped into a clean, chlorine-scented room in which gray daylight screamed through a panel of windows. The walls were bare, the plastic floor polished. A small table was flanked by two chairs, one of which held a curiously bright assortment of toys. To their left, reclined in tranquility against the head of a metal-framed bed, sat a patient. Slim, ruddy, dusty blond, with a thick cable-knit sweater draped around his shoulders, the man looked as if he'd just returned from a hike in the Harz.

"This is Martin," Witzbold said, jovially, as if introducing friends at a pub. "Martin, this is a friendly colleague. He'll be listening in today."

"Of course," said Martin, his face brightening. He scanned Zeiger, sat up a little straighter, and folded his hands in his lap, preparing himself with the excitement of a child about to learn an elaborate game. In the harsh daylight his skin gave the impression of uncooked chicken.

Witzbold sank into a chair, rested his fat palms on his fat belly. Zeiger collected the pile of toys—a ruby-red ball, a frayed stuffed animal of indeterminate genus, a rattle of some sort—placed them on the table, and sat in the other chair. Martin and the doctor began chatting—a football score, the lunch selection, a nurse's incorrigibly philandering boyfriend—and even though Zeiger had avoided doctors all his life, abhorred the look of them, their condescending remove, their devastating notepads, their delicate fingers, he started to feel at ease. Witzbold's head, he noted, was the shape of an eggplant.

"It's your last day with us, Martin," Witzbold finally said. "Tell me, how do you feel?"

"Doctor, I feel fantastic." Then, glancing at Zeiger, he said, "Don't look at me like that, I don't bite," and he burst into laughter.

Witzbold joined in, a high-pitched cackle. "Who are you?" the doctor asked buoyantly, coaxing Martin into what appeared to be a practiced routine.

"I'm Martin!" Martin exclaimed.

"And what are you?"

"A person," he said, throwing his arms up in cheer.

"What are you not?" Witzbold said with a smile.

"A retriever."

"Good," Witzbold said.

Martin eased back onto his bed. There was a pause, a subtle shift. "I understand every last bit of it, Doctor. I'm not a retriever, and not any other type of dog, either."

Witzbold labored himself back to standing. Zeiger followed suit, rising from his chair and inching, like Witzbold, toward the door.

"And neither are you," Martin said, pointing at Zeiger and raising his eyebrows as if imparting the most important news.

"Let's not meet again," Witzbold said. He bowed one last time at Martin and funneled Zeiger back into the hallway, where he instructed him to return to Martin's room in one week's time, then escaped again into the cavernous ward.

Zeiger stood alone at the staircase, his nose watering, his head afloat in the ward's peculiar odors: the germicidal soaps, chilling coffee, and piss; the sad footnotes of safe, hygienic lunacy.

For Lara, here in her apartment, Zeiger had styled Martin as a distant acquaintance he'd visited at St. Hedwig's, omitting any mention of Witzbold.

"I knew a guy once who took a pill someone brought over from the other side," Lara said, in a teacherly tone, "and ended up thinking he lived between the wall and the wallpaper. Someone who knows he's not a dog is far from insane."

Zeiger's laughter died quickly and replaced itself with a dryness so clingy he reached for the water Lara had set at his feet.

"I shouldn't have said that," she said. "Pills from the other side."

"It's all right," Zeiger said. "By now I've heard it all."

"It was a British guy who brought it over, the same one who smuggled Die Toten Hosen over here to play at the church." Lara pulled up her legs, crossed them at the ankles, and sat blinking at Zeiger somewhat expectantly, her hands cupped in her lap. "Aren't you going to write that down?"

"I have no interest in that."

"I see," Lara said, stiff with confusion. After a silence, she asked him what had happened to his friend who knew he wasn't a dog.

"Not just any dog," Zeiger said. "A retriever."

When Zeiger returned to the ward at St. Hedwig's, a week after meeting Witzbold, he found no sign of the doctor, predictably. After pacing in wait for quite some time, he decided to try Martin's door. He'd hoped for the bed to have been stripped and scrubbed, for everything to be cleansed and quiet and sane. But when he peeked around the corner of the door, nothing had changed but the curtains, which were drawn, drenching the room in grave amber light. On the metal-frame bed, under the covers, curled and still like a corpse, lay Martin, his cable-knit sweater piled under his head. Zeiger stood motionless, gauging the option of escaping, noiselessly, back through the door.

Martin, choking, near pleading, spoke. "The doctor said you would come, so come."

His words prompted Zeiger to step forward, toward the foot of the bed. "We'd better wait for Dr. Witzbold," he said.

"The doctor just left. Told me I had to talk to you. Who the hell knows?"

Zeiger was afraid of disturbing whatever fragile psychic

equilibrium was keeping Martin coiled on his bed, but he moved closer.

"I was home for four days but came back," Martin said.

"I see."

"Even though there is nothing wrong with me."

"I'll let you sleep."

"I still know I'm not a dog, you know." Martin removed the covers, throwing them, impatiently, down the length of his legs, which were naked and nearly hairless under his paper hospital gown. "Not a retriever, not a terrier, pincher, collie, poodle, or whatever those mean-faced furry ones with those blue tongues are called."

"Pekingese," Zeiger tried.

"Chow Chows, I believe," Martin said, lying on his back.

Silence ensued, thick and inhospitable. The room was infused with substratal layers of noise: a murmur of voices caught in the walls; invisible water pipes tinkling like bells; moist, productive hacks in the courtyard below.

Martin wheezed heavily. "I'm a songwriter," he said. "I'm not just a nobody." And he rattled off a series of song titles: "My Wagon Has Four Tires," "Dance, Dolly, Dance," "We're Going Hiking Today," "I Hear the Soldiers Sing"...His voice trailed off, tapered into a hum. "Until one line, *Freedom, Freedom beyond Mortar and Stone,* and that was it for my writing career. That's not even what the line meant, but life has become very literal these days."

Zeiger asked him what it meant.

It was a metaphor, Martin said. The walls of our minds. Our hearts. "You wouldn't understand," he told Zeiger. "Nor does it matter now. They even scrapped my royalties, which I'm entitled to, as you know." He'd been forced to take a job at his father-in-law's paint shop, he said, but it turns out that fathers-in-law have big ears and even bigger mouths, and the man, who was originally from

Warsaw, had never liked Martin anyway. Then, eventually, his wife left him. He couldn't explain how it happened, but with his wife moving out and his friends staying away, and with his own brother telling him their mother didn't want him coming around anymore, Martin had something of a break. The next thing he knew, he said, he was here at St. Hedwig's, howling and pissing and eating dried tripe from a bowl on the floor.

Zeiger stood there with his chin in his hands, attempting to convey an air of professional regard as Martin gesticulated frenetically from his bed.

"I really, honestly, was convinced I was a retriever of some kind," Martin said. "That I liked to swim and fetch balls."

"Sometimes I feel like nobody is real," Zeiger offered.

"That's normal."

"It isn't to me."

"I've eaten dog shit I found on the street," Martin said.

"I once beat a dog with a rock till it died."

"A few months ago, at the Konsum, I bit into a woman's hand and didn't let go."

"But you said yourself you know you're not a dog," Zeiger said.

Martin grunted dismissively. He sat up in his bed, narrowed his eyes at Zeiger, let a full minute pass. Then he lifted a hand, pointed at the door, and whispered in a voice both worried and sly, "I know I'm not a dog and so do you. But the real question is, do the cats know that too?"

Lara's eyes grew wide, her mouth slowly, prettily unlatching. "You beat a dog till it died?" she said, and down the sleek slope of her nose she eyed the porcelain setter on the table.

Zeiger didn't answer. His back was crawling with sweat. He

removed his overcoat, glanced at Lara, and, seeing no hint of apprehension, folded it over the back of his chair.

He could not recall having spent more than a few minutes in the same room with Witzbold during the days of conceiving the Manual. The process had dragged on for months, years, throughout which Zeiger had begged the doctor for guidance with the pathetic urgency of a forlorn child. In return he received the occasional audience with patients such as Martin, convoluted case-study files, and textbooks as thick as bricks, all with little explanation on the part of Witzbold, whose aloofness and inconsistency produced in Zeiger both wounded attraction and homicidal fantasy.

Over time, Zeiger gleaned only the most rudimentary knowledge with which to standardize the Manual. A few years later, during his fateful involvement with the physicist Johannes Held, with the Manual at last complete and Management content, he came to realize that his knowledge had not by much exceeded the two things he understood upon exiting Martin's room that day: that something as trite as uncertainty would suffice in producing and maintaining an ailing psyche, and that insanity was a rather reserved state of mind, pedestrian and often banal, that could be classified as delusional only by those whose reality continued as agreed upon by all.

None of which he could convey to Lara, who had bounced quite suddenly from the bed and launched herself toward the door. Zeiger, reflexively and just in time, took hold of the sweet, sturdy bone of her wrist. He yanked her backward, harder than intended. Lara twisted around, wrenching her arm, and the two faced each other, staring in awe and confusion, as if something valuable had been dropped and now lay shattered on the floor.

"I wanted to get a bottle. I thought you might want some," Lara muttered, grasping her wrist. "I don't know why you're telling me these things."

"I'm sorry," Zeiger said.

"I promise I haven't done anything," she said, her voice breaking.

If there were tears in her eyes he couldn't detect them in the dim, aimless light.

She stood over him, small, proud, as erect as a sapling. "Matter of fact," she added, "I don't think you have either."

"Why?" Zeiger asked.

"I don't know," she said. "Just feels that way."

"You shouldn't trust people based on how you feel."

"Ha," Lara erupted, bending at the waist as if kicked. Her hair poured over her shoulder, covering the side of her face.

For an instant Zeiger feared she'd been injured, an invisible fist to her gut, but when she raised her head again, she was truly giggling, first breathlessly, then with a shrill piercing sound.

"Now if that isn't some fatherly advice," she said. "Trust is good, but control is better. Am I right?" Still laughing, shaking her copper hair, she disappeared into the kitchen, leaving Zeiger to stare into the cool darkness of the anteroom at the impossible entanglement of shoes and overcoats on the floor until they grew dim and muddled and seemed very far away.

When she returned, she looked tired, as if she'd been drained all at once of her elements. She moved sluggishly, her shoulders slightly hunched, as she set a bottle of schnapps and two tiny glasses on the table.

It occurred to Zeiger that she could have fled, and had she decided to run, he wouldn't have been able to catch her. She flopped back onto the bed and leaned against the wall, her knees tucked up high in front of her, and she kept them together like that, peering into the gloom.

"What about your family?" Zeiger asked.

In the dim light and deep shadows Lara flinched and for a moment betrayed a frown. "I have none," she said.

"No mother, no father?" Zeiger pressed.

Lara shook her head.

"I was an orphan when I was your age," he said.

"Really?" she said cautiously. "What happened to them?"

"One was killed by the war, the other by herself. Which is the same thing, if you think about it. Both were suicides."

Lara stretched out her legs on the bed, then bent forward, hinging at the hips, and took hold of her toes. An elegant, acrobatic motion designed for an audience. She yawned elaborately. "I used to think," she started, "that my father came to visit me at the orphanage. Lots of people came to look at us. We were looked at all the time, little zoo animals we were. Some would come and pick one of us for the day, take us somewhere. Even though we knew they weren't really our parents, when we were very small we always somehow believed they were. There was one guy in particular—"

—who, so Lara remembered, seemed to materialize out of nowhere every once in a while, just outside the fence of the orphanage play yard. He was dressed all in one color—monochrome, you'd call it—with dark hair that would have been disheveled had it not been combed and pomaded, and something like a sharp nose and sallow skin and sunken eyes, but he was always just a little too far away for her to see him clearly, and she'd never dared approach him, so she could never tell what he really looked like. In fair weather he'd stand there staring at her with his hands in his pants pockets, or, when it was winter, in his overcoat pockets, surrounded by a gentle white cloud of his own condensed breath. She never saw his hands, or at any rate she couldn't remember them, which was disturbing, and his presence always seemed to coincide with the discovery of something dead in the yard—a bird, a cat, a hedgehog with bleeding nostrils—but that may have been nothing more than childish superstition, because in truth the orphanage was always afflicted with filth, whether he was there or not. But she was sure, quite positive in fact, that he came there to look at her, specifically her; so whenever he appeared and the children huddled and pointed, cracking wise about how they'd heard he was a pervert or liked to catch children, skin them, and eat them alive, she would shush them or kick them in the shins, and tell them all proudly that it was her father who'd come to visit. Of course she had no evidence to support that notion, and he never came inside the fence, yet something about him seemed familiar. It was something she couldn't explain—quite literally she had no words to describe it—but his presence was, how should she put it, *scented* somehow.

"Scented?" Zeiger asked, trying hard to follow her.

"Scented," she repeated. "It was an electric smell, dusty, like static. Whenever he disappeared, which he always did very abruptly, it was gone."

2.3

Zeiger rose from his chair. The room quivered, just for an instant, like a heat shiver, a refraction of light. This wouldn't be easy, remembering everything in minute detail. But he felt warm and energized, absorbed and alive. He had prepared for this, he reminded himself as he paced—small circles, large circles—in front of her bed. He sat back in his chair. It was time. He paused to glance at Lara, who was watching him intently, her head angled and propped on one hand. Then he told her the story of Held.

At a certain time of the day, Johannes Held had explained to him in his apartment with mesmerizing calm, when the sun swallows all shadows and drenches those ancient dunes in sick, skeletal light, it is as if one can hear the desert howl in agony, an entity both dead and alive. He parachuted his arms out to his sides, nearly knocking the shot glass of Mampe from his armrest, then fixed Zeiger's face with the sincerity of grave inebriation. The Arizona desert, he continued in a hushed voice, is like a corpse underground, expired yet conscious with invisible life. Among the biblical creosote bushes and scorched shrubs, the armadillo carcasses strewn about like shipwrecked boats, and the taxa of blooming cacti one never thought existed in real life, a war is raging between massacre and birth; an anxious, unsolvable state of infernal ambivalence. "But really," Held said, "the heat just poaches your brains."

He downed his liquor. He had been at it all night, and now, as dawn approached, early-morning light illuminated the smoke between the two men in a cold and cheerless dance. Held looked depleted. Lack of sunshine, isolation, but as Zeiger understood, sliding halfway down the lounge chair on the opposite side of the seating arrangement, something more terminal—inoperable heartbreak.

It had been late in the spring of 1965, and for Zeiger the memory of this particular talk in Held's apartment was like a delicate specimen preserved behind glass. It was to be their last conversation, one final push. A Ministry meeting to discuss the results of these sessions was scheduled for the following day. Held had worn a thick, braided pullover in forest green that added girth to his otherwise dainty frame. It was the only pullover he'd ever seen Held wear, and the musty, mortal odor it emitted signaled he'd had no reason to wash in a while. Zeiger stretched out two fingers, prompting Held to toss a cigarette into his lap.

It had taken Zeiger only a few weeks of work to notice the particularly softening effect that hard liquor had on Held's tongue. Under prophylactic house arrest after his retrieval from the United States, these late nights were Held's only social engagement, save for regular interrogations at Hohenschönhausen, which of course didn't count. Every other night over the last several weeks, Zeiger had pounded their shared wall—an alert to Held that it would be him, his neighbor, about to ring his bell, and that it would be safe to open the door—then made his way over, wearing a pair of convincing paint-splattered overalls and holding a bottle of Mampe. It was a ritual that Zeiger took great comfort in, since their friendship, unbeknownst to Held, was otherwise closely monitored.

Held seemed to have accepted his house arrest as if he'd chosen it himself, never failing to greet Zeiger with a bow and a comradely smile. Even when his lids, bloodshot and blue from the beatings, struggled to open, even when the gaps in his teeth grew as wide and black as holes in the sky, Held was happy to receive the dull, proletariat neighbor he believed Zeiger to be.

With great effort, Zeiger hoisted himself upward and took hold of the bottle of Mampe that sat on the table. Held leaned forward, carefully pinching the end of the cigarette between his lips. Squinting a little, he offered his glass for the pour. Then the physicist shrank back into the folds of his couch. With one arm extended over the armrest, his lower lip shelving forward in sentimental absorption, Held gave the impression of an elderly man, a geezer awaiting a nurse's prophetic blood-pressure gauge.

"It is puzzling to me, the American desert," Zeiger said, gingerly, so as not to disrupt Held's confessional mood.

"Many things are puzzling, Bernd," Held said, staring into the gelatinous air above Zeiger's head. "Five-year plans and people buying items in bulk, matter-of-factly, rolls of toilet paper by the dozen, as if they were guaranteed to outlive such items. I'm a man of science, Bernd, but the day I was promoted to head the lab in Berlin, a crow dropped dead on my windowsill."

The Technische Universität's quantum-physics lab here in Berlin, Held explained, had not been exempt from the cleansings. Some scientists were purged, some were promoted, but unless you were shot in the face on the spot, it was hard to tell which of the two was happening to you. Of the ten taciturn fellows he'd worked with at TU, five were called in, never to return; four were moved to labs in other towns; and one was put on leave for bouts of insomnia—leaving only one, Held himself, to head the laboratory and the ten fresh pimple-faced research fellows culled from who knows where across the Eastern Bloc. He never asked for the promotion, nor did it add up, he being by far the most junior of the lot.

They were hard workers, his colleagues. Many of them weren't assigned vehicles, so lacking transportation they took to sleeping on cots in the labs. Despite the language barrier, a respectful, fraternal mood unfolded among them. And even though their exchanges could take quite heated turns, they were all limited, as far as Held's meager Russian, Hungarian, or Czech allowed him to discern, to the parameters of science, the passion they shared.

One of them, a certain Popov, presented Held with a clipping from the *Journal of International Scientific Discourse* advertising a fellowship placement at an American laboratory, somewhere in the Arizona desert, for researchers in the field of quantum entanglement. The implication seemed to be that one among them ought to apply. Held, unconvinced, tucked the clipping in his desk and nearly forgot about it until, a few days later, Popov returned and in so many gestures inquired about his decision. In the subsequent lab meeting that Held called, it was unanimously decided he should give it a try. A few months later, after the application process had long given way to more immediate concerns, a letter arrived. Out of hundreds of applicants the Americans had decided on Held. They'd even sent a check to cover travel expenses.

With the fellowship just six months away, Held began sorting his paperwork and designated an interim team leader—Popov, of course, a token of his gratitude—and everything seemed to be in order. But then the letters arrived, and calls from the dean, and visits from district committee members all advising him—imploring him, rather—to join the Party to secure his career. Although he was ambivalent about politics, he joined, thinking that would put an end to the bother. But then he was summoned to the Science and Technology Unit in the Ministry compound and he knew joining the Party had been just the beginning.

He was received at the Ministry by a colossal man, tanned like an outdoor athlete, unlike any scientist he'd ever seen, and two officers, both perplexed-looking fellows with unblinking eyes. They inquired about his research, his position at the lab; applauded his decision to join the Party at this point in time; then forced him to acknowledge the mistakes he had made. Just what mistakes, Held never knew, but he confessed and repented, and neither the tanned fellow nor his two owl-eyed friends requested anything more specific from him.

Then they gave him coffee and fed him fresh *Schweinsohren* and candy so tacky it stuck like cement to his teeth, and when the room fell silent and Held gathered his things, the three officers, smiling thinly as if there was a joke he'd missed, ordered him to sit and so he sat, and that's when they revealed their knowledge of his fellowship in the American desert.

Two weeks later he flew off to America. The Ministry's objective in supervising his placement, the periodic communications they had ordered, the detailed reports—the purpose of all of it would remain hazy to him until long after his return.

"Three months I was there," Held said, slack-mouthed. "You know what happens in science over the course of three months, Bernd?"

"Unthinkable things?"

"Nothing. Absolutely nothing happens in science over the course of three months. Life is quite a waste of time." Then Held seemed to rally with a glimmer of wakefulness. "Have you read much, Bernd? Our own poets, Georg Herwegh, comrades of that sort?"

Zeiger shook his head and cupped a hand against his face, concealing the hot flush rising in his cheeks.

Held waited a beat, averting his face, a gracious gesture, then asked if Zeiger would've been happier if he'd lived long ago.

Zeiger stirred in his chair, opened and closed his mouth a few times. He strained to find a response, his wet palm suctioning his cheek, and was quite relieved that the recording device Ledermann and his unit had stuck to his ribs had turned cold a long time ago. "I think I would've been doing the same thing," he said. "Trying at a better life, I assume."

"As would I," Held said. "As would we all. Something no book, poem, pamphlet, or Party member can change about people. Unless, of course, they somehow find a potion to make everyone content as they are." Held smiled and stared into his glass as if something quite comical were happening inside it.

Upon his arrival in the U.S., Held was picked up at the airport by a fat young man who talked so rapidly that his splendid American jaw should have unscrewed right off his face. He drove Held first through a flat, people-less city—a toy town, inappropriately colored for the dwelling place of adult human beings—then beyond city limits and into the desert. About two hours later they sloped around the bend of a steep, brush-riddled peak, behind which Held spotted the institute floating with the calm of an iceberg in the sprawling sea of dust and dirt. It was a small compound, all things considered, comprising only three faux-adobe buildings, one of which had a telescope dome attached like a tit to its side. The place was the whitest thing he'd ever seen, a fierce, eye-splitting white, and also the most desolate. The small workforce at the institute would turn out to be a shy and shade-loving people.

The fat American led him down a pathway behind the main building complex and on to a row of bungalow-style housing units, all as white as sugar and fronted by two identical entrance doors. His apartment, though a square, sparsely furnished one-bedroom, was larger than any home Held had ever called his own. There was a sofa unit and beechwood coffee table of shaky American make, a heavy door that seemed to connect his unit to the apartment next door, three thick porcelain cups in the cupboard, a coffee machine, and a pouch of ground coffee. The American pointed at the bed and said "Queen." Held stared at the crude floral bedding, wondering what, if anything, American sleep had to do with monarchies, then followed the man from the kitchen unit into the bathroom. The American turned on the faucet, let the water run, and shot Held a meaningful look. Unsure what was expected of him, Held arched his eyebrows in marvel, which pleased the American, who handed him a schedule and took his leave.

As soon as he was alone, Held tried the adjoining door. It was locked. He removed his shoes and, for quite some time, stood barefoot in the middle of his living room. He lifted his left foot, then his right, sensing the soft, synthetic carpet bulge between his toes. Fierce and sudden nightfall drenched the room in interstellar dark. It wasn't until a faint knock and scrape came from the apartment next door that he was certain he'd not been hurled into space to die a lonely, lunar death.

He woke before dawn. The coffee machine looked complicated and he did not dare touch it. Tentatively, he opened the pouch of coffee and inhaled. Once, twice, a third time. He lifted the curtain and squinted into the vast and empty distance, where morning sunlight oozed like egg yolk along the edge of the sky.

It was on his way to the cafeteria—a small x in the hand-drawn map on the back of his schedule—that he saw the first child: a tiny figure no more than one meter ten in height, flitting with bobbing strides in the shade of a building that flanked the path, until it disappeared around a corner and out of sight. Perhaps he was imagining things. He paused and lifted his hand to shield his eyes. He pivoted slowly on his heel, scanned the path, the strips of bland desert dirt along the buildings, and turned back just in time to catch a second figure, even smaller than the first, dashing with small, speedy steps through the shade. This was a child, no doubt about it, a boy no older than four, his hair a mop of tousled black curls. He too bolted around the corner and disappeared.

Held traced the boy's steps along the wall and peeked around the corner. The building was set at the edge of a dune opening onto a shallow, bone-colored valley punctuated by spikes of spindly cacti. Treacherous terrain, reptilian territory. At the bottom of the slope, not a hundred meters off, impossibly, a gaggle of five boys huddled together over something on the ground. Some were crouching while others, wielding long crooked sticks, were jabbing at an object in their midst. They did not notice Held, and for a moment he had the urge to shout. Had they never heard of coyotes? Had their negligent parents never read them Karl May's novels about Winnetou's desert adventures and the vicious fauna he braved?

Held took a step forward, but just as he was about to call out, one of the boys, hectically and somewhat robotically, began stomping the earth. One after the other the boys followed suit, until all of them were trampling the ground, throwing their arms about, and shrieking and laughing in a terrifying dance. Then the first black-haired boy Held had noticed—all of them, he now discerned, were black-haired and golden-skinned, like tiny Aztec icons—picked up a rock, lifted it with both hands high over his head, and let it crash to the ground with a *crack*. As quickly as the commotion had started it came to an end, and the boys dispersed, darting like startled chicks up the slope and into the grounds of the complex. Held descended, unsteadily navigating the mounds of brittle stone, until he reached the abandoned spot, where, next to a rock about the size of his own head, the sleek, broken tail of a rat twitched as if still alive.

He arrived at the cafeteria fatigued and nauseated. The space was enormous, polished, and dentally white, divided by rows of steel tables, one of which was occupied by a small group of people. Three vents as large and round as airplane turbines blasted arctic air from the ceiling, adding a morgue-like chill. With unexpected embarrassment Held noticed that he was the only one not wearing a sweater.

There were five of them, four men and one woman, and by the time Held approached the table, all of them had dropped their utensils and risen to greet him. They bowed and shook his hand, exuberant, seemingly genuinely happy to see him, and Held was reminded of people he'd encountered—in doctors' offices, in Ministry foyers, at music recitals—who'd been stuck waiting together for something vaguely unpleasant.

"Hungarian?" asked one man, plump, with a nondescript feminine face, dressed in a plush tan pullover that was shedding hair. "Scottish?"

"German," Held said. "East Berlin."

"Ah," the group howled, throwing up their arms.

"You see," the man said, "they told us there was one Hungarian on the list, one Scot, and one man from East Berlin. We made bets about which one would actually show up, and only one of us said it'd be you." He pointed across the table at the woman.

She was wrapped in an indigenous-looking poncho, brightly striped in turquoise and pink. She uncurled a small hand and extended it to Held. Her face was so pale it looked to have been emptied of blood. "Katja, thermodynamics," she said, adding quietly, "East or West, it doesn't matter. German either way—and so reliable that clocks have been set after us."

"Doomsday clocks," said another of the men, Austrian by the look of his collarless, wood-buttoned cardigan. Hook-nosed and corpulent, he was the oldest of the group.

"I'm from Munich," Katja said, smiling.

Held shook her hand. In the brutal halogen light, her hair showed traces of chestnut red.

The Austrian appeared unimpressed by the addition of Held. He remained silent, intently concerned with his food.

The other two men, Jan and Herman, were Dutch, both as tall and slim and white as flagpoles. They resumed a discussion that, in their strangled tongue, sounded like a vicious quarrel.

It was Rodolfo—Italian, he clarified—in the shedding pullover, who told Held to sit. "Long way from home. Very hot here, very dry," he said without looking up from his tray. "Vultures every-where. They always seem to know something about you that you don't. The food here—how should I say?—is something we feed our dogs from cans. Very much gelatin."

Held mentioned the cold.

"It's always cold inside," Rodolfo said. "Like they're penguins or something. Bring a sweater. Good work, though, very much free-dom." Rodolfo looked as though he was about to say more, then paused to ask Held whether he'd seen them.

Yes, he'd seen them, Held was about to say—the children, their horrific dance. What were they doing here with no adult in sight? Here, in a murderous desert that would swallow them whole?

Before he could speak, a woman in a hairnet appeared and set a tray before him.

"An American," Rodolfo pressed. "Have you seen one?"

He'd been picked up from the airport by one, Held said.

"That's nobody," Rodolfo said. "A low-level American. I mean the real Americans, the team."

Held conceded that he hadn't. It struck him now that the cafeteria was empty, save for the six of them, foreigners in sweaters.

"Neither have we," Rodolfo said.

"That's not exactly true," Katja said.

"What she means," Rodolfo said, his voice low, "is that we see them sometimes, in the distance, bolting across the dunes in their Jeeps. We think there must be some off-site compound they don't want us to see."

Abruptly, with the vigor of a pub-hall drunk, the Austrian shoved his tray aside and pointed his fork at Held. "You," he shouted across the table, narrowing his eyes as if deciphering small print. "I ask you, in your own biased, indoctrinated opinion, what is the biggest difference between these Americans and us?"

Jan and Herman fell silent. Katja's lips, faint in profile, settled into a sour, omniscient smile.

"These Americans here, specifically?" Held asked, lightly.

"All of them, the American psyche versus ours."

"Historically, there are obviously—"

"Historically, please," the Austrian growled. "They have no monarchy to mourn. Sure, what else is new, *the sky is blue*? I mean emotionally, spiritually. What's the difference?"

Held sought Rodolfo's face, but the Italian, evading his gaze, was applying himself to arranging the rinds of a nectarine on his tray.

"Imagination!" the Austrian bellowed. "What we lack—or rather, has been beaten out of us—these people practice as a religion. Look at that land they built. A whole land dedicated to a mouse. Imagine!"

"Disneyland, in California," Katja whispered, leaning in close to Held.

"If it can be imagined," the Austrian caterwauled, "here it shall become reality. They could, for example, and probably will—why not?—exchange their entire government for speaking bonobos. Why? Because if they already thought it possible to colonize us, or to invent a bomb vicious enough to darken our skies, or endless soda fountains and self-made men, or a pill that ends all procreation, why not teach bonobos to speak and let them lead the government?" He glared and thrust his neck forward, making the hawklike hook of his nose even more pronounced. He had long stopped orating only to Held and was addressing the room. "But imagination is, what was the term?"

"A self-destructing system," Rodolfo offered under his breath.

"Yes!" the Austrian exclaimed. "Bless Kaiser Franz Joseph. An empire, neither fish nor fowl, but healthy, skeptical, and morally sound, obliterated by the childish imagination of a few. Done with *Bildung, a wholesome education,* they said. Or you"—he gestured toward Katja and Held—"look what one of your men's imagination brought you in the end. And don't start with me, Rodolfo, the *Führer* wasn't one of ours."

"They prohibited the consumption of alcoholic beverages on site," Katja whispered to Held. "One of their arbitrary rules. We've observed some sentimental leanings in Hans since then."

"We're done with imagination," Hans continued. "It's been scorched, bombed, and raped out of our silly minds. And I say let it stay that way, let us never again underestimate the perversion of possibility. Let us now sit back and watch how the great American empire imagines itself into its own personal oblivion!" Hans's last note echoed through the cafeteria as if through an empty barrel. He looked around, startled, seemingly only now becoming aware of his silent audience. He lifted himself, revealing for the first time a cane at his side, and stalked, one leg dragging, toward the door. "And let me tell you directly, you, what should we call you?" Hans yelled back across the cafeteria at Held. "*Comrade.* Our comrade over there. These Americans trust us about as much as we trust them. That's why we're here and they're over there. We're nothing but pawns in their lethal imaginings and God only knows what for."

It was Katja who offered to direct Held to his office. As soon as they stepped outside, she wiggled out of her poncho, swiftly and effortlessly, like a snake exfoliating its skin, then set off down the narrow path at such speed that Held had to jog to keep up. She stayed close to the buildings, avoiding patches of sun, and steered away from the paved pathways, along the backs of buildings, where the heat glimmered like water among the desert slopes. Absent the poncho, Katja's body looked childlike, her naked arms like two chicken wings gnawed to the bone. The back of her neck was covered with a sheet of translucent freckles so dense it resembled a tan. The two of them angled around a corner, and just as Held darted after Katja into the building, there, topping a bald hill, were the five boys, waving at him as if he were one of their own.

"I burn in the sun. I have to move fast," Katja said, not the least out of breath.

She ushered him down a bland, frigid hallway and pointed him into an office. It was windowless and sparsely equipped with nothing more than a desk and chair, a filing cabinet, and one dim light attached to, but not quite centered in, the ceiling. The piercing stench of pipe smoke hung in the air like an abandoned soul.

"It's all on there," Katja said, gesturing at a slip of paper on the desk as she backed out the door. "It's all any of us got as to instructions. It's a comfortable life. A paid vacation in charred paradise. Don't mind Hans, he's a monarchist."

"On my way to the cafeteria," Held mumbled, "and just now, I saw, I don't know what I saw, there were..."

But Katja had already made her way down the corridor.

The instructions, as she'd suggested, were simple, outlined by hand on graph paper. Held was to perform, record, and supply his calculations daily, the contents of which would be defined as needed through written correspondence to be found on his desk. There were apologies for any disappointment as to the lack of equipment they could provide for applied-theorem tests. He was invited to eat liberally, socialize freely, and meditate with abandon on the sublime natural beauty of the desert grounds. The signature was ornate and illegible.

Held, gripping the paper with both hands, let himself sink into the chair. A lightness that he could not name overcame him, and suddenly he had little recollection of how he'd come to be sitting in this place, so many unthinkable miles from a home to which nothing and nobody could force him to return. He performed his calculations, placed them on his desk, and left his office around twilight. He walked at a leisurely pace, stopping occasionally to gaze into the brainlike face of a succulent blooming along the winding path. He spotted first one and then dozens of small, algae-colored lizards flitting among the gravel or basking atop stones, pumping their tiny forearms in calisthenic exercise. Colorless shade had descended among the dunes, along with a chill, the desert's macabre nighttime breath.

He was veering toward the dormitory path when a movement to his side, something aflutter, made him pause and inspect the deepening shade, where two birds as large and black as hunting dogs were looking back at him. Held could describe what followed only as a brief moment of mutual regard. The vultures, cocking their stupid arrowed heads, peered at him lidlessly and with a degree of sadness, causing Held to do the same. Just then a shriek interrupted his reverie, and from behind a far corner the boys came charging, laughing hoarsely and flailing their arms. Some tilted around him to his right, some to his left.

"You!" he yelled. "Hey, you!" And he reached to grab a collar, something, an arm, but none of them paid him any mind. When he looked again into the darker shade, the vultures had noiselessly fled.

"They're Mexican, they don't speak English," someone said behind him.

Held turned, coming face-to-face with Hans, who had propped himself nonchalantly on his cane not a meter behind Held. "Why?" was all he could think to ask.

Hans lifted his cane, beckoning him. "We walk together," he said, and they began to walk, silently at first, keeping their eyes on the ground. Then, with a smile in his voice, Hans said, "Entanglement. *Spooky action at a distance* some call it, am I right?"

"It's become quite a catchphrase," Held acknowledged.

Was it the position of Held's field, quantum mechanics, Hans wanted to know, that an object, whether micro or macro, exists in various states at once? That it's both a wave and a particle, or a combination of the two, and its actual properties merely a set of possibilities?

"That's our assumption, yes," Held said.

"Until the object is observed," Hans said, "at which point it collapses into something definite? Meaning, one couldn't observe or, say, copy and transmit an object without, at the same time—"

"—disturbing its natural state and thus destroying some of the information it contained," Held said. "Correct."

"But that's where you come in," Hans said, and gestured his cane toward a cactus at the side of the path.

"Technically," Held said. It was true, for example, that when an object A and an object B were made to interact, their information transferred from one to the other. Just what information no one knew, but from that point forward, even when those two objects were kilometers apart, whatever was done to object A was registered also in object B. "They have been, as we say, entangled."

"Spooky," Hans said.

"Mathematics," Held countered.

They had passed the dormitories and, after turning a corner, found themselves at the foot of the colossal telescope dome. Hans stopped, knocked its hollow side with his cane. They raised their heads up the length of its body and toward its bulbous tip, where the last rays of sunset had gathered in red, smoldering heat. They stood for a while, craning their necks.

"What I said this morning is, of course, all humbug," Hans said. "Without imagination, what would there be? Evolution: imagination. Love: imagination. The miracle of conception: pure cellular imagination. I like to get a rise out of that group. That's my place. You'd better start thinking of what yours ought to be."

He scrunched the sun-molten folds of his eyes, and they embarked again along the path, strolling as twilight turned into darkness, the desert dunes beyond the buildings a cold, galactic black. A row of gnomelike electrical torches twitched to life along the edge of the path, dimly lighting their way. There was calm in the silence of the two men, but also shared bewilderment, the quiet perplexity that Held remembered only from childhood, when the thought of an impenetrable vastness, the gnarled textures of untouched moons, was still capable of arresting his mind.

When they returned to their dormitory lane, Hans paused and rested his hands on his cane, some grim realization clouding his face. Scowling into an undefined distance, he said, "Object A is now entangled with object B. Consequently, if one would copy, transmit, and thus destroy parts of object A, one could use object B to transmit its remaining information, as gleaned from their entanglement, thus completing the object's transfer in its entirety, is that not so?"

"Theoretically."

Hans was a geophysicist, he said. Radiometry. He'd come here on a grant to study radiant energy. Atmospheric gases, greenhouse gases, various wavelengths of the sun's rays. There were plenty of those around here. But that wasn't the kind of radiant energy the Americans seemed to be interested in, he said with a glare.

They peered up again together into a flat sky punctured by stars.

"And you?" Hans asked. "Your entanglement research, what is it for?"

"For theory," Held said. "A thought experiment." Seeing no reaction on Hans's face, he added, "Computing and telecommunication."

"Teleportation," Hans said.

Held had to laugh, a meek snort. He waited for Hans to join in, but the geophysicist remained quiet and merely nodded at the sky in a grave manner, as if something calamitous and long-awaited were finally hurtling their way.

"The sky," Hans said, without elaboration.

The two men stood like this, in humorless stillness, until they bid each other good night.

Back in his apartment, Held found that the refrigerator had been stocked with blocks of cheese, an iridescent orange, and a loaf of seedless bread, which he ate standing and without much appetite from a pristine plate. The refrigerator whirred, whispered like a person, then fell silent. Despite the dark, the curtains had been drawn. His bed had been made, tucked in tightly on all four sides, and a glass of water stood on the nightstand along the right, the side on which he'd slept. It crossed his mind to sort his things. But he opened the lamella-door closet to the discovery that his personal effects had already been sorted and his clothes folded and stacked among the shelves. With some effort he untucked the sheets, then peered at the glass of water until he dropped off to sleep.

It must have been long past midnight when he seized awake at an unfamiliar sound. He strained his eyes into the darkness and waited. Something had happened. He searched for his limbs, stiff and knotted among the intricate layers of sheets. That hum was the refrigerator. That purr, the monstrous appliance attached to the window exhaling insufferable heat. Then the sound came again, a *click,* the adjoining door closing. The darkness was luminous, charged now with meaning. Held had often imagined a nighttime intruder, a pulsing black contour at the end of his bed. His visions had entailed room for reasoning with the person, a touching moment of shared humanity, or else swift and efficient violence, an object, heavy and blunt, thrust into the faceless dark. But this was paralysis.

The noise that followed was soft, like a fist kneading wool. Footsteps grazed rather than touched the ground, and then an outline materialized. Slim and hunched, it stood by the door, where it seemed to hesitate for a moment. Not viciously, not intently, but sideways and with clear reluctance it stepped forward and paused at the side of the bed. By the sharp angles, the long, witchlike bend in her neck, it was Katja. She bent over, her small bare breasts adangle. Calmly, mechanically, she pushed aside the covers and positioned herself next to Held. Her naked body radiated cool and damp, like a gust of cellar air.

He did not dare turn his head. Then his throat emitted something awful, something strangled, cracking the silence, and Katja jerked forward with a flash of loose, light hair, her skeletal shoulder piercing his ribs. Her lips, hard and dry and heavy, first pecked, then suctioned, seeking his mouth, and it wasn't until she grabbed hold of him, yanked and pumped, as furious as a frustrated child, that his own body stirred.

Despite his growing discomfort, there was nothing for Zeiger to do but let Held go on. The living room had lightened considerably, conveying an atmosphere of easy cheer. With the bottle of Mampe long since killed, Held had interrupted his story, disappeared into the kitchen, and returned now with a tin pitcher of coffee. They split an old bun between them.

"They do feed me," Held said, chewing methodically. "Bring food every day. Should show up any moment now."

"They want you alive," Zeiger said. "I hear they can be quite hospitable when they need someone."

"What do you know about them?"

Zeiger thought for a moment, softening the bun in his mouth.

"No," Held continued, "never mind. We all know more about them than we'd like to. I've kept you all night. It's a workday."

"It's a Sunday."

Held bobbed his head, eyes glazing. "Sunday," he said. He stopped chewing, stared out the window in absorption, as if only now understanding a pertinent truth about the sky.

"Is it true?" Zeiger asked.

"Not many things are true," Held said.

"What you said before, about those Americans and teleportation."

"What do you know about teleporting?"

"Nothing."

Even now Zeiger could see in Held's face the remnants of a strong and weathering sun. His complexion was the unnatural color of cod-liver oil. Held stripped off his shoes, stretched his legs, wiggled his toes, and inspected his socks. Then, with a competent and faraway look, he rose and advanced toward the window, his back to Zeiger.

"What have we gone and done with that Wall?" he said.

"Keep people out," Zeiger said.

"And people in. Between us, I don't care. Go ahead, build a Wall. Wire the entire Harz woods with spring guns. Set up odor-sample cans for every last citizen, see how they stink." Held's silhouette convulsed, a silent laugh. "They think they're in this to learn about teleportation. I mean, think about it, can you imagine the exodus? *Poof* "—he hurtled his arms out in a mock explosion—"and thousands of citizens vanish. See how a Wall holds up against that."

"You're saying this will happen?" Zeiger said. "It's possible?" He could sense the room brighten with cellular clarity.

"You're missing the point," Held said, turning. Against the window, his face was black and illegible. "Everyone's missing the point. They worry about teleportation, but it's something far more common. People's penchant for dying. Something as trite as imagination. The root of alcoholism. The need for procreation. The feeling of regret. Love. What do all these things have in common?"

Zeiger sat motionless.

"It's a semantic issue," Held said. "People don't want teleportation. They want transcendence."

Zeiger stared for a while at Held's indecipherable face. His ears were backlit, like two pink sunsets. Calmly, evenly, as if outside himself, Zeiger said: "You can teleport people?"

Held returned to his story.

Days passed in the desert like infernal clockwork, monotonous, mucinous, hot. As night fell the sky snapped from deafening blue to darkness by the switch of some heartless mechanical hand. Mornings were spent in the cafeteria, where the only attendant, a rotund middle-aged woman with fried hair, set their trays and cleared them, acknowledging them with mute, conspicuous stares. Like schoolboys, like prisoners of war, the group breakfasted in silence, each absorbed in private astonishment. After their late-night walk, Hans had grown quiet. Jan and Herman didn't whisper in Dutch. Katja kept to herself. Even Rodolfo, though with visible effort and after a delightful greeting, refrained from whatever he might have to say. Held had learned to bring a sweater.

One nondescript morning they passed among them a flyer that had been left on the cafeteria table. A shuttle had been organized for a trip into town, where they had been invited to purchase necessities, get a haircut, pay a visit to the Apache museum. Later that afternoon, they convened at the compound's entrance rondelle and waited, silent but skittish and somewhat disconcerted by the irregularity of this plan, but the shuttle never appeared and they dispersed again into the compound, all of them into their own monastic cell.

The mathematics on which Held was working had grown intricate and convoluted, with little applied purpose. Only occasionally did Held deduce a vague relation to equations he'd delivered in the days before, but any connection seemed far-fetched and tangled, and despite his best efforts he could not conceive just what the equations were for. Reflexively and with little aspiration, he performed his daily tasks and placed them on his desk. Then, with equal dispassion, he fashioned his secret dispatches to the Science and Technology Unit at home. After conveying in detail the utter lack of anything to report, he addressed the envelope to a paint shop in West Berlin, and dropped it in the ground-floor mailbox.

With nothing left to do, he strolled the compound, encountering nobody but an audience of bereaved-looking vultures. The occasional abandoned sock, a rock tied with string, or a browning apple core alerted him to the boys' presence, and sometimes, there in the shade of an overgrown portico, he spotted them, all five of them, thrashing about in a semicircle, consumed by savage play.

But Held did not puzzle over time's odd amalgamation, nor could he worry about the boys. Something else, something quite alarming, had started to take place. He roamed the grounds for hours, alone and unobserved, each step among the bleached stones a ridiculous revelation. Once in a while he would stop to gape into a smoldering dune, where suddenly, insanely, and with a goatlike eruption he found himself snorting with laughter. And just as abruptly the air would abandon his lungs, and as he spotted a procession of industrious ants on the ground, or a lone swift in the sky, or the curled and dried remains of a lizard in the brush, a surge of hot tears would flood his eyes, and he would stand for a while and cry. For a brief moment of lucidity, he saw himself: Held the soft and sorry animal, with its ceaseless, deeply absurd efforts to contain life's entropy. He was, as he knew, incorrigibly in love with Katja.

Every night, shortly after midnight, Katja had been announcing herself by the *click* of their adjoining door. After advancing on light tiptoe through the carpeted living room, she would hover for a moment in his bedroom doorway, sway with reluctance, then finally slip into his bed, where she lay silently and straight as a dash until making her move. Only once had Held ventured to sit up and whisper her name, whereupon Katja had contracted spasmodically, backed out the door, and not appeared again for several days.

By the time she returned, Held had learned to control his breath and to limit his startled response to a soundless shift of his eyeballs in the dark. Katja, seemingly pleased by his efforts and no longer hesitant, approached his bed swiftly and immediately set to work. What followed was an act of dry and regimented violence. First, she mounted him and seesawed vigorously and somewhat painfully a handful of times. Then, by a shove to his torso, she turned him on his side, backed against him and attached herself laterally, and grew perfectly limp. Frenzied, Held obeyed, thrilled at catching glimpses of her obscured face, her mouth stretched as if disgusted over her slanted teeth, her eyelids pinched, the ropes of her neck taut, until suddenly, sorely, and out of sheer terror it was finished, and he quietly detached.

Katja lay next to him for a while, her back curved fetally against his side, and he noticed with relief the ordinary flux of breath in her shoulders, the faint glisten of sweat on her neck. It was then that he experienced something like joy or deep sadness, but also tenderness, regret, and a mind-splitting lightness. He watched Katja's back until she got up and left.

Love turned out to be a tediously unpleasant experience. A long time ago, when the war was nearing its end and a platoon of jug-eared Amis had taken over a wing of his school, a prankster bunkmate stuck a wad of wet gum in his hair. He treated the lump with talcum powder, borrowed a fine-toothed comb from the nurse, even placed his head in the icebox in hopes of freezing the gum off. He finally resigned himself to extraction by scissors.

Afterward, as he stared down at the malignant wad of hair in his hand, he understood that this was what love would be like. He would never have a more accurate thought in his life.

Katja—arid, voiceless, fleshless Katja—infested him like a disease. Nothing was normal. Everything, including his feelings, seemed unreasonable and new. That first ray of sunshine between those vertical blinds was Katja. Katja the puckered mouth of a cactus flower by his door. There, on the blank cafeteria floor, that perfectly round splatter of syrup, Katja. Katja the equation drawn elegantly and by hand on a sheet of chlorine-white paper. Appalled and nauseated, he tried to return to reason, but with every attempt, Katja, barnacle-like, attached herself somewhere else in his mind.

In the morning, en route to the cafeteria, or on his way back, when Katja sprinted past him through the patches of shade, nothing suggested she had any desire to acknowledge his existence. Once, in the cafeteria, he ventured to slip his hand under the table and place it on her thigh, but her jaw locked and she set her vacant eyes on the table, and he retrieved his hand, consumed for the rest of the day by thoughts of ending his life quickly and violently.

The more he sought her in daylight, the more elusive she became. He began spending early evenings crouched on the floor, with one ear pressed against their adjoining door, hoping to catch just a shuffle, a sneeze, a symptom of Katja beyond what she could control. When he heard something, he knocked, once, twice, to no avail. Then he cowered in bed, one moment ravished by murderous heat, the next overcome with clarity. This was it, it was ruined, she would never return. But every night, shortly after midnight, there was Katja, wordlessly, damply slithering in next to him.

The weeks bled into one another. Held stopped eating, was afraid of the dark, and began hating himself with a dark and boring rage. It was in this condition that, one early evening, Held found himself sitting at the edge of a steep, brush-riddled dune. The desert vista before him glowed with apocalyptic color: howling pinks, chattering reds, contagious and counterfeit emergency hues emitted from somewhere just beyond the brink of the sky, where someone without feelings was roping in the night. Amazed, terrified, he watched a gang of determined vultures traverse a ridge on foot. It had gone on too long, he had tried it all; if his heart was plotting to kill him, it should get it over with. Most worryingly, he was not unhappy. There was a glow in this surrender, something triumphant. He could do nothing but let the pain pass through him, mangle him, until it faded again, as it invariably would. This was an insight of mild hilarity, and he was in the midst of letting out a burst of bleating laughter when something, a noise like radio static, caused him to turn.

A few paces behind him, leaning against his cane and wearing, to Held's astonishment, a double-filtered gas mask in olive green, stood Hans. His chin angled high, his eyes narrowed behind his fogged visor, he was beholding the vista with the calm air of a critic.

Held asked him what he was looking at.

"Many millions of years ago," Hans shouted through his mask, "this sprawling bone-dry desert was home to sea creatures the likes of which we cannot—"

"Please, I can't bear it," Held said.

Hans fell silent. Wheezing robotically through his mask, he hobbled toward the edge of the dune and positioned himself next to Held. Together they looked out over the bedazzled desert.

"I've been seeing spots," Hans shouted. "Are you seeing spots?"

"No," Held said.

"Are you having soft stools? Pins and needles in your toes?"

Held shook his head.

"Mood swings?"

Held cast his head upward, his gaze lost for a moment in the complicated contraption suctioned like an extraterrestrial claw against Hans's face. "I've been crying a lot," he said.

"What else?"

"I wet my bed the other day," he admitted.

"That's concerning."

Held asked what it meant.

"Simple regression," Hans yelled. "Don't worry, it can happen to anyone. At the end of the war about half of my platoon was sucking their thumbs."

Something mammalian cried out from beyond the dune, a blasé, nocturnal scream. They listened together, slanting their heads, until the echo died.

"Come with me," Hans shouted.

They retraced the narrow footpath, sloped around a boulder, passed the murmuring electricity box where someone, long ago, had left the orthodontically complex remains of a gopher skull, and returned to the main path. With sternness and some degree of urgency, Hans led him through the compound and finally on to the entrance rondelle, where he stopped and pointed his cane. Held saw nothing out of the ordinary. To the left, slotted at neat 45-degree angles, was a row of dust-covered cars nobody had moved since the day he'd arrived. To the right, a dense wall of blooming cacti. Beyond it, all around them, stretched the dull, anemic desert, gray in the impending nightfall.

"Look," Hans shouted, jabbing his cane as if stoking a fire.

And then Held saw them. In the middle of the rondelle, high up in the rough-leaf tree, perched among its branches like strange, plump fruit, the boys sat staring at them with long, saddened faces. Nobody moved. A stillness unraveled, metered only by Hans's mechanical breath at his side, until one of the boys lifted a hand and waved.

Held waved back. "I've been trying to tell you people," he said. "They're alone here, roaming about like stray dogs."

"They're not," Hans said. "It just looks that way during the day. At night they're with them." Hans lifted his cane again to indicate some odd direction beyond the desert plains. "They come to pick them up at nightfall. I've been watching it happen since the day I got here."

Another boy, posted higher than the first, lifted his hand and waved as well.

"What does it mean?" Held said. "Why are you showing me this?"

"Are you blind? Look," Hans repeated, his eyes popping behind his milky visor. "There are only four left."

Held tallied the number of tiny bean-brown faces among the branches. Hans was correct. The smallest—the shaggy-haired four-year-old whom Held had spotted the day he arrived—wasn't there. He scanned the surroundings, into the compound, searched uselessly for a whole empty minute for a sign of the boy. When he turned again, Hans was waddling back up the path at an unnatural speed.

"I have a spare if you want one," Hans yelled over his shoulder, tapping a finger against his mask. "You really never know. What sort ends a war in that godawful manner?"

With that he was gone and Held was left to face the boys on his own. At first he stuffed his hands in his pockets, kept his distance. Then he veered to his left, pacing a semicircle, and drew closer until he reached the foot of the tree. Though the sun was down, out of habit he shielded his eyes with his hand. "Play monkey up there?" he said, trying his English.

Peering down at him with perfect, unblinking eyes, the boys

looked neither startled nor surprised, and Held was reminded of some of the more discomforting avian encounters he'd had in the area.

"I forgot," Held said, "you can't understand me."

He was turning to leave when one of the boys spoke from the tree: "We understand you okay," he said. "We're Mexican, not stupid." He was the oldest of the group—seven, maybe eight years old. He was dressed, like the others, in a white T-shirt and shorts. He shifted his legs, breaking his squat, and sat down on the branch, from which he dangled his legs.

Held asked him where their parents were.

Grinning, the boy mumbled something in Spanish, and the group erupted in cackling. "We don't have any," he said. "Why you think we're here?"

"You were five the last time I see you," Held said. "Where's your friend?"

The boys stopped laughing. They hung their heads, began picking at nearby branches.

"Six months ago," the boy said, "when they brought us here, there were nine of us. A month later, seven. By the time you first showed up, we were only five. And now..." The boy lifted four dirty fingers.

"The coyotes," Held said. "Is that it? He's hurt and lost in the dunes?"

Again the boy erupted in rolling Spanish and the others giggled in return. "The desert is a playground compared to where we go," he said.

"The void," a thickset boy chimed in.

"The Nothing," said another from the very top of the tree.

"Crashing sounds and bolts of lightning," said the oldest. "Never to be seen again."

Skipping from one grim little face to another, Held felt his legs quiver. Nerves, Katja, lack of sleep. But there was something wild and otherworldly in these smart little faces. "What does it mean?" he said. "I'm sorry, but I don't understand a thing."

With a thump the lowest-hanging boy jumped off his branch and ran furiously toward a van now idling at the far side of the rondelle. The other three boys followed suit, dropping like ticks from the tree, one after the other, and sprinted toward the van. The oldest was the last to descend, and Held, his hand still senselessly shielding his eyes, watched as he leaped and dangled, then came to a halt, swinging with apelike agility just a few centimeters from the ground. They locked eyes.

"They don't kill them, I don't think," the boy whispered. "Don't be afraid. We think they just make it so they go somewhere else." Then he dropped from the branch and ran—his knees knocking, feet kicking dust—to join his friends in the van.

Just a few moments later Held found himself hammering against Katja's front door. He rattled the handle, then darted into his apartment and began pounding the wall. He pressed his ear against the adjoining door, heard nothing, then tried the knob. It was unlocked. This he had not expected. As soon as he stepped inside, he lost all sense of urgency. His mission to tell Katja about the boys in the tree, their preposterous purpose in this impossible place, or, come to think of it, anyone's purpose anywhere, all dimmed somewhere in the back of his mind.

It was his own apartment, mirror-inverted. The same beige wall-to-wall carpeting, the same lamella curtains, now swaying serenely in the sudden gust of wind. The kitchen counters looked polished. The coffee table, the sofa, all cleared and clean. He opened the refrigerator, which was empty and reeking of chlorine. In the bedroom, an exact replica of his own, floral-patterned bedding lay in a heap on the floor. The mattress had been stripped. Propped at its center was a note, the last mortal evidence of Katja.

Held launched himself toward it, grabbed it, nearly tore it in two. Blinking violently, he deciphered the words: *Work is done,* it read. *Had to go back. Thank you for everything.* In block-lettered English, it added, SORRY.

Two days later Held was recalled to Berlin.

There was a knock at Held's apartment door. The physicist, now reclining lengthwise on his couch, made no attempt to answer the call. Since he'd finished his story, he and Zeiger had been sitting like this, mutely, for nearly ten minutes, with Held's tranquil eyes fixed on the ceiling, and Zeiger, though fully aware of the events that had followed for Held when he returned to Berlin, watching and waiting with something like childish suspense.

"Provisions," Held said, with an aura of finality. Just then there was another knock, and Zeiger rose from his chair. When he opened the door, a peculiarly tiny man was lifting a large box of provisions with two equally tiny arms.

The man blinked at him with dumb irritation, scanned him top to bottom, lingering for an open-mouthed second on his paint-splattered overalls. "Now who the hangman are you?" he said in a rough, deep-East drawl. "I don't know many things, but I know you're not Held."

Zeiger pointed his chin inside.

The man pushed past him, glanced into the living room, and dropped the box on the floor. "Nobody tells me anything," the man muttered to himself. "Now all of a sudden, prisoners are allowed company. Why not let them throw a party? Why not throw them a party ourselves? I have a bag of *Schrippen,*" he said, and began unpacking various items on the coffee table. "Two cans of Kaffee Mix, a bushel of kale. No, two bushels of kale. Cooking oil, tomato soup. A few bottles of beer. We're not monsters, you know."

The man stood back up and looked around, first at Held on his couch, then at Zeiger, who stood by the window taking in the proceedings with mild alarm.

"That's it, citizens," the man said, his voice trailing off into a hum.

Then he narrowed his tiny eyes and widened them again in stupid surprise. And just as Zeiger understood what was happening within the man's feeble mind, the conclusion he was coming to, the man grinned, stuck up his thumb, and broke out rambling again.

"I have Coca-Cola in the van, for our special guest," he said, and nodded toward Zeiger. "And maybe a few rolls of toilet paper for our esteemed prisoner? Anything. Special pastries, chocolate. Whatever you'd like," he said. "Comrades," he added, "of course."

2.4

Even though he knew just where Lara sat in the corner at the top of her bed, how she had drawn up her legs even closer to her body and rested her head on her knees, he had the distinct notion that she was somewhere else. A raw and empty stillness had unfolded between them. This had been a lot to tell her.

It was late now, he did not know how late, and they sat in absolute quiet, until finally, and with gusto, Lara burst out, "You're saying this man, Held, whatever you said his name was, knew how to teleport people?" She jerked her head up and tilted it at him, as if just now growing aware of what he'd said.

It took Zeiger a moment to realize she was looking outside, where the red lights of a police car had flared against the dark foliage, then disappeared. "He never told me," Zeiger said.

"You lie," Lara said. "You know."

The bottle of schnapps Lara had brought in from the kitchen stood on the coffee table, taunting him. He had refrained, wanting to remain lucid and recall all that was needed, but now he leaned forward and poured himself a glass. There was space on the bed, and it was possible, plausible even, for him to make his way over and sit close to her.

Lara had heard people discussing it at the church, she continued. Little fringe groups that didn't really mingle. They talked about astral bodies, the transformational power of love, transporting themselves, and whatnot.

Zeiger asked what she knew about them.

"Nothing," Lara said, her voice looping, "other than that they give me the creeps. Whatever's wrong with a place can be measured by the delusion du jour of its people. My best friend is absolutely convinced our air is contaminated. What do I tell him? That he's inventing it? You want me to give you names, strike up conversations, find you the leaders? Is that what you want?"

"That's not why I'm here."

"Then why are you telling me all this?"

"I'm dying," Zeiger said, surprising himself.

"Of what?"

"I don't know." There was no stopping this.

"Who says so? The doctors?"

"Old things look new. New things look unrecognizable. Something's changing. Sometimes I want to break my head open to see the inside of my skull. There are urges. I can't tell what's happening."

"I'll tell you what's happening. Look around you," Lara said, pointing out the window. "Look at you people. With your five-year plans and your stupid birthday parades. It's like trying to carry water in a sieve."

"Some things are bigger than you can comprehend," Zeiger said.

"My point exactly," Lara said, jerking her head forward in an unnatural way. "Things are going to be very different. Maybe it'll take another decade or two, but..." She gestured at Zeiger's cigarettes on the table.

Zeiger stretched painfully to retrieve the pack, cradled it for a moment in his hand, then threw it on the bed next to Lara. He tested his nostrils. The blood had dried.

Lara smoked hectically. "What did you do to this Held?"

Zeiger set his shot glass down and folded his hands in front of him. "It's not what," he said. "It's why."

"Who cares about why?" Lara said with venom. "Does knowing why make it less evil? Nature doesn't ask why. Ask why and you dissolve all meaning." With a jeering smile she added, "Scared little boys is all you guys are."

Zeiger seemed to observe himself drawing each individual breath. It was as if he watched the air itself accumulate, cling to his lungs, and lift him out of his chair. He felt buoyant and light, weightless and blank. An unfamiliar sensation, something astronomical and hot, planted him square in front of Lara's bed.

She raised her palms, half shielding and half begging.

"I brought these," he said, fully outside himself now. The box of *Kalter Hund* cookies hung like a club from his fist.

A look had crossed Lara's face two, maybe three times, throughout that night. In hindsight, he could tell it had been loaded with great significance. Indifference tinged with pity, disgust. She knew what he was and she was bored by violence.

She glared for a while, then snatched the box from his fist and tore at the cardboard, splitting it open. "You take yourself very seriously," she said. She placed a cookie on her palm, then threw it into her mouth. "If you were my father I'd tell you to lighten up."

Zeiger closed his eyes, rubbed his face with the flats of his hands, and began pacing. She was exasperating, as slithery as quicksilver, absolutely exquisite. With an air of vexed determination, he continued.

*   *   *

For a brief period in the summer of 1965, Management had ordered a Ministry-wide dress code to exclude all shades of gray. Gray, according to Ulbricht's wife, Lotte, was not a color; it was the sustenance of skeptics, not of socialist good cheer.

Due to the lack of specific guidelines, hushed and flustered discussions ensued on the nature of gray undertones, the temperament of gray, its true, defining essence. Without an explicit agreement, Ministry employees nevertheless soon concurred that hues of brown, black, beige, and light blue could also be deemed dissentious, so they avoided those colors as well. For a few weeks, comrades were seen wandering the courtyards in outfits of staggering creative breadth: high-waisted blue tracksuits, borrowed from athletic friends; shift dresses in dazzling primary colors; striped socks. Some darted down the corridors, ashamed of their garish ensembles, while others, with new purpose and joy in their eyes, sauntered with casual ease.

Zeiger had not received the memorandum. Fatigued and stale-mouthed from his late night bearing witness to Held's desert experiences, he arrived at the compound Monday morning dressed in a solid gray two-piece and a collared shirt in light beige. On the paternoster, a group of nightmarishly dressed comrades gaped at him in variations of shock. In the hallway of Ledermann's unit, a man in an aubergine sweater grabbed him in passing and, grinning bizarrely, assured him that all would be well. Zeiger did not register the color scheme so much as the mood in the air; something courteous, kind, and subtly volatile, as if everyone were sharing an embarrassing secret.

At the end of the hallway, Ledermann was pacing small circles in front of the conference room. He wore a short-sleeved dress shirt in clownish red, offset by a colorful patterned tie that hung from his neck like a bib. With his massive arms folded over his chest, his shoulders hunched, and his neck telescoping forward in animated distress, he looked much like a circus bear, a wild animal entertaining to all but itself. He shot his arms up when he saw Zeiger at the end of the hall, a gesture to indicate he'd been waiting for a while. Zeiger glanced at his watch—which, he now noticed, he'd somehow forgotten to wind—and approached Ledermann, who came to a halt and stared at him, open-mouthed and clearly alarmed.

"But we don't believe in gray," he said.

"In what?" Zeiger asked.

"The shade."

"The color?"

"The concept," Ledermann said.

"What do we believe in?" Zeiger asked.

"That's not what matters now," Ledermann said, then whispered: "You're late, someone is here." He pointed at the conference-room door, wiped a hand over his face.

The meeting had been scheduled as an update on Held. There would be concluding remarks and a rundown of the confession the Manual had promised to produce.

Zeiger looked at the door. "Who?" he asked.

Ledermann reached out and grabbed his shoulder, lightly, not violently, and asked how things stood with Held. The look in his eyes was one of pure and soft desperation.

Zeiger assured him that all had gone well.

Ledermann relaxed, seemed to search the ground for the next thing to say, then grabbed Zeiger's shoulder again, quite tightly this time, and explained that they were going to go into the conference room and speak to the person inside. But—and here Ledermann squeezed and shimmied Zeiger's arms—it was of utmost importance that Zeiger not laugh. Not a chuckle, giggle, grin, not so much as the whiff of a smile. If he found something funny, there were ample tragedies to which he could turn his mind: African children with potbellies and flies in their eyes, genocides, homicides, extraterrestrial life, whatever private humiliation he liked.

Zeiger promised, and after repeating himself once more, Ledermann opened the door and pointed him inside.

A nutty scent, the thick and earthy smell of real coffee, hung in the room. The remnants of a lavish coffee break—brown layer cake on dainty porcelain plates—lay strewn about the table. Three things caught Zeiger's eye: a tiny china bowl brimming with whipped cream, untouched by the evidence of its delicate white peak; next to it, a tin box of ornate white pralines, by which he was momentarily transfixed, having not seen its kind in years; and leaning over the box, one fat finger poised for extraction, belonging to a corpulent man in the garb of a general.

The General snapped a praline into his mouth, hauled himself back into his chair, and waved both men inside. His face was broad and unfazed. What remained of his hair had been gelled back over the globe of his head. This was Management.

Zeiger recognized him immediately as the hardened and humorless type, those grown from industry unions, with coal dust baked into the lines of their palms and possessed of impeccable ideological hygiene. Something deep in Zeiger's gut gargled, and he coughed with violence.

Ledermann sat down next to the General and ordered Zeiger to take a seat across the table. Zeiger began arranging his things. The notebook to keep track of his visits with Held, a pencil sharpened at home. From his pocket he pulled the recorder that Ledermann had taped to his chest for his last visit with Held, placed it on the table, and fanned out its wires. All this happened in silence. Zeiger glanced at the General, who watched without affect. His was the type of obesity that obliterated all trace of feeling from a face.

The General leaned forward, toward the pralines, and his chin buckled over his collar. This in itself would have been quite comical, but then he smacked his palm on the table, and in a voice as clear, high-pitched, and lovely as a choirboy's, he exclaimed: "We no longer believe in gray!" His body contracted and thrust upward as he spoke, as if straining to propel air through the narrow tip of a flute. It was an inconceivable voice; angelic, soprano.

Zeiger looked at Ledermann. Ledermann stared down at the table as if something magnificent were happening there.

"I understand," Zeiger said.

"We have found it necessary," the General squealed, "to encourage a positive outlook. We have ordered a more colorful garment-production cycle. It may take a few months to a year."

"This may be useful for the Manual," Zeiger tried.

"The what?" said the General, striking, impossibly, an even higher pitch.

"Comrade Zeiger here," Ledermann interjected, "has been standardizing demoralization techniques into a manual. Our new XX Unit. He has been assigned to this case to test the techniques in the field."

The General blinked.

Zeiger considered his ears, which were potato-shaped, their lobes creased and buoyed by the mounds of his cheeks.

"Now who would come up with something like that?" the General said, turning stiffly to Ledermann. "What a monstrous idea."

A pause hung in the air, then abruptly the General broke into a laugh. A piercing, suffocated shriek. Unsure of what was expected, Zeiger joined in and they laughed together until the General fell silent again.

"This is funny to you?" he asked Zeiger. "I'm funny to you?"

Something was happening to Ledermann's mouth so that his lower lip dropped. Out of the sheer necessity of having to look somewhere, Zeiger looked at the bottom ranks of his coffee-stained teeth. "No," he said.

"I advise you to dress more appropriately," the General said. "Everyone or no one. You're no one, of course."

"Of course," Zeiger said.

Yesterday Held had predicted that Management would appear. As soon as the deliveryman had left, he sat up on the couch, poured schnapps into their coffee cups, and said to Zeiger, "You think I didn't know, comrade?"—and he stressed the word with a grin. "You people, you Stasi, are peasants like the rest of us. Orphans, handymen, masons, or, as you'd like me to believe, hardworking painters in overalls. You're no different. It's a national sport to believe others are idiots." He smiled when he told Zeiger this, free of animosity or fear. "You'll tell your superiors everything I've said. And your superiors"—here Zeiger, in a daze, at last retrieved the cup from Held's hand—"will do what they must." Held raised his cup, seeking a toast.

"But you're my friend," Zeiger said.

And that was the last he would see of Held in free form: soaked in silvery light, peering over the rim of his cup with one arm extended, toasting to free will and choice and, he added, their opposite: love.

"I was made," Zeiger said now, to the General. He dropped his notebook, shoved it aside.

The General stopped chewing. Narrowing his fat lids, he turned to Ledermann, who stared at Zeiger with a ghastly look on his face, his nostrils flared and white.

"A deliveryman came," Zeiger continued evenly. "He recognized me, for whatever reason, as not an ordinary citizen, then offered us Coca-Cola and began addressing us as *comrades*. Naturally, Held caught on."

His two superiors took a moment.

"Go on, now," the General said. "What is it that Held said?"

"If I may," Zeiger started. Something had come over him, an unfamiliar recklessness, a dim sort of hope. "I have a bit of a philosophical question. Rudimentary, as pertaining to this man's predicament. Legally speaking, what if he confessed?"

"To what?" the General asked.

"To conspiring with the Americans and lying about it."

"Why, that's treason and espionage. He'd be going to prison."

"And if he didn't confess?" Zeiger asked. He was succeeding, he thought, in striking a speculative tone, a straightforward, fundamental curiosity in the metaphysics of it all.

The General leaned back in his chair and leveled his eyes. A simple man eager to display his competencies. "That would be espionage and treason," he said.

"If he had reported from the desert," Zeiger ventured, "about supposedly successful teleportation technology on the part of the Americans, what would have happened to him?"

"Well, comrade, he's but a scientist with questionable loyalties. If he were in possession of such knowledge, he'd be a threat to national security. We would have taken him into custody. But that's a redundant scenario."

"Why is that, Comrade General?" Zeiger asked.

"Comrade," the General said, chuckling, "someone who would like us to believe that teleportation is real is clearly best kept in a nice, padded cell."

Zeiger paused, admiring the elegance of the equation. There was nothing as simple as fate in this system. "Held confessed," he said. "And he very much believes that teleportation is possible."

Confession—a good word, one that mattered. It was an odd moment to consider its complexion, taste its flavor and weight. The Manual now felt painfully short of defining its breadth. Was confession a leveraging tool, a bonding device, a cleanser, a death sentence? All of the above? Crimes were confessed, love was confessed. He thought of China and its "struggle sessions" for the Communist cause; wondered if Father had been made to confess, kneeling on sharp pebbles in that labor camp's barren yard.

"How?" Ledermann asked.

"With the techniques outlined in the Manual," Zeiger said.

"The teleportation, I mean," Ledermann said. He leaned in expectantly and pointed at the recorder.

"I was in there for hours," Zeiger said. "I'm afraid it died."

"I see."

"Go on, now," the General said in the same shrill voice. "How'd you do it?"

"I told him about our informant, Katja," Zeiger said. "How she'd related everything about his secret dealings with the Americans."

"Good," cheered the General, squealing and clapping his hands.

"How she'd said it was him and only him," Zeiger continued, "who knew about teleportation and that he'd kept it from us, purposefully and traitorously."

"And then what?" the General asked.

"Then I told him that she was pregnant and has given birth to their child."

"Did you tell him it was a girl?"

"I did," Zeiger said. A clean and uncluttered lie. It was all he could do.

"Splendid," the General said. He swiveled his massive head

toward Ledermann and coaxed from him a hazy smile. "And what did he say?"

"He cried."

"That's only natural."

"He's a human being," Ledermann said. "I can relate. I just had a son. Rudi is his name."

"Ah," the General said. He screwed his eyes open, absorbing this trivia with genuine surprise. They exchanged a congratulatory nod.

It was only now that Zeiger considered the panoramic view behind their heads, a long, rectangular slice of white sky. A gang of black swallows darted into the frame, rising and scattering in dramatic pursuit of a larger, less athletic bird; a crow, he assumed.

"Did he confess to conspiring?" the General asked. He pulled the plate of layer cake toward him and began shaving off thin slices and throwing them into his mouth.

"Just the teleportation."

"It seems one is inevitably tied to the other, Herr Comrade. What exactly is it he confessed?"

This Zeiger had expected. He opened his notebook, leafed through to the corresponding page, and began tallying the bullet points he had prepared. The desert, its deathly hot breath, the vultures and lizards and toxic sunsets. He paused for a moment, collecting his thoughts, then told them of the tree and those Mexican children who had been disappearing.

Both the General and Ledermann looked on sedately: the General, a bloated, featureless, moon-shaped head; Ledermann, a blank face cast red in the sheen of his clownish shirt. They stared for a long time, for what felt like hours, long enough for Zeiger to witness the damp imprints of his hands warp and vanish from the sheen of the teak table.

"Well," the General said. "This Held has clearly lost his mind."

"Clearly," Ledermann said.

"Utterly mad. Teleportation. Mexican children."

"Complete lunacy," Ledermann agreed.

Then the General emitted a strange noise. All that was loose on his face puffed out with toadlike buoyancy and he appeared to be holding his breath. With small, desperate eyes he searched Zeiger's face, then turned to Ledermann, who was already rising to reach for his arm.

The General's mouth pursed and, like a broken valve, in a sharp piercing sound he burst out: "I had a great aunt who couldn't be convinced her husband was real. She swore he was a stranger wearing an Onkel Friedrich costume—a husband-costume, you understand? God knows who she thought he actually was. It made for awkward family outings. How is that for insane?"

"Given the subject's obvious mental instabilities—" Zeiger started.

"Such odd people in the world. Teleportation," the General squealed.

"Yes, Comrade General," Zeiger said. This was his moment. "Because of this insanity," he continued, "paired with the fact that oppositional individuals are seen as martyrs when incarcerated, may I suggest, rather than Hohenschönhausen, that we consider the ward at St. Hedwig's a more appropriate place to keep Held?"

Flushed still, catching his breath, the General picked up the tin box of pralines and extended it across the table. Zeiger hesitated for a moment, catching Ledermann's indecipherable eye, before removing a piece and placing it on his tongue. It dissolved with difficulty and stuck to the roof of his mouth.

"As you wish," the General said. "You've done good."

Zeiger asked what had happened to Held's child.

The General said the woman had given her up for adoption in Leipzig and had been sent back to West Germany and barred from returning. "Good riddance, for all we care, we don't need her anymore. Sodom and Gomorrah. What kind of mother would give up her child?"

As soon as they had extracted the General from the Ministry conference room, shaken hands goodbye, and sent him waddling away down the hall, Ledermann ordered Zeiger to attend Held's final interrogation at Hohenschönhausen jail. The science, he stressed with a crazed look in his eyes, might not be of any interest to Management, but it should be to them. It would be the last Held was to confess before moving on to St. Hedwig's.

Zeiger had paced as he talked, had not so much as glanced at Lara. He gesticulated, pointed, fanned out his arms. He took large steps and small ones, moving in tiny, deliberate circles in front of her bed. All of this he had told her in minute detail. He felt warm and energized, absorbed and alive. Until he looked at Lara and saw the ghastly look on her face.

"I don't mean to bore you," he said.

At first Lara said nothing. She sat and stared. "This Held," she said, finally, "he's at St. Hedwig's?"

"Has been for decades."

"Because of you?"

"In a manner of speaking. No more questions now."

"But I have many."

A car rumbled over the cobblestones below. Rapid, hollow artillery sounds. The world outside was alive. It was the most impossible thing Zeiger had ever heard.

"It's unforgivable," he said.

Lara absorbed this, narrowing her eyes. Then she straightened her back, and with a grave nod she said, "It seems like you spared him the worst."

The puzzle of his lifetime, decided in minutes. "I acted like I was God," he said.

"God is the most terrible thing in the world," Lara said. She was smiling, but it was dejected somehow rather than glad.

Von Horváth, Zeiger thought, feeling light-headed, though it was unlikely she knew that writer. He returned the smile but said nothing, then found a way to continue.

An hour after their meeting with the General, Zeiger stood in an airless observation cubicle, facing a two-way mirror that looked into the interrogation room where Held sat hunched, naked, but in apparent good cheer at the long end of the T. Viewed from behind the glass, the room was all shadows, murky and damp but for the cone of light spilling from a lamp that dangled from the ceiling like a spider over Held's head. Behind Held, in shadow, the Russian waited, meticulously picking a scab on his arm, his mean eyes obscured under the prominent, prehistoric ridge of his brow. Sitting at the roof end of the T, his back to Zeiger, Ledermann motioned emphatically. To hear what he was saying, Zeiger would have to press the intercom, but Ledermann's inquisition was of no interest to him. He watched the proceedings with vacuous attention: the glistening back of Ledermann's head; his shirt, now tinged purple in the lackluster light; the Russian, glaring at him through the two-way mirror.

Only when Held opened his mouth did Zeiger press the lever. He suctioned his ear against the speaker. Through the machine Held's voice sounded secluded and hollow, distilled as if through vast expanses. He spoke of those dogs strapped to torture machines who even when unharnessed somehow refused to leave. Between beatings he inquired after Katja. Periodically the Russian roused himself like a windup toy and continued the beatings, but Held remained unfazed. He did not confess to knowing anything about teleportation and he would not confess, but smiled, calmly, as if something intimately funny were happening instead. From the stifling darkness of his cubicle, feeling somehow light and not quite in place, Zeiger smiled in return.

After a while he left and fled through the low maze of bunker-like corridors. On reaching the entrance landing, he skipped down the stairs and bent over to vomit onto the clean patch of concrete. When he was finished retching, he looked up, and, through watering eyes, scanned the empty courtyard. A sapling had recently been planted at its center. He considered its planting, the multiple layers of Management that such a request would have survived, the piles of paperwork like strata of earth. The young tree tipped in the robust evening wind, its flimsy arms reaching and grasping as if in escape.

Days later, as was protocol, Zeiger was summoned to discuss his thoughts and feelings, as if they were the measurable symptoms of a chronic disease. These were informal talks, performed in the cozy quarters of the Ministry Management Kantine, to create an easy, off-the-record ambience designed to confuse both parties about exactly whose thoughts and feelings were being examined.

At the designated time, Zeiger made his way into the Kantine, where he found Ledermann alone and wedged in a deep cushioned chair. He looked sorry and misplaced, like an outcast boy, his massive knees angling high above the low marble table. The room was empty but somehow dense with cigarette smoke. Ledermann waved him over and slid a sweating pint of beer across the marble table. For a while they drank in silence. They could have been two strangers in transit at a train-station pub, or nemesis brothers with nothing to add.

At last Ledermann set down his glass. "We know about as much as before," he said, spreading his hands, his eyes wide. He'd pressed Held on the mathematics, the physics, the engineering, anything related to the mechanics of what was going on at that American institute, but Held claimed to know nothing at all. "He did speak beautifully about the desert, however," Ledermann finished.

"Boys in a tree."

"Some Austrian who lost his mind. You're our only witness to his confession. How does that make you feel?"

"Burdened."

"You're a fraud," Ledermann said. "There's something wrong with you."

"There are a lot of things wrong with all of us," Zeiger replied.

"It doesn't scare you that there's someone running around fully aware of how to teleport people? Don't you know what that could do to this nation?"

"He'll be in a psychiatric ward," Zeiger said. "Nobody will believe a word he says. Besides, even if he knew how, he doesn't have the equipment to teleport anything anywhere."

"But what if all he needs is his mind?" whispered Ledermann, widening his eyes in childish enchantment.

They gaped at each other in stupefied silence. This Zeiger hadn't considered.

"I think you never told him about Katja or his child," Ledermann continued.

And if that were the case, Zeiger said, which he wasn't admitting, how would Ledermann feel about it?

Ledermann stared at his glass with great concentration, rotated it clockwise, inched it sideways and back, as if its precise placement were of grave importance. He then checked his watch. With some difficulty he dislodged himself from the chair and jerked his head at Zeiger to follow.

Together they drove to Hohenschönhausen jail, where Held was waiting for transport to St. Hedwig's. In the loading area, the driver, a large, bug-eyed type, leaned lazily against the van that contained Held. He made no effort at a salute when they arrived. He lifted a foot and extinguished his cigarette on the rubber sole of his shoe, then shoved a clipboard at them. Both men signed it, and all three of them climbed into the cab of the van. Zeiger wound up lodged in the middle. As soon as the engine started, music blared from the radio—a coarse, agitated tune.

It was a short drive with a rural feel, the roads lined by the quaint, inoffensive housing units that Zeiger had come to know over the years. Once in Mitte, the driver followed prescribed protocol: left turns into one-way streets, stops, reversals, unnecessary U-turns, zeroing in on St. Hedwig's in what he must have deemed the most erratic route imaginable.

"He knows where we're going," Zeiger said.

The driver grunted, rolled down the window, and began smoking aggressively. "My van or yours?" he said, and they drove the rest of the tour in silence.

Zeiger turned in his seat and unsealed the square peephole behind him. He peered into the darkness. For a hot and hollow second he thought they'd left Held behind, but then he spotted him, in the far corner, sprawled on the plywood bench, his head tipped backward, eyes closed. His hands were shackled and fastened by a chain to the floor. He appeared to be asleep. The smile on his face was one of utter serenity, something calm and strangely elated.

Zeiger wanted him to scream. But Held was perfectly still. What would have been a scream if not hope?

A pale sunset announced itself against the low-hanging clouds. Just there, at the center of the boulevard's funnel-like end, a radio tower would soon be erected, 370 meters in height. *Nu, comrades, you can clearly see, this is where it belongs,* then–General Secretary Ulbricht had said at the plan's unveiling, tapping the spire of the tower model in the same way Zeiger pictured *Dornröschen,* Sleeping Beauty, pricking her finger on the tip of the spindle. He locked his eyes on the distance, imagined the beast.

At St. Hedwig's the driver ushered Held out the back of the van and into a double-doored side entrance, where a male nurse and two nuns with illegible faces guided him into the hospital. Zeiger hoped with foolish anticipation for a look from Held, a gesture, a flare of anger. But nothing came. Held let himself be guided through the doors, his head high, inspecting his surroundings, as if he were entering a place of great wonder.

In the years that followed, Zeiger often considered paying Held a visit, continuing the friendship somehow, forging a new one if necessary. But he couldn't bear it. So there Held remained, neither wave nor particle, in the tombs of St. Hedwig's psychiatric hospital.

2.5

It took weeks to register, validate, and archive the completion of the Manual. There were forms to fill out, which required other forms to acquire, which, in turn, nobody knew how to obtain. Signatures of comrades with hypertensive faces and unfamiliar names. Rubber stamps from departments buried in faraway compound corners. Zeiger performed these duties meticulously and thoroughly. There was comfort in typeset words on paper; a dotted line signed, a questionnaire filled out. As his stack of forms proliferated, each one stapled in the upper left corner and inserted into its own manila casing, so did their validity and irrevocable truth. Here was something to outlive him.

It was late summer, months after Held's transfer to St. Hedwig's, by the time the process was finished. The Manual was multiplied and distributed to Ministry personnel. One copy was assigned for archiving at the *Archiv für Hermeneutik und Literarische Unterfangen,* a perplexing, unfitting home for his Manual, as it was not a work of fiction, but he didn't question Management's reasoning. To deliver the document, he carried it down into the compound cellar where the archival unit was located, losing himself briefly in the complicated twists of its corridors. At the end of a narrow passageway, marked by a wheezing submarine light, he finally found a door marked ARCHIV and knocked; once, twice, a third time with force, until finally, in some intricate mechanism, it swung open and revealed its vaultlike entrails.

There were several archival units in the compound, some of which he had already visited on his paperwork quest. They were dense, windowless rooms, populated by haggard comrades who gave the impression of having lived there since they were born. Keepers of records and posthumous fate constituted a very particular species, one bred to survive without sunlight or rest.

At the reception desk Zeiger encountered one such individual, a deathly pale clerk with a bony head, dangerous cheekbones, and a skin condition that made his scalp shed. He was dressed, as was the custom now, in a pastel-green button-down. A colorful tie was roped around his neck. He made a great show of ignoring Zeiger as he walked through the door. Zeiger cradled the Manual, fondled its smooth surface, as if it too felt damp and nervous, and looked into the dim rows of filing units behind the clerk's desk.

From an adjacent room came the yapping of a group of people watching a football match. *"Eigentor!"* someone yelled. An own goal, following a terribly missed pass. Other voices chimed in, murmuring in agreement.

"What's this?" the clerk said.

"Can I deliver my document here?"

"If I filled this room with water you could even take a swim," said the clerk, scowling at the stack of forms as if they were a personal offense. "What do you want?"

"For its registration," Zeiger said, and presented the stack of papers.

"Yes, but what is it?" the clerk asked.

"Forms," Zeiger said, helplessly.

"I just want this one. I don't know what the rest is for." The clerk leafed through the stack and extracted the form that was needed. Breaking a rule was never as bad as presenting a rule someone didn't know had been instated. The clerk shoved the remaining forms across the desk at Zeiger, swiveled toward his typewriter, and began typing in clipped, efficient strokes, his eyes heartless and barren. Flakes of scalp dotted his shoulders like a light blanket of snow.

The chatter in the adjacent room continued, now quiet and serious.

"What is this?" the clerk said after a while.

"A form."

"No, this," the clerk replied, pointing at the Manual in Zeiger's arms.

"*The Standardization of Demoralization Procedures.* It says so on the form."

"Why is it being put in my archive? Is it a fictional work?"

Zeiger considered this. "No," he said.

"An essay, dubious literary criticism, a problematic dissertation, a poem?"

"I wrote it myself," Zeiger said.

The clerk retrieved the Manual and opened a page at random. He moved his lips as he read. "Very irregular," he said, and resumed hacking into the typewriter. He wrote for a long time, glancing at the Manual, glancing at the form, avoiding looking at Zeiger all the while, then rose and summoned him to follow.

Together they ventured into the tunnel of shelves. At the far end of an aisle, Zeiger spotted the source of the commotion. Crammed into a glass-fronted conference room, four elderly men lounged around a long, snack-filled table. The match, apparently, was over. The men wore knit vests and crocheted sweaters. The Hermeneutics Department, Zeiger gathered; a unit of grim notoriety. They had an air about them—trusting looks in their eyes; clean, childish smiles; an old-age softness mistaken for innocence. A layer of cigarette smoke hung above the table like a churning false ceiling.

The clerk directed Zeiger into an aisle, told him to wait, retrieved a fresh box from a shelf and began labeling it by hand.

"*Every Saturday,*" someone recited from the conference room, "*the nice fat father goes—*"

"*—to fetch a bucket of coal,*" a muffled voice continued. "*From the cellar, for the bath / So that stain / So that stain / So that stainless children he may have.*"

A long pensive silence followed, then the sound of paper being shuffled.

"I don't get it," someone said.

"A clear stress on *stain,*" said someone else.

"*Stainless,*" said another.

"*Saturday,* I would say," a quiet voice chimed in.

"Utter nonsense, Dietrich, you don't understand a thing about modern lyrics."

A quarrel ensued, a cadence of voices.

"He puts his kids in the bathtub, after them his wife. *And with his wife he plays / Blue, blue Mediterranean.* Do you see what I'm saying, Dietrich? *For a few weeks in the forties he was there / as Adolf Hitler's major—*"

"I still don't understand."

"Fine," someone said. "For fuck's sake, it's *stain,* then. I need to piss."

There was a creaking of chairs, then footsteps. The room fell silent again.

The clerk was bending over the box, licking and affixing various handwritten labels. Zeiger resisted the urge to dust the flakes from his shoulder. The clerk removed the lid, dropped the Manual inside, and closed it. He taped it tight around the edges, then lifted it and shoved it in among the rest with one vigorous movement.

"There," he said, rubbing his hands in conclusion. "Anything else?"

"That's it?" Zeiger said. He looked up at his box, plain and nondescript.

"No, of course not," the clerk said. "The brass band is on its way and Ulbricht himself will be coming in person." With a withering look he turned and disappeared down the aisle.

Zeiger needed to touch the box. He stretched onto the tips of his toes and patted its soft cardboard front. Identical boxes—bland, oatmeal-brown—extended to either side of it, above it and below it, in neat, symmetrical lines. He listened for a moment, quickly scanned the aisle, then shoved the box backward, just a few centimeters, pushing it out of alignment. He was shuffling toward the exit when he heard someone yell.

"You, yes, you with that beer-mug tie, come here."

Zeiger stopped and glanced into the glass-fronted conference room, where all four men had turned to look at him, sucking their cigarettes with primatial calm.

"We have a question for you," one of them said. "Help a few old sacks out." The man had a bulbous red nose and a very long neck and was beckoning with a swirl of one hand.

Zeiger approached.

"We need an amateur's ear," the man said. "Listen." He adjusted his glasses, lifted a crooked finger, and read from his papers. *"Suddenly a shark appears / Suddenly the wife is gone / And the bathwater reddens / When the father has murdered!"* The man lifted his head, appraised Zeiger standing there with his pomaded hair, and cupped a hand around his chin.

"Konrad," one of the men said, kindly, soothingly, "he's just a young lad."

"No, he understands. Tell us, what is it you think has happened here?"

"The father has murdered his wife in the tub," Zeiger said.

"Or the shark?" the man said.

"They're one and the same."

"Said so!" bellowed one of the men, throwing up his arms.

"But really," the man said. "If the father has turned into a shark and murders his wife, who can we hold accountable?"

"Nobody," Zeiger said.

"I see. I see." The old man scanned his papers, nodded pensively, taking it in. "Essentially, the author has absolved the father of murder."

"I think so," Zeiger said. "We can't help it if we turn into sharks."

The men stirred, whispered among themselves, lit fresh cigarettes, seemed to forget Zeiger was there.

He watched them for a while, unsure if he was free to go. "Is that good or bad?" he finally asked.

The man turned his long neck, opened his mouth, cocked his head as if surprised to find Zeiger still there. "Why, it's heresy, son," he said. "You did good."

Outside, in the Ministry lot, Zeiger hesitated, considering his options. He wanted someone to tell him what to do. In a stroke of atypical impulse, he exited through the Ministry gate and set off toward Lichtenberg Park. He encountered few people on the way: a secretarial type with sonorous heels, angling into an entryway; an elderly couple, bickering in subdued tones over a dropped set of keys. Zeiger's steps were brisk, but when he arrived at the park's forked entrance, the destination he'd had in mind, he didn't know which way to turn. Many decisions had been made. Held was gone. Life meant verifying one's effect on the world. He turned right. The air among the shrubbery was cool. Above him and to all sides oak trees dominated, their gnarled branches joined into canopies. Another fork in the road, another right turn, and soon he merged onto the park's main path, where benches dotted the edges and order was restored.

Something in the air, sharp and textured with dust, stung his nose, and he stopped. He retrieved a handkerchief from his pocket and was honking with vehemence when he recognized a man of vaguely familiar heft and build, dressed in a pastel-yellow tracksuit, seated on a bench a few paces away. The man detected Zeiger and twitched, skimmed the area with a flustered twist of the head. He lifted his globular backside from the bench and hurried down the path. The ducklike waddle and wisps of gray hair gave away Dr. Witzbold attempting an escape. He was carrying something, a thick volume or a book, that flapped against his leg with every step. It was the Manual, Zeiger realized, trotting in pursuit. The two men cantered for a strenuous minute, Zeiger pleading with the doctor to stop and the doctor cupping a hand over his eyes as if to render himself invisible. Finally, Witzbold slowed and the men walked side by side, both of them panting, as if merely on a vigorous stroll together.

"You're everywhere," Witzbold said, and veered toward a bench, where he rested, pigeon-toed and clearly exerted. He laid the Manual across his knees.

Zeiger sat down next to him. A patch of mowed grass, designed for leisure and athletic activity, stretched out before them. In a weak beam of sunlight a cloud of frantic gnats swarmed as if suspended on invisible string.

"Look at me," Witzbold said. He opened his arms wide and inspected his outfit. His tracksuit was made of terry cloth, a pale paschal yellow.

"You got a copy of the Manual," Zeiger said.

"The tyranny of color," said Witzbold, tugging at his pants legs. "What's next? What is happening?"

"We don't believe in gray," Zeiger said.

A woman approached, dragging behind her an unwilling Dachshund on a leash. The dog strained against its collar, rowing its crooked forelegs in the dirt in an attempt to sniff the men, who waited until the woman and her dog had disappeared down the path.

"The Manual," Zeiger said.

There was a windswept quality to Witzbold's face. The wisps of gray hair were tousled wildly over his bald head. Several days' stubble tarnished his cheeks. He stared into his lap. "Did you know, Zeiger, I wasn't always a psychiatrist," he said in a distant, musing voice. "I was a socialist once."

Zeiger turned around and scanned their surroundings. They were alone. "Can't one be both?" he whispered.

"Of course not," Witzbold said. Assuming a scholarly tone, sweeping and Socratic, he continued, "Do we first have to create a good society in order to produce good people? Or the opposite, do we have to create good people in order to produce a good society? Have you answered this for yourself?"

"I haven't thought about it."

"Naturally," Witzbold said. "Once you do, you'll know what you are, socialist or psychiatrist. I assume you're neither. The same is true of me."

Zeiger couldn't help detecting a note of dejection. "Maybe you should get some rest," he said. "I suspect you don't know what you're saying."

"In the end," Witzbold went on, unperturbed, "both fail to predict anything at all about a person in life's extremes. Or perhaps it's the wrong question to ask. Maybe it should be: *Are people good?* You know, I have four sons. The youngest is roughly your age. I haven't seen them in twenty years, since before the camps—"

"The Allies?" Zeiger asked with dumb surprise.

"Our own," Witzbold said. "We had our own—you do know that?" He paused and eyed Zeiger gloomily. There was an officer in his camp who distributed prisoner mail, he said. It was rare to receive correspondence, but one morning he came in with a whole packet of letters. When he read out the names of the addressees, to Witzbold's surprise his own name was included. The officer finished reading the names, said now the prisoners knew they'd received mail, then dumped the letters onto the floor and set them on fire. "Save for one," Witzbold said, raising a finger in the air. "Mine." And he poked his own chest. "My letter," he said, "the officer opens and reads in silence. Reads it for a very long time. The barrack room was so quiet you could hear the hay sighing. My wife has written me, this officer says. Says one of my sons has died. A gruesome death, typhoid. Then he takes out a lighter and lights it on fire. Says it's up to me to guess which one it was."

The sky had darkened considerably. A streetlamp above them jumped to life, spewing an aura of sick orange light.

"When he burned that letter," Witzbold said, "it occurred to me: the only thing deadlier than denial is hope in the goodness of men."

Zeiger tried to stop himself but couldn't refrain. "Which son was it?" he asked.

"I have no idea."

"You never saw them again?"

"I haven't so much as spoken to them. They left for America

with their mother before the end. They're probably off fighting that nonsensical war with the Vietnamese." Then Witzbold buried his hand in his pocket and from somewhere underneath the flap of his gut generated a pouch. "Dried plum?" he offered.

Zeiger dislodged one from the pouch. It burst in his mouth, oozed its contents, stung the hollow of a tooth.

Witzbold hefted the Manual from his lap into the light of the streetlamp. He looked at the cover for a very long time. "I do like the title. It is…" He paused and pursed his lips, squinting at the Manual as if it were a small piece of art. "Lyrical," he finally said.

"It's mainly theoretical," Zeiger said.

"On the contrary, it's insightful. A slap is much worse than a broken face—so you say in the preface—because at least there's something manly in severe suffering."

Zeiger squared his shoulders, drawing in his breath, deeply flattered by the meticulousness with which Witzbold had examined his work.

"What's the most basic freedom we have?" Witzbold asked. An earnest expression dominated his face.

Zeiger extended a hand and fished another dried plum from the bag. He chewed, reflecting. "To end our lives when we want to," he said.

"Even that can be controlled," Witzbold said. "No, it's the freedom to feel what we feel. You're right in this preface. Infants know only what their parents want them to know. They would remain infants for eternity if they couldn't self-determine. True existence begins when we can make choices. Feel what we must and think what we may. Men stripped of that are nothing but children, as you say. When was the last time you had your own feelings?"

"I lied today," Zeiger said. "To Management."

"How does that make you feel?" Witzbold asked.

Zeiger couldn't answer. They were silent for a while, enveloped by the damp nighttime breeze. He studied the side of Witzbold's face, his sad, baglike cheeks. "How did you survive?" he asked. "The camp?"

"It wasn't happening to me. Not to the man who loved his children. This is important, Zeiger. Are you listening?"

Zeiger stared at Witzbold with blank anticipation, resisting the urge to shout *Yes!* as he'd been ordered to during his school days.

"Numbing yourself makes some people fearless," Witzbold said. "Others it turns into murderers." He lifted the Manual, laid it softly on Zeiger's knees, and placed the bag of dried plums on top of it. Then he zipped his tracksuit up to his neck, rose, and said, *"Gute Nacht."* He shuffled down the darkened path, his body bent and luminous in the patches of ill orange light.

It was the last time Zeiger would see Witzbold. Three days after their night on the bench, an anonymous tipster called the Ministry accusing him of antisocialist sentiment. When the officers arrived for his arrest, they found him dressed in his best black suit and sprawled on his bed. Dead, they said, for at least three days. *What shall not be cannot be,* Mother had said on the day Berlin fell. The record would indicate that Witzbold had died of natural causes.

A few months later, the Party lifted the ban on gray, in a fit of collective regression. What had been planned as the 11th Zentralkomitee plenum on their New Economic System developed instead into a scorched-earth campaign to obliterate all liberal and progressive sentiment that had developed that year. Comrades returned to work in old muted suits and colorless ties and avoided one another. As quickly as the clouds had parted, they were shuttered back into a low-hanging mass every bit as deep, impenetrable, and, some would argue, even more gray than before.

2.6

Lara snorted in some private amusement. She crinkled her mouth into a lazy smile, opened an eye, shot Zeiger a look, then closed it again. It was clear he had overdone it. Too much detail, things that didn't matter to her. He'd had her attention when he was talking about Held, but he'd lost it. His hands grew sticky with shame. What a sorry lunatic he'd become. The vista outside had not changed. It was as dark and impervious as it had been for hours. Day would break soon, he estimated.

One woman, Zeiger shouted—and he had to shout now, because Lara's head was again tilting ever so slowly down the wall toward her shoulder, and he couldn't have her sleeping now, because this would be, for her, the most important part, and so he shouted until she smacked her lips together a few times, lifted her head, and strained her eyes at him in a daze. One woman stuck out with clarity in his mind—white, frail, and queerly arousing, even though their encounter had never been physical. She'd appeared roughly fifteen years ago, during the mid-1970s, when the Manual had long been completed and Held put away. At first he'd thought he was seeing things. One morning, after he left the corner café, he climbed into his Trabi and as he was checking his rearview mirror, a figure, a vague shape, flitted spasmodically out of his vision. When he turned, no one was there, but as soon as he'd composed himself and gone on his way, there it was again, a damp sensation on the back of his neck and a squirrelly shadow vanishing into the ether.

This happened with increasing frequency over the course of a week—an erratic movement in a darkened doorway as he looked outside his window, a soggy footstep between the hedges on his way to the market—until one morning, quite spur-of-the-moment, he decided to lure the phantom out into the open. As he stepped out of his building, he turned not right toward the café but left down the street, and broke into a sprint. He skidded around the next corner, came to an abrupt halt, and just as he swiveled around, there she was, stalling unsteadily a few paces behind him.

A moment passed. She was small, pale, freckled, her large, watery eyes rimmed red like those of an albino rabbit. She moved backward, jerking into herself. "What?" she asked with an air of defiance, crossing her arms. "What are you looking at?" There was a lull in her voice, something fuzzy and removed.

"I know you," Zeiger said.

"What do you know?"

"I don't know. What do *you* know?"

They gaped at each other, scowling with confusion.

"Never mind," she said then, "I've made a mistake."

"Are you drunk?"

"I suppose I am."

Zeiger relaxed. This was not the work of the Ministry. He advanced a few steps, showing his palms. The woman was wrapped tight in a bulky down coat, expensive-looking, of West German make. The ethanol on her breath smelled sharp and fresh. He marveled at the fine lace of capillaries over her lids, which she squeezed shut periodically to focus her gaze. From the depths of her sleeve she extended a hand. It was small like a child's and fracturable. This was how he met Katja Grün.

Her time was limited, she explained. Her visa was based on false papers. The Ministry had banished her. She didn't understand. They'd promised her a position at the Technische Universität in East Berlin, research grants, promotions. She had done as she'd been told back in the American desert. Instead they had taken her child.

"How would you know who I am?" Zeiger said.

Katja's stare grew distant.

"I could tell them you're back," he pushed.

"I could tell them he told you how those Mexican boys disappeared," she said.

"Did they?"

"I want my child," she said.

For a moment they scanned their surroundings. Nobody was watching, they were alone. Then, somewhere up above, a *crack* sounded, a door falling into its lock or a window whacking closed. Katja ducked, as if from an invisible fist, turned, and sprinted down the street. Zeiger pursued her, trotting in a soft-focus daze. There was no plan. Puffing laboriously, he followed her into a cross street, along the curved, unkempt lip of the Zion's Church lawn, into the gray mouth of an entranceway, and from there into a courtyard, where she stopped and beckoned him inside.

He found himself in her stove-heated bedroom, which she had rented, she explained, from an old university acquaintance. It was cold and sparsely furnished. There was a single window, against which a family of houseflies was hammering with futile purpose. From a bottle on the nightstand she poured them both a shot of vodka. At first he declined, then accepted and downed it. There were no chairs in the room. They sat on the bed. Silence followed, and a clearing of throats.

She had the humorless demeanor of single-minded people—priests, new mothers, quack healers with questionable motives. She poured herself another glass, sloshed it lovelessly down her throat. "Where's Held now?" she asked.

"I thought you would know that," Zeiger said, genuinely surprised.

"He's not in Hohenschönhausen, that much is certain."

"Did you love him?"

She stalled, then winced and twitched backward as if he'd spit in her face. "What does that mean for someone like me? They make you hate yourself. After that there's nothing else."

Zeiger considered this. Outside, the pigeons cooed and flirted, rustling their paper wings. "There's evidence to suggest that Held loved you very much," he said.

"It's just a matter of time before they disappear."

"That's a bleak prospect. There are couples who stay together for—"

"You misunderstand. Hans the Austrian, Rodolfo the Italian, the pair of Dutchmen, Jan and Herman, they've all vanished—*whoosh!*" She mimed a small detonation. "Nowhere to be found after the desert."

"Like those Mexican children?" Zeiger said. He leaned forward, elbows on knees, surprised at the animation he felt.

"I'm more concerned about my own," she said, and bending over the edge of the bed, she slid out a suitcase from which she retrieved a tattered notebook. She handed Zeiger a laminated photograph. A black-and-white portrait of a perplexed-looking newborn with extraterrestrial eyes. "Find her," she said. "If you can do that, I'll tell you everything."

*   *   *

It wasn't difficult to locate the child. In the footnotes of the case file—stored away now in a Ministry archive—he found a mention of an orphanage in Leipzig, which he set out to visit a few days later.

It was noontime when he arrived. A gusty day spritzed with wet snow. The orphanage, a dilapidated structure with a hazardously overgrown yard, was surrounded, much like a prison, by a chain-link fence. He parked in the lot, and, in the rearview mirror, watched for a while as a slow stream of children trickled from the back of the building and into the yard. Like tiny drunk people in over-size jackets and mittens, they waddled into a corner and huddled together, hiding from the cold in the slipstream of the building. It was playtime. The operation was simple: go inside, use his Ministry ID card, persuade the director to let him see the child.

The director didn't need convincing. The children ranged from two to sixteen years old, he said as he guided Zeiger through the barren hallways and toward the back of the building. He was a soft-spoken, soft-faced young man, corpulent but with long, effeminate hands. The younger ones, he said, those from six to eight, enjoyed "handiwork assignments," for which their nimble little fingers suited them well. Others could serve as decoy kin. "Most of your officers seem to have an issue employing their own offspring for such things," the director said. "Depending on the children's age and assignment, fees vary."

"I just need to see the one I mentioned," Zeiger said.

"Naturally," said the director, ushering him through the back door and into the yard.

The noise was deafening, bestial in pitch. About three dozen children swarmed the yard, shouting, sprinting, chasing, quarreling in varying degrees of murderous play. From among a cluster of leafless bushes, a group of boys rattled a burst of gunfire at Zeiger, pointing their makeshift wooden rifles at him with surprising skill.

The orphanage had found that an hour of unstructured play decreases dissociation and aggression, the director explained, though he acknowledged that they'd been experiencing some difficulties with the formation of hierarchical structures. Their goal, of course, was the implementation of a collectivist mindset. He asked Zeiger if he'd gotten around to reading *Lord of the Flies*.

Zeiger shook his head. He was searching the multitude of small, hungry faces, attempting to detect in them some vague resemblance—to Held, to Katja—but the children struck him as altogether generic, a conglomerate of miniature people, each equipped with a miniature being.

"There," the director said and lifted a forefinger.

Under a tree on the far side of the yard, a circle of crouched children was picking with curiosity at something in the mud. Uneasy, it seemed, about whatever they had found, they were cocking their little heads, deliberating with secretive frowns.

"Where?" Zeiger said.

"There, in the black wool coat and brown mittens." Then the director squinted at the children's activity. "Excuse me, comrade," he said, and shouting and shaking his fist in the air, he stomped toward the tree.

The circle of children screamed and scattered. Only one child remained, a girl about nine years of age, who wore a black coat with mouse-brown mittens. Cupped in her hands was the limp body of a crow wrapped in a shawl removed from her own head. The girl was white-blonde with a tinge of copper, and, like Katja, exceptionally pale and copiously freckled. She had Held's chin, but not quite as regrettably receding.

Towering over her now, screaming with impatience, the director attempted to dislodge the bird from her hands, prying them open with such force that the girl nearly toppled forward, screeching in pain. The image froze, blue-white in the glassy winter light, and for an instant Zeiger thought he would charge at the man, grab his baby-round skull, and crack it open. But he did not. The bird plummeted into the mud.

Yanking the girl by the ear, the director hauled her toward the building. "This one and animals," he explained as they passed. "All sorts! Don't let her even close to dogs. She'd give them all the food we have left."

The girl's jaw was set, her thin mouth curved into an unreadable smile. She did not look up at Zeiger.

He let a few days pass. When he returned to Katja's apartment, her things were no longer there. Only a faint odor of stale liquor remained. A little digging revealed that she'd been detected, or rather, a few neighbors had found her presence suspicious and reported her, along with her university friend—who, to this day, has been residing at Hohenschönhausen for subversive sentiments—to the relevant authorities. She had been deported again, Zeiger's Ministry contact explained. It was unlikely she would ever again succeed in crossing the border, and as far as Zeiger knew, she never did.

Later that week he found himself back in Leipzig, staring once more at the image in his rearview mirror of the cackling, sprinting, sometimes screaming figure of the girl. She was now, unbeknownst to her, even more alone than before. With increasing frequency and against all reason, he continued driving the two hours to the orphanage lot, searching always for a sign of the girl—in the low-hanging fog, or later, in spring, among the budding fruit of the snowberry bushes—until his visits became a reflexive, self-governing system, as unconscious and essential as breathing.

As she got older, she stopped running, screeched less, began spending more time congressing with her girlfriends while leaning fashionably against the brick wall of the building. More than once, Zeiger watched a group of gangly boys approach and try to catch her attention with taunts and ridiculous games. She kicked them in the shins, an action he approved of. She grew, but not excessively. Her hair never darkened. When she turned sixteen, she was released from the orphanage. She moved to Berlin and started work at the café. By this time she was a fully formed being. A microcosm of private thoughts and untouchable feelings—their child, Held's daughter, his Lara. He would make sure she didn't disappear.

He'd regained Lara's attention with the story of Katja. There were shadows around her lids, and her usual taut composure was slack, but she was listening. She stared at him quizzically, computing the narrative. Earlier, when her eyes had been closed and her face burrowed into the tops of her knees, it had been easy to turn and pull the key out of the bedroom-door lock, then slither it into his pocket. He fondled it as he wandered over and took a seat on the bed, neither too close nor too far from her. He leaned his back against the wall, let his heavy feet dangle off the side of the bed, and tested the whining box spring under his weight. It was an unnatural position, agile and young.

Lara studied him, her expression impassive.

What reaction had he expected? He opened his mouth, closed it again. Drops of rain studded the window. They sought one another, merged, and drained in long weeping streams. The porcelain setter stared from the coffee table, its flat canine mouth stretched into a grin. Zeiger tried to speak, but nothing came. He waited. Surely there would be a hint of something, anything. A sliver of grief, confusion, or hate. But there was nothing. No punishment, no divine judgment. Of all the things he had done, the most contemptible was this: creating a generation, an entire nation, immune to monstrosity.

Without warning, Lara catapulted herself from the bed and lunged toward the door. She stretched out her arms and grabbed the knob, rattled it savagely, murderously, her body bent, her back turned.

Zeiger experienced a moment of dreamlike relief. They had not been truly alone until she knew the door was locked.

She continued rattling the knob for a while, then dropped her arms and tilted her head, as though seeing a door for the very first time. Once more she drew up her hands, gave a final, weak jolt to the knob, then turned around.

To Zeiger's surprise, she was smiling, whether with shrewdness or insanity, he couldn't tell. In the matte darkness broken only by the dim lamp in the corner, it was hard to gauge if the smile was for him.

"This feels like a metaphor," she said.

"You give life too much credit," he said.

Then her body began swaying. She shifted her weight from one foot to the other, shimmying to some inaudible tune. With slow, feline steps she walked toward the bed. She crossed her arms and clasped the seam of her sweater, lifted it, revealing the rumpled waist of her leggings. "I understand now," she said, unnaturally. "I've heard of guys like you. You could've just said this is what you wanted. We'd have been out of here a long time ago." She stopped at the edge of the bed, wriggled out of her sweater, and dropped it on the floor. She wore a brassiere of some modern, strappy sort that covered the whole of her breasts. Her milky skin was pied blue from the cold. She arched forward across the edge of the bed and placed a hand on his shin. It rested there, small and warm. "Is this what you want?"

She was right there, her sweet, angled eyes the length of an arm away from his own. This was Lara. Leaning sideways, away from her face, he tugged his coat from the chair and rummaged its pockets until he found Mother's Walther, which he held up for Lara.

She let out a cry that sounded like a question.

He placed the pistol on his palm, presented it to her like seeds to a bird. She stumbled backward and knocked the coffee table, causing it to shiver, then raised an elbow like a shield. It was for this reason that he had locked the door, to prevent her from fleeing while he gave her the pistol.

"What is it?" she shrieked.

"I have no children and this is of value."

"What is it?" she cried again. With one quick dart she stole toward the window, where she groped her bare shoulders crosswise, covering herself.

"When I'm dead it will be all they see," he said. "This also." He lodged the Walther under his arm as he launched back into his coat pockets for the small velvet box. He snapped it open to reveal Father's pin, the bright grinning skull.

She glared into the box from afar. "Is this a joke?" she said. "Whyever the fuck would I want that?"

"To remember me by," he said. He placed the box on the table and rotated it slightly, so that it caught the dim light. She could sell it if she wanted to, he told her. The Americans offered rewards for them, or so he'd heard. They called it *paraphernalia*. But he hoped she would keep it, if that was all right.

He didn't wait for a response. He retrieved the porcelain setter, placed it next to Father's pin. Then would come Mother's Walther. He moistened its handle with his breath, polished it with the sleeve of his coat, and aligned it nicely next to Father's pin. He cocked his head, taking in his composition. This was what would be left of him. Propping his hands on his knees for leverage, he hoisted himself off the bed. Lara's sweater lay in a pile at his feet. He bent over, gathered it, folded it, and put it on the bed. At the door he retrieved the key from his pants pocket and fumbled it into the lock.

"Did he ever find out?" Lara said. "That you lied?"

He turned in the doorway. "His life was already ruined," he said.

"Did he know?" she asked.

"I don't know."

"How to teleport people?"

"I like to believe that he did."

"Why, because that would make you less of a criminal?"

"For the same reason you want to believe you can topple this system," he said.

Lara opened her mouth as if to speak but held back.

It was time to leave. He stepped into the anteroom, circumventing the tangle of shoes on the floor.

Just as he reached the front door, Lara appeared in the doorway, clutching her sweater. "Don't," she said.

"See you tomorrow? Before the parade?" Zeiger asked. "At the café?"

She looked at him and the whites of her eyes appeared somehow lit from within. "I just wanted to say..." She paused and he could see that her mind was grasping. "Nosebleeds can be a symptom of a serious condition." She hunched, shivering now, her naked shoulder blades jutting like wings from her back.

She had never looked more like a child to Zeiger, not in all his years of visiting the orphanage. Though he did not yet know it, that would be the last time he ever saw Lara.

*   *   *

As he stepped outside, a gust of wind hit him sideways, spitting rain. The street was quiet, indifferent, aglow with damp early-morning light. He wrapped his coat tight, flipped up his collar. In his car he lit a cigarette and smoked for a while. Eventually, in a haze, he drove himself home. Failure and shame; iron and steel. Some things were bound not to change. Tomorrow morning, just as he'd been ordered to, he would report to observe the parade. He would stand among his fellow citizens, the good German coward that he was, and watch them with duty and stone-faced vigilance.

3

3.1

The punk coughed, which drew Zeiger's attention. The young man was sitting on Lara's bed, elbows propped on his knees. He hadn't moved from this position over the last half hour of monologuing about Zeiger's age, Lara's vanishing, ever-new angles on the irreversible results of radioactive air pollution. Finally he'd fallen silent, and it was the absence of the sound of his voice, followed by his cough, that had startled Zeiger out of narcosis and into the present.

Like a child, tongue rolled and chuting from the circlet of his lips, the punk coughed again, beating his chest as if he were gravely ill. *Radiation pneumonitis or something,* he explained in a thick voice.

The girl sighed with annoyance from her spot on the floor. She had come to lie beneath the window and was reclined in a position often assumed at the beach, an arm draped over her face, one leg dangling over the other.

The punk stirred and began inspecting the room: the bed, the messy pile of clothes in front of the closet, the coffee table. He seemed to be confirming their existence, the general reality of the room, that it was here Zeiger had last seen his friend.

Then the punk spoke, quietly but with a degree of force. "Did you kill Lara?" he said. "Are you a pervert?" He was not looking at Zeiger but at his own hands, which he was massaging as if they were cold. "You want me to believe she just—*wham!*—vanished? I think this is all one of your—how did you call it? One of those *demoralization* things you people use on everyone."

"I thought we had established I'm not one of them," Zeiger said. "You said so yourself. I'm too old. And as I told you, I haven't seen Lara since I spoke to her here, a month ago." He considered the punk, whose eyes grew soft and distant, as if straining to compute a difficult riddle. Then Zeiger said he was thirsty and would like to get something to drink.

The punk jerked his head backward, quick and turkey-like. "Am I an idiot? No, you're staying right here. You," he said, jabbing the girl with his foot, "get this man some water."

The girl jolted up as if out of a trance. "What the hell, man?" she said in a cotton voice. She spotted Zeiger, and, after a long, confused second, slumped her shoulders with bored recognition. "Don't tell me what to do," she said, but she pushed herself up and disappeared into the kitchen.

"I'd be careful with tap water," the punk said.

"Lead," Zeiger said.

"Cesium 137 in the soil, the air, our water."

"The Russians already acknowledged the accident, on television, for everyone to see. That's the difference between us and those Americans."

"That our system values life?" the punk asked.

"Their system values it so much they believe there's more of it after they die."

"Afterlife," the punk said, and chuckled heartlessly, gazing into space. "Heaven. We all get the hell we've envisioned."

"It's not all so terrible here, considering the alternative, is it?" Zeiger said. He straightened himself, leaned forward emphatically. Now he was getting somewhere. "Why would you want this to end? You want us all to become like those Americans?"

The punk's face brightened in genuine surprise. The Americans couldn't even admit to their underground tests, he said. No, nobody here was interested in getting in with the West. "It's nothing but constant babble over there," he said, flapping his fingers like the bill of a duck. "So much noise, and war, and noise, and television. For all the afterlife they believe in, they're sure afraid of dying." The punk paused, musing. "We're not so different, you and me. You people can keep your Wall for all we care. That's what you don't understand. You always think we want this to end, so you gag us"—he strangled the air with both hands—"but you know what happens to kids with overbearing mothers?"

"I do, actually," Zeiger said.

"They become impotent, secretive motherfuckers. Go under-ground with their sickness and perversion. We're not shooting people dead on the street like those cowboys do over there. No, worse, we lock our daughters in basements and make them eat their own hair. If you think our resistance is just some sort of political thing, you're all deafer than I thought. We don't mind our system, it'll be around for another hundred years. It's not the *what*, it's the *how*. Let us be."

"How," Zeiger echoed.

"We're not stupid. We know someone like Lara doesn't just disappear. You did something to her."

"So why don't you call the police on the fucker already?" said the girl, who had shuffled back into the room. She stopped in front of Zeiger and handed him a glass of water.

He clasped it but his hands were so numb and heavy that he could hardly feel the glass.

Dragging her feet, the girl padded to the window, took a seat on the floor, and eyed them both dully.

"You go and call," the punk said. "No way I'm leaving this guy here alone."

The girl inhaled sharply, then expelled the air with a sigh. She closed her lids and massaged her eyes in small circular motions. "Nobody has to leave," she said under her breath.

"Yeah, nobody's leaving," the punk confirmed, fixing Zeiger with a stare and crossing his arms bouncer-style.

"You dimwit!" the girl burst out. "Nobody has to leave because there's a phone in here."

A lag followed, a moment of confusion in which both Zeiger and the punk appraised the girl, who sat cross-legged and hunched, her eyes as round as coins.

"You're drunk," the punk said.

No doubt he knew, as Zeiger did, that neither Lara nor anyone else in his general aura would ever have been allotted a personal phone.

"Don't believe me?" she said. "Go look for it."

The punk hesitated. He rotated, examined the room, then extended a foot and upended a pile of garments in front of him. It toppled and spread across the floor. The punk crouched to peek under the bed, then vanished into the closet, where he foraged with impatient grunts.

Zeiger suggested that if there was one in this unit, it would be attached to the wall.

The punk emerged from the closet, stood for a moment with

dumb indecision, then dropped on all fours and began casing the walls with rodent-like speed.

"It would be a little higher—right about here," Zeiger said, indicating his midsection.

The punk glanced up at him, then stood, circled the room once, and returned to angle his arm into the space behind the closet.

Zeiger observed the operation with levelheaded remove. He checked his watch. Just after six. He remembered Schabowski. The press conference was starting this minute. He closed his eyes, squeezing them tight. The day had derailed hopelessly.

"Oh," the punk said, his voice echoing from behind the closet. He tugged at something and emerged holding the black loop of a cable, which he inspected before dropping it on the floor. Then he walked to the other end of the closet, foraged for a while, and resurfaced with a lime-green phone with a black plastic dial. It looked polished, new, and inhumanly real. He and Zeiger must have stared at the contraption together for a whole silent minute.

"You're surprised," the girl said, her round eyes flitting between the punk and Zeiger.

The punk twitched. The phone's metal innards jangled in response.

"You can't imagine that Lara had an inner life," the girl continued. "Something private that had nothing to do with you. Well, they got her like the rest of us. Recruited her a long while back, gave her a phone to call them with. She didn't tell me everything—didn't want to get me too involved—but this much I knew."

"But—" came out of the punk's mouth.

"*Ja,*" the girl laughed, "that's right. So either he offed her or finally let her out of the deal."

"Me?" Zeiger said, the word surfacing slowly, like a methane-gas bubble from a swamp.

"You? No, that guy who's been coming around to see her. Maybe he finally let her go."

"Go where?" the punk asked.

The girl narrowed her eyes, worked out a smile. "Out," she said. "Out of the country. She must've finally given them what they wanted or something."

"What guy?" Zeiger asked. "Who're you talking about?"

Exasperated, the girl threw up her arms, extending her open palms as if in a plea to the sky.

"Some blind guy has been coming round," the punk said, his voice tinged with a wonder that suggested the implications were only now dawning on him. He frowned deeply at the phone in his hands. "Handsome guy, jaw cut like a movie star, but blind as a bat."

"Brings her presents," the girl said.

Nausea crawled, millipede-like, from the sour sack of his stomach up the length of his throat. He remembered Schreibmüller and his companion—the porcelain shop in Meissen—and thought of Held's explanation of synchronicity, how events could be connected and meaningful even without a causal relationship. Zeiger had believed him. He'd believed that something as precious as coincidence could exist in this system. But there was no such thing. For a moment he felt as though he would relieve himself on the floor, but even that seemed laborious and futile. He considered the phone in the punk's hands, then the file on the floor. Lara's existence assembled in a stack of paper no thicker than the nail of his own little finger. That alone should have made him suspicious. No one's life was so thin.

"Why the presents?" the punk asked. It was a general question, pitched with quiet desperation not to the girl but into the room itself.

"To get her to do a number on someone," the girl said. "From the look on this old sack's face"—the girl flicked her chin in Zeiger's direction—"I bet he was the mark. Seems like it's working."

The punk lifted his head. He was still clutching the phone with both hands, holding it away from his body now, as if it might detonate at any moment. "Why you?" he said to Zeiger. "Who are you to her?" His eyes had turned sad, emptied of all hate or anger.

The punk's question came as if from a great distance. They had recruited Lara like the rest of them. How had he missed that? What else had he missed? Zeiger's mind felt like a searchlight, capable of illuminating only one sorry fact at a time. The whole picture, the backdrop, was much like the cosmos Held had described: cold and dark, ruthless and blind.

The girl and the punk had started conversing by the window, their foreheads so close together they nearly touched. Occasionally they paused to glance at Zeiger, slitting their eyes, thinking, shooting looks, plotting. He had compassion for their problem. Soon they digressed into a squabble. *"Tod,"* he thought he heard the girl say, or *"Brot."*

"We'll be locked up in Hohenschönhausen by midnight if we let him go now," she whispered hoarsely. "The first thing he'll do is report us."

"Look at him," the punk replied, gesturing at Zeiger as if at a thing. "Does he look like someone interested in reporting someone right now?"

"We can't just go," she said.

"What do you suggest?"

"We kill him."

"You again with the killing."

"We could suffocate him," she said, pointing at a pillow on the bed.

"You have any idea how long that would take?"

"He's too fat to strangle," she said impassively. "We could push him out the window."

The punk seemed to be picturing this, eyeballing first the window, then Zeiger. "No," he said. "Look what they've done to him. The poor fuck is all—"

A crash sounded outside the window, followed by a second of crystalline silence. Then, with one enormous, human-like screech, a car horn erupted from the street. The punk and the girl froze mid-flinch and turned to Zeiger, their eyes screwed open with soft, simple fear.

Zeiger rose, wedged himself between them, and looked through the curtains. He saw nothing at first. The sidewalks, fissured and sprouting with dead weeds, were calm and unpeopled. Fallen leaves in varying degrees of decay dotted the street like an intricate mosaic. He pressed his forehead against the cool glass, scanned the cars parked sporadically alongside the curb. Then he saw it: below them, parked on the opposite curb, an eggshell-brown Trabi, its headlights and taillights ablaze. It took Zeiger a moment to understand the delicate arrangement of car, lights, horn. He crouched, spotted the driver, who was slumped in his seat with the whole of his face resting against the steering wheel, causing it to blare uninterrupted. His arm, the one visible from this vantage point, dangled motionlessly at his side. He had the posture of someone prepared to receive a massage.

"He's dead," the punk said. In the chlorinated light his profile was sharp and inscrutable.

"Can't be," the girl whispered.

Nothing stirred. Not the driver, nor Zeiger and his companions, who stood perfectly still, fogging the window. The car horn was reaching a strained, inconsolable pitch.

"Isn't anybody going to help?" the girl asked.

"Heart attack or stroke," the punk replied. "Not much you can do."

"How do you know?"

"Look at him, he just keeled. Something must've startled him."

They craned their necks, speaking to each other around Zeiger, their tone calm and clinical, then fell silent for a while.

"What an odd day to die," the girl said finally.

At last people began to emerge from their doorways and circle in on the car. Some turned their heads as they approached. Others cast their eyes up into the clouds, as if the car and its driver had fallen from the sky and another such miracle could occur at any time. A woman in a printed housedress searched the vehicle. Behind her trailed a boy no older than six, nibbling on his coat sleeve. His mother flung open the car door, then jerked up and stumbled away. She bolted back into the building, leaving her gape-mouthed child to stare into the vehicle. More people congregated at a distance, wagging their hands or cupping the sides of their heads. All the while the car horn continued its vile cry.

It crossed Zeiger's mind that the man wasn't dead, and that they were all partaking in some sort of play.

The little boy whose mother had left him shuffled toward the car. He seemed to reflect for a moment, then extended a finger and poked the man in the shoulder.

"We'd better hurry up," the punk burst out, lunging toward his jacket on the bed. He hastened toward the door, then turned to shout at the girl. "You coming?"

"I'm not stealing from a dead man, if that's what you have in mind."

"But you're okay killing this one?" the punk said, pointing at Zeiger.

"This gnat obviously isn't innocent."

"Nobody's innocent around here. Let's go." With that, the punk swiveled on his heel and a few seconds later was out the door and tramping down the stairwell.

The girl let out a moan. She picked up her jacket, combatively inserted her arms into its sleeves. Halfway out the door, she stopped and looked at Zeiger. "We wouldn't have killed you," she said. "None of us are evil, you know."

"Who else?" Zeiger asked, advancing a step. "Don't go. Who other than the blind guy has been around to see Lara? Was there a large guy, very tanned, athletic? Perhaps a man with a setter?" The girl stared at him blankly, chewing her lip. She stared for so long that Zeiger took another step forward and repeated himself to make sure she'd understood. "Who else has been here?" he said.

She gave a tight, girlish shrug. "Fuck do I know?" she said and banged the apartment door shut behind her.

Zeiger returned to the window. His eyes sought the little boy, leaning against the front of the building, his mouth ajar, arms hanging by his sides. A distant, idle look covered his face, as if he were absorbed by some riveting show. Two men who had split from the group of onlookers were walking toward the marooned car. They inspected the vehicle, gesturing and nodding to each other with amateur expertise. Apart from the unending sound of the horn, it was a casual scene, familiar and relaxed, like nothing more than a friendly curbside chat. They shifted the body and the blaring stopped, replaced by the metallic echo of the car radio, which was blasting the press conference at full throttle. Schabowski's voice was the last the dead man had heard. One of the men switched off the radio. A silence unfolded, so sweeping and clean it was as if it were the first moment of silence in the history of time.

A few seconds later the punk bolted across the street, flapping his arms as if to scare away crows. He had draped his leather jacket over his head like a veil, shielding himself, Zeiger understood, from the air's intangible contagion. The two men by the car observed this ludicrous debut with something like amusement. When the punk arrived and began puffing out his chest, they retreated, sideways, in good German fashion, back toward the circle of neighbors. The punk searched the car, then the glove compartment. The girl, whom Zeiger hadn't seen outside until this moment, appeared by his side, and after a short exchange of words, she looped around to the driver's side, where she busied herself. Their movements were quick, practiced, and methodical. Nobody intervened.

Zeiger directed his attention toward the man at the wheel, whose head, now leaning back and sideways on the headrest, was facing Zeiger through the passenger door. A trickle of blood bisected his forehead in one clean, unbroken dash, giving the impression that someone, maybe even the man himself, had perfected its placement for theatrical effect. This was death, a performance of itself. The man did not return Zeiger's stare.

What came to Zeiger's mind was the waiting room on the Ministry compound to which comrades were summoned for loyalty interviews. It was a small, square room, with an overhead light that threw its occupants' eyes into shadows; wooden chairs lining the walls gave it a forum-like feel. One after the other, comrades would be called by name, prompting them to enter through a black, handleless door, behind which they vanished for an hour or more. The remaining comrades waited, evading one another's gazes, clearing their throats, with a nervous type always whispering in an attempt to engage a stone-faced neighbor, until finally the door opened and the comrade resurfaced, his collar loosened, his hair in disarray, as if he had just concluded not an interview but harsh manual labor. A ritual silence would befall the room, a tribute to the one returned, and it was then, as now, that Zeiger experienced a swell of awe for the man emerged from the underworld, who was now a custodian of great secrets, someone who had not only glimpsed but also grasped that all this would end. Someone like the driver below, someone like Held.

The punk had pulled a briefcase off the passenger's seat and onto the ground, where he squatted, strewing its contents, unfazed by the little boy, the six-year-old, who had somehow materialized again close by. It seemed, at first, as if the boy were merely curious, but soon he started stomping his feet, pulled the jacket off the punk's head, and began assaulting him with small, impotent kicks to the leg. The girl's head emerged above the roof of the car. She glanced first at the punk, then at the boy, then at the group of onlookers, now reduced to a small group of men huddling like sideline football coaches a few paces away.

It occurred to Zeiger that he was free to go.

He wheeled around to face Lara's room, which appeared new and foreign. It was November. Night did not fall, it plunged with finality. The air was motionless, electric with meaning, as in an ancient tomb or at the scene of an unwitnessed murder. His gaze landed on the coffee table and its relief of objects: coffee-crusted mugs; spineless books; ashtrays filled to the brim; a pair of broken glasses; cosmetics jars; bottles of nail polish, some toppled and leaking, others leaning in strange equilibrium. He took in the arrangement for a whole stupefied minute, not the objects so much as what was missing: Mother's Walther, Father's pin, and the porcelain setter. Until now he had failed to notice their absence. Lara had taken them with her.

Any room, he realized, can be a torture chamber. It need not be titled as such to become one. A bedroom, a pretty house, a state, one's own porous skull.

He picked up Lara's file from the floor, dropped it again—what did it matter? In semi-darkness he felt his way toward the exit, found the anteroom, then the door. The stairwell was hard to navigate. He gripped the banister, sought the edge of each step with his foot, and shuffled blindly around the landings, an eternal descent in the dark.

By the time Zeiger reached the street an ambulance had arrived. Its roof lights flared red, illuminating house fronts and faces, cobblestones and windshields, as if by human pulse. Two paramedics in billowing white slacks were in the process of rearranging the driver in his seat. They did so calmly and with competence. Across the street, the woman in the printed housedress was conversing with a policeman who seemed to have arrived on foot. Some onlookers leered from the sidewalks, others were leaving. The punk and the girl had long since disappeared.

Zeiger searched for the little boy. The boy was important. He found him standing alone at the edge of the ambulance. Legs spread and fists balled at his sides, he was scrutinizing the paramedics' attempts to remove the driver from the car. In a practiced maneuver of hoisting and leveraging, the men finally succeeded in extracting the body. They grabbed it by armpit and ankle, letting it dangle in the air for a moment. The little boy twitched and lunged forward from his post by the ambulance. The fate of the nation was entrusted to children.

3.2

One winter during the war, Mother had taken him to Lake Müggelsee. She wore a black wool service coat and a side cap, just as black, and had it not been for the puffs of their breath or those white pins on her coat, he would have thought the whole world had been frost-swept in black. Mother had marched him at a punishing pace along the forested path and down a trail toward the lake, and there, at the lake's edge, between the shrubs and weeds that stuck like skeletal fingers from the ice, Mother ordered him to strip. Down to his socks and underpants he stripped, and before he could look up at Mother, she shoved him into the water, which sliced his skin, slashed his face, submerged him entirely. It was his first conscious moment, his first awareness of being a soul in a body. He didn't know how long he remained underwater, but just as quickly as she had pushed him in, Mother retrieved him. "Men don't catch death," she said, and began rubbing him down with the starched wool of his sweater. He ran a fever for a week but never again contracted a chill. According to Mother, she had made him invincible.

He steered, the tires of his car quaking with exhaustion, away from Lara's apartment, onto Leninallee, and toward the Ministry. He accelerated and the sad plastic parts of his Trabi shivered. Clusters of people engrossed in hushed conversation lined the street. A pair of women with shopping bags at their feet stood on a corner, one weeping, the other paralyzed with furious laughter. The lanes opposite, leading west into Mitte, were chaotic and heavily clogged with cyclers and vehicles. It was just after eight. This was highly unusual. It took him a moment to realize the streetlamps hadn't been ignited.

He sped. He passed crumbling facades, house fronts torn open to expose bowels of wire, shelled lots and jungles of weeds, all decay and ruin. Nothing had changed, this was his home. Always a void, his childhood and home. If only he could bring it all back—Mother and Father. But it occurred to him that although he had once been a child and there had been a childhood, it was amorphous and blank, an emptiness designed to torture by vanishing.

A group of teenagers with rucksacks bolted onto the street. They ran, light and buoyant, toward the median. Zeiger swerved but did not brake. He ran a red light at Strausberger Platz; nobody noticed, nobody cared. All yield to the maniac maimed by betrayal.

Schreibmüller, his virile and beautiful neighbor, had been in on it. Worse, of course, was Lara. Her hand on his shoulder had been the Ministry's hand on his shoulder. On his life. Ledermann—who else?—must have finally baited Management with Held's illusive confession. He must have used Schreibmüller, used Lara, to draw out Zeiger and his ancient involvement. But why? Precisely the question designed to drive subjects to madness. One always looked for meaning in monstrosity.

Zeiger, flying with lunatic speed, blurted out a cackle. Had this been the order of things? An intricate procedure? He thought of betrayal—betrayal of State, betrayal of Party, betrayal of self—and whether it was betrayal that turned boys into men. He would have to ask Ledermann. He would have to ask Held.

The Ministry came into view. Its concrete-slab face loomed dark over the intersection. He stopped at the light. It would be impossible to turn left across Leninallee into the lot. Traffic into Mitte had come to a halt. People had exited their cars and were conversing with other drivers. One family—complete with grandparents, parents, a couple of teenagers, and toddlers—piled out of their Trabi, gathered their things, and continued on foot.

Thunder caught Zeiger's ear, followed by a screech like breaking metal. For an instant he wasn't sure if his legs were quaking or if the pavement had started shaking beneath his car. Then a tram ground to an earsplitting halt just short of the intersection. A middle-aged man, about his own age, dressed smartly in a fitted coat and pressed trousers, stood on the tracks gaping at an unlatched briefcase in his hand. Manila files, snippets of paper, three-ring binders, and colorful booklets had spilled from his briefcase onto the pavement. There was a baffled, indignant look on the man's face, as if he were witnessing not a personal mishap but some great cosmic punishment. Zeiger immediately recognized him as one of their own.

It was a regular occurrence, a near miss, tram versus person, and knowing his fellow Berliners, Zeiger understood how the encounter would continue. The conductor was a short, beefy man with a choleric red face, and as he climbed from his cab, it was certain he was preparing to launch into a violent rage. What came next hit Zeiger with such peculiarity that he could only watch in awe. After studying the chaos, the conductor stretched out an arm, shook the man's hand, and together, like comrades, like the greatest of friends, they began collecting the papers from the ground.

Communal lunacy, low-pressure weather, something was happening. Zeiger left his car at the curb on Leninallee, navigated the intersection on foot, and crossed diagonally into the Ministry lot. Just as he began to slow his pace, the streetlamps clinked in unison, illuminating the gate before him with timid cones of light. The gate was ajar. He approached the guard booth, which was empty and locked. Nothing short of a nuclear strike would leave this post unmanned. Only a few cars lined the lot.

As he entered the foyer, he was relieved to spot a woman rummaging through a stack of boxes piled haphazardly and for no apparent reason around the lounge area. Dressed in block heels and a pantsuit, tending to her boxes, she spelled order and maternal propriety. Zeiger approached, treading firmly to announce his arrival, but she did not so much as look up to acknowledge his presence, as if he were both invisible and soundless.

He encountered nobody on the paternoster. It wheeled him past corridors that were lit and empty. In the Science and Technology Unit, the silence quickened, grew thick and vibrant. A few loose pieces of paper were scattered on the ground. Zeiger peered through open office doors, saw no one. The entire Unit had vanished. The break room was deserted. The TV on top of the refrigerator was switched off, its glass screen as black as the back of a mirror. Panic whirled from the centrifuge of Zeiger's chest. Ledermann was gone, his door wide open. Zeiger would enter, confirm its desolation. There was a draft, a slight pull of wind, diluting the dirt scent of burned papers and ashes. Whatever gizmos and contraptions had buzzed and blinked during his morning visit lay dormant. They looked like toy things now, harmless and phony. Zeiger would advance a few steps more, absorb the odd silence of Ledermann's empty office.

"Someone turned the main power off," a voice declared.

Zeiger swiveled, saw nobody. He looked about hectically; the door, the desk, the metal closet, behind which he discovered Ledermann. He was sitting on the floor, wedged between closet and wall, his knees drawn to his chest.

The generator had picked up after a while, Ledermann said, but now everyone was gone and he was all out of matches. Did Zeiger have any? Or a lighter? He wasn't quite finished burning these papers yet. Ledermann's voice was low but firm, the coarse whisper of someone hoping not to disturb a sleeping child.

The two men studied each other for a while: Ledermann, his massive elbows propped on his knees; Zeiger, paralyzed and mute, standing quite erect in the middle of the room. It was unclear whether Ledermann understood the irregularity of this occurrence. He was looking at Zeiger with kindness, a little blurrily. A weak, sad smile quivered on his lips. Piles of paper were scattered around Ledermann's feet, some shredded, others singed or burned to ashes. Whatever they had done to Ledermann, it had come to fruition. There was tenderness in his face, an air of comradely sympathy.

Zeiger took a step forward. "What have you done to me?" he said.

Ledermann cocked his head, his face docile and limp. "You found Rudi already?" he asked. He was unreachable.

"Who?"

"My son."

"No," Zeiger said. It took him a moment to recall who Rudi was.

Ledermann seemed to digest this, then turned his attention to a stack of documents in front of him. He retrieved a few papers and began shredding them lengthwise, at once deeply consumed by the process.

"You told them everything?" Zeiger said. "About Held, how I lied about his confession? Management knows?"

"Maybe. Yes, maybe I did," Ledermann said, his voice far away.

"Look at me. What they've done to me." He was crying now—slow, lifeless tears. "I don't even know what day it is."

"Was it all part of it?" Zeiger said. "Part of the procedure? Lara at the café? Everyone else at the café? Her file? Schreibmüller, my neighbor? Has he been watching me ever since he moved in? Why a blind man, for Christ's sake? And Lara—what did you tell her, what did she know? Where did she go? What was in it for her?" He could not stop himself. He didn't wait for answers. Though his voice echoed majestically, he felt shameful and desperate.

"The more intently we watch someone," Ledermann said, "the less we notice they're watching us. Isn't that true, Bernd? You wrote the Manual. Listen, I had to give them something to take the pressure off, you understand? Ever since that goddamn megabit-chip fiasco, what they've been doing to us, to Rudi? I couldn't bear it anymore. And Nadine, she's dying, you know. They told me, 'Give us something. Give us someone.'" Ledermann paused, panting feverishly, then continued, "So I thought of you and Held and that whole scenario. I have to admit, I never forgot about the guy. Maybe that's because we never did find out what he knew about those Americans. In reality, I'm not sure he knew the first thing about teleportation. But—I'm ashamed to say it—during my darkest hours, searching, waiting for Rudi, it's Held who crosses my mind. And I wonder, is it possible? Could he have—"

"I know," Zeiger said.

Ledermann stared, smiling with relief and commiseration. "Be that as it may, I told Management about your little situation back then, the creative license you took reporting on Held's confession, and what do you know, they loved it! The devil knows why, it was all so long ago. But it was worthless without your confession, and that's when I remembered Lara and how you've been tracking her."

"I have not," Zeiger said, pointlessly.

Ledermann waited a beat. He leveled his eyes and tightened his lips. Regardless, Ledermann said, he knew that if they played it right Zeiger would eventually talk to Lara. It was bound to happen. "Don't look at me that way, Bernd. I also made them give you more assignments, involve you a bit more. Didn't you like it? The press-conference observations, the interrogation at Hohenschönhausen this morning? Aren't you happy? You were practically retired. Even today I asked you to find my own son. I made all this happen for you. You should be grateful."

"I told Lara everything," Zeiger said. "Every last detail. She knows it all."

"You're cute," Ledermann said. "She knew the whole thing already. I told you—we just needed you to confess. The only thing we didn't tell her is where Held was taken. It's what we promised to give her if she participated. Where her father is now. Everything else was old news to her, including that weird desert business."

Zeiger advanced another step toward Ledermann, but something shifted. Dark spots drifted across his vision like dead leaves on a glassy pond. "I'm very confused by all this," he said.

"So am I, actually," Ledermann said, his eyes growing distant, his voice trailing off. "So am I. Constantly. Thoroughly."

"How am I still here?" Zeiger asked. "You have my confession. You've had it for weeks. Why am I not at Hohenschönhausen jail?"

Ledermann raised his head. "Look, we always do our best, don't we?" he said. "Plan every last detail. What we can't control is people. Lara disappeared. She gave us nothing, *nichts*. Maybe she thought you did the right thing, keeping her father out of prison. Maybe she was screwing us all along." Ledermann was staring into the distance with the glazed look of a Renaissance portrait. "And now she's gone. Like my Rudi. Like the rest of them. And

Management has other problems. Nobody cares. It was all, as you know, for nothing."

"I want to know why," Zeiger started.

"Why," Ledermann echoed. "Why what?"

Zeiger couldn't respond. He gripped the edge of the closet.

Ledermann was sprinkling the pulverized remains of a document onto a pile. He retrieved another, starting anew. "Why what?" he repeated, and looked up at Zeiger, bleary-eyed, an expression of pure insanity. "Why torture? Why torment? Why cruelty? Why naivete? Why evil? Why good? Why a million orphaned children? Why war? Why Jews? Why some but not others? Why us and not them? *Why* is one hell of a question, Bernd. Narrow it down somewhere, would you. And what does it matter, anyway? If you knew why, what would you do? My wife, Nadine, she's dying. Did I say that? So tell me. Why happiness, then death? Some things are so atrocious that *why* doesn't exist. Why are we like this? Who made us like this? It doesn't matter now. It's over. There is no why, Bernd, just how."

A jangling slashed into the silence after Ledermann's last words—the clatter of a telephone on the floor. Zeiger kicked it. It skidded but didn't stop ringing. He stomped on it, once, twice. It cracked, then fell silent. Ledermann wasn't paying attention.

"You believe all that nonsense?" Zeiger said.

He waited but no answer came. Then he lunged at Ledermann and teetered, nearly falling on him. He grabbed Ledermann's monstrous shoulders. Ledermann yelped. Papers launched into the air. Ledermann shrank into himself, shielding his face.

"No *why*, you say?" Zeiger shouted, spraying. "All of this, all that we've done, has been us asking *how* and not *why*?"

He stumbled and lost his balance, then caught himself just in time to slide in controlled slow motion down the wall and onto the floor.

Impeccable blackness inked his vision. Brilliant dendritic shapes cracked and fissured. He touched the back of his hand to his nose and it came away wet. Something had burst. He was bleeding again.

Something simple crossed his mind: He did not want to die.

His eyesight returned, revealing, in lieu of darkness, reality in sharp and vivid color. Ledermann's large head had lolled sideways against the wall. He shut his eyes, opened them wide, shut them again. Then he started crying. It was soundless at first, a dry and asphyxiated croak. Then his mouth fell open, formed a terrible *O*, and emitted a squeal, horribly loud like a seagull's. He cupped his hands over his face, hiding its contortions. He fell silent, remained quiet for so long he might have stopped breathing, then erupted again into hideous screeching.

"Come," Zeiger said, but Ledermann didn't respond. "Come," Zeiger repeated, extending a hand. Ledermann slapped at it.

Using the wall for leverage, Zeiger raised himself to a standing position. He paused, wiped his nose with his sleeve. It had stopped bleeding. Ledermann needed help. He would get him to the hospital. His old friend was enormous—both fleshy and mountainous. Zeiger secured the crook of his arms under Ledermann's pits and yanked futilely. Then Ledermann softened, became rubbery and compliant, and let himself be hoisted onto his feet. Together they traversed the desolate hallway. With every empty office they passed, Ledermann discharged a kitten-like cry. Zeiger guided him by the shoulder. The foyer was deserted.

Out on the Allee, Zeiger maneuvered him with difficulty between bumpers and spluttering exhausts, through the stream of people migrating like a herd of dazed cattle toward whatever was happening in Mitte. He organized Ledermann in the passenger's seat of his Trabi, where he sat slumped, his face flaccid, too far gone, it seemed, to notice the scene.

*　　*　　*

They arrived at St. Hedwig's in a state of wet exhaustion. The streets had been teeming with cars and people. More than once Zeiger had had to brake sharply—nearly propelling the limp, pliant body of Ledermann through the windshield. Whatever was happening, it was happening quickly.

Zeiger turned off the engine. They sat in darkness for a while, adjusting to the silence. Ledermann had stopped crying and was staring catatonically through the windshield. Zeiger examined his profile. In the dark, it looked foreign and grotesquely disfigured. He did not blink once. Then Ledermann opened his mouth, let his jaw hang loose for a while. He inhaled sharply, preparing to speak. Zeiger waited.

"I don't want to go to school," Ledermann said with finality.

It took a few tries to extract him from the car. In the distance, back toward the way they'd come, car horns blared in strange unison. Zeiger draped Ledermann's beefy arm around his shoulder, looked left, looked right, saw nobody and nothing, and ferried him across the street.

He had forgotten the startling effect of the hospital's ecclesiastical complexion. Stained-glass windows, praying-angel icons, pointed arches from depressed to flamboyant, all spared during the war by the Allies or whatever God they believed in. The hospital was a masterpiece, a Gothic work of art. In charge of the hospital were the Sisters of Mercy of St. Borromeo, a religious congregation dedicated to healing sick and orphaned children. He had spotted the nuns on previous visits with Dr. Witzbold, during which they had floated like black ghosts down the hallways, instilling in him a sense of deep, unknowable terror.

The hospital lobby was a perfect square. It was quiet, save for the echo of their steps, which caused Zeiger to look up and examine the complex mouth of the domed ceiling. The staircase was a massive, ornate construction. Zeiger strategized for a moment, latched Ledermann's hand onto the railing and guided him onward. They passed first a small and queerly luminous painting of a naked infant Christ—a grim and mocking smile on his face, the sharp and weathered features of a grown man—then a life-size marble Virgin Mary, smooth, white, lidless, her head tilted sideways in a manner suggesting perplexity rather than transcendent repose.

As they reached a landing, Zeiger was assaulted by the acrid, somewhat sulfuric scent of wound dressings, drainpipes, and hygienic supplies. He'd been remiss to believe that a place unchanged for centuries would have somehow modernized in the twenty years since he'd deposited Held here. The psychiatry ward was a cheerier section of the hospital, upliftingly decorated with crude but tranquil paintings of meadows, seafronts, and harmless animals. There was a murmur in the air like the hushed blanket of voices in a quiet café. Somewhere toward the end of the main hall a television set was blasting unrecognizable noise. Zeiger glanced into one of the offshoot corridors, where decades ago, behind that thick oak door, he had spoken to Martin—the man who had not been a dog.

He grabbed Ledermann by the elbow, intending to steer him forward, but Ledermann balked. He was now refusing to walk. Zeiger leaned in, brought his ear to the humid hole of Ledermann's mouth.

"I don't want to go to school," he was whispering.

They passed patients in the main hallway conversing quietly in the open doorways of their rooms, dressed in identical rubber slippers and white robes. They craned their necks, acknowledging their passage with curt, closed-eye nods. Zeiger found Reception at the end of the hallway, just where he'd remembered. It was a single room, lined on two sides by wooden chairs, with the head psychiatrist's office, Dr. Witzbold's old quarters, behind a heavily secured oak door. Two men dressed in business suits, their faces despondent but otherwise unruffled and sane, sat waiting. They lifted their eyes when Zeiger and Ledermann entered, then dropped them again to study their hands.

Zeiger guided Ledermann inside the room. The oak door opened and a nurse appeared. She stomped toward her desk, tended to something with quick jots of her pen, then approached the two businessmen, and instructed them to find the intake room two doors down the hall. They gathered their things and disappeared.

"Intake for two?" Zeiger heard the nurse say.

"Just him. His name is Ledermann."

Ledermann had slipped behind his back in a futile attempt to hide.

The nurse looked on with detachment. A professional assessment; she could tell what they were. "You're not the first of your kind tonight," she was saying. "You'll be in good company, Herr Ledermann."

His eyes flitting about, Ledermann said, "I didn't do my homework."

"That's all right," the nurse said.

She produced a clipboard, handed it to Zeiger, and asked him to fill out the form it held. Then she sidestepped and lunged forward in an attempt to grab hold of Ledermann, who retreated, snatching his arms away from her fingers. After a brief dance she succeeded in capturing him. She held him for a moment and he seemed to relax.

"I'd like to talk with the doctor," Zeiger said. "Official Ministry business. I'm here to see a patient."

The nurse blinked at him. A few seconds passed. She seemed to be computing the boundless occupational intricacies of his request. "And I'd like to be on a shopping spree on Ku'damm right now," she said, turning Ledermann toward the door. "Not tonight, you're not. Come back when all this has passed."

As he was led through the door, Ledermann looked back at Zeiger. His face was expressionless, his demoralization complete.

Zeiger took a seat. There was a portrait of Honecker. He stared at it blankly. He waited, though he did not know for what. The logical conclusion. The wisest next step. He rose and crossed toward the oak door. The door would be locked but he tried the handle anyway. It was not.

He recognized the office—long, rectangular, spartan, with high vaulted ceilings. It had been difficult for Dr. Witzbold to hide from him here, and with a pang of queer nostalgia, Zeiger remembered how he had once found him cowering, there, behind that high buffet table. The room was oddly lit, the floor covered by a frayed Persian carpet, little more than a mildewed memory. There were no rubber exam tables, syringes, strips of gauze, skeleton models, or any other equipment to hint at the room's depressing objective. Directly opposite the door was the dome of a high Gothic window, now black with night. Beneath it, flanked by two blinding lamps with trumpet-like shades, sat a wooden desk, a Biedermeier, placed with the symmetry of a sacrificial shrine.

Zeiger took a few steps into the room, raised the clipboard to shield his eyes from the glare, then spotted her, the doctor, reclined in a high-backed chair. She was plump and small, like a well-fed child, her hair gray and intricately coiled atop her head. Her white coat was draped around her shoulders, its sleeves hanging limply beside her. She said nothing as he approached.

"The door was unlocked," Zeiger said.

"It's been a long night," the doctor replied. "I'm taking a moment."

Zeiger approached the chair across from the desk. He attempted to lower himself, but the chair was much shorter than normal, and he dangled for a moment, squatting awkwardly as if above a soiled toilet seat, before finally plunking himself down. He shifted to make himself comfortable, his knees angling high. The doctor's desk was clean, with only a few ornamental features: a desk pad, a small vase clasping a poinsettia branch, a vague porcelain bust with phrenological markings in black. Another desk. Hadn't he spent his whole life taking a seat at a desk?

The doctor observed him with level eyes. It seemed important to her for him to speak first.

"I was acquainted with Dr. Witzbold," he said after a while. When she betrayed no recognition, he added, "You might not have been familiar with him."

The doctor patted the pockets of her white coat and produced a pen. "You've been here before?"

Her hands were soft and white, the skin on her face covered in a thin coat of fuzz. Mother's age, Zeiger surmised. She scribbled something onto a pad, then placed the pen on the table and nudged it until content with its alignment. His mind still and light, Zeiger considered how satisfying it would be to cup the bottoms of her loose, fleshy cheeks and knead them like batches of dough.

"The clipboard?" she said.

Zeiger looked at the clipboard in his lap. He'd forgotten he was holding it. "That's not why I'm here. I want to visit a patient. Someone who's been here for a while."

The doctor jotted words onto her pad. "You want to hide here. I know what this is about. You and your ilk. Well, I can't help you if you don't make this easy," she said without lifting her eyes. "You're hardly the first person wanting to admit themselves tonight, Herr...?"

"Zeiger."

"Herr Zeiger. And given how this night seems likely to progress, you won't be the last. I need to assess if you meet the criteria."

"You misunderstand. His name is Johannes Held." Zeiger retrieved his ID card and placed it on the desk. "This is an official request," he said.

"They all are," the doctor said. She gathered the card and studied it, squinting myopically. Contorting her mouth, she said, "That Manual, is it? It's on a shelf somewhere here. I didn't know that Unit was still operational."

"It was," Zeiger said, then amended: "It is. Most aren't aware."

"It accounts for three-quarters of our patients in here."

"I merely wrote it. Nothing more."

The doctor dropped her pen, frowned at Zeiger, leaned back into her chair, and for a long, befuddled moment studied him as she had his ID card. "You've done nothing, of course," she said.

"Most don't even know it was me."

With one wizened finger, she slid his card back across the desk. "Of all people, I understand why you're here," she said.

Zeiger had stopped listening. Between the red-blotched folds of her breasts, a silver crucifix had captured the light.

The doctor followed his gaze, and, bunching the pleats of her chin, looked down to inspect the pendant, as if she herself were surprised to find it there. "After the Second Vatican Council," she said, "we're no longer required to wear habits. They tell us we're more approachable this way. Some still like the dress, of course. It does make the mornings faster and easier. I suppose we've also lost interest in pushing an agenda about uniformity and poverty, especially in this region, where marketing is key—"

"Where do we go when we die?" Zeiger asked.

She did not look surprised by the question. She fondled her cross, rubbing it absentmindedly, as if for good luck. "That would very much depend," she said.

"I mean in general. Is the soul connected to the body? Is there some sort of tether? Does it hurt when it's severed? Is there something we can do to make sure the cessation goes smoothly?" Zeiger spoke in a rush. He leaned forward, out of breath.

The doctor resumed writing on her pad, her blue veins slithering like worms across the back of her hand. "Where do we go?" she said in a pensive tone somehow laced with levity. "Heaven, paradise, some version of hell, I don't know. Whatever you chose to believe while alive."

"What do you mean you don't know?"

The doctor rested her arms on the desk. Closing her eyes in apparent contemplation, she said, "We're not so different, you and I. Socialism, religion, medicine—they're ideas conceived to end all uncertainty. It's only when they fail us, Herr Zeiger, that we understand our true desire: to be taken care of as children." She remained in this position, a quiet smile lingering, then fading from her lips. "What exactly is the purpose of this proposed visitation?" she asked.

"I would like to consult"—his tongue caught at his throat, a heavy swallow—"I will be consulting Herr Held on matters of disappearance."

"Disappearance," the doctor said.

"Some people have vanished and Herr Held, as it happens, is a valuable expert on such situations."

"Teleportation," the doctor said. "I've gathered."

"The transfer of matter from one place to another."

"Which he can perform?"

"The evidence was there."

"Yet this success, I was informed, was the reason Held was charged with conspiracy, is that right?"

Zeiger acknowledged that it was.

"And what would've happened if the research had failed?"

"He'd have gone to jail for treason."

"Conspiracy, teleportation—do you believe all that?"

Zeiger shifted in his seat. His legs felt cold and lightly carbonated; they'd fallen asleep. No, he didn't believe that Held had conspired with the Americans, he told the doctor.

The doctor lifted a finger to her lips, held it there as if to keep herself from speaking. She lifted her pen, seemed to think better of it, and dropped it back on the desk. She asked Zeiger if he believed teleportation was real.

"It would be a threat to national security."

"So are cartoons, Herr Zeiger. What does it mean to you?"

"It would be a momentous contribution to science."

"But to you. What does it stir in your soul?"

"Hope," he admitted.

"That could be a symptom," she said.

"Of what?"

"Psychosis. Magical thinking."

"Where is Held?" Zeiger asked.

With a wooden *screech* she pushed back her chair and rose from the desk.

"Don't go," Zeiger said.

Her legs were as thin as winter twigs and too long for the compressed bulb of her body. Zeiger felt the urge to hold on to her.

She wobbled around the desk, and with the decrepit, slightly forward-leaning locomotion of a turtle made her way toward the door. "Held," she said as though in passing. "Let me see about something."

Zeiger turned around to watch her go and the door fall shut. He was alone. Had Held ever been afraid? Of illness, lightning bolts, the false hope of health, himself? Zeiger spotted himself in the window: a hunched, translucent figure, a colossal human in a tiny chair; the sharp bones of his head; the two vacant holes where his eyes should have been. He lifted a hand, waved at himself, then tucked it back between his knees and stared at the ground.

The doctor returned, followed by a shuffling male nurse in white V-neck attire. He was tall and bald, with large puffy lips and an expressionless face native, usually, to the exceptionally observant or possibly dimwitted. It was immediately clear he did not want to be there. Zeiger hadn't known male nurses existed. With a sigh the man crossed his arms and positioned himself next to the desk, between the doctor, who took her seat behind the desk, and Zeiger, who cowered in his little chair.

"Say what happened," the doctor said.

"*What happened,*" the man said.

"No," said the doctor, "say what happened."

"*What happened,*" the man repeated.

"Good God," the doctor said with exasperation, "a month ago, the irregular situation."

The man was breathing audibly. He seemed to consider this for a while, his face motionless, his eyes blank. "*Irregular* is a bit of a loose concept around here. You'd better be more specific. You mean the spoon incident?"

"Not the spoons," she said. "About Held. The physicist."

The name registered with the nurse. Briefly he stirred, widening his stance. He tightened his arms around his chest and glanced at Zeiger, who smiled weakly, a little insanely, he guessed.

"What's it to this guy?" the nurse said. "Am I in trouble or something?"

"Tell him what happened," the doctor said, impatience rising.

The man sucked in his breath. "This was a month ago," he started, "a day after the birthday parade. Easy to remember because days after any kind of public festivities are worse around here in terms of lunacy than any full moon, you follow?"

Slowly, tonelessly, as if for the hundredth time, the nurse explained how, on the day after the birthday parade, in the evening, a young woman—a girl, really—had appeared in the ward. She was a small, flitty thing, he recalled, quite pale in the face, with red-blond hair. At first, as she'd crept around a corner, and even later, when he spotted her again, slipping from doorframe to doorframe, he thought he was hallucinating. It was a late night, and the place was conducive to seeing things not there, so he thought nothing of it. Until—the man raised a finger and pointed didactically at the ceiling—until he caught her sneaking around the mesh-wired doors of the closed ward for criminals. Then he grabbed her by the arm and dragged her to the nurses' station, where he sat her down. She wouldn't say a word, though, just chewed her nails. Until finally she said she was there to see her father, Johannes Held. The nurse told her to wait while he went to find him.

"That's not irregular?" Zeiger said. "Letting criminals have visitors?" The doctor wasn't interjecting and he wanted objections. He felt increasingly agitated, confused, and hysterical.

"Held is no criminal," the man replied with an air of superiority. "And he hadn't had one visitor in all the years he was here. I thought someone may have finally had mercy on him, ordered him a girl, you know what I mean—"

"I do not," Zeiger said, his eyes darting toward the doctor, then back to the nurse.

For the better part of a decade, Held had inhabited a single two-by-four-meter padded cell, according to the male nurse, who had adopted a tone full of antiestablishment venom.

Zeiger inquired as to why the cell was padded.

"One thing you have to understand about Held," the nurse explained, "he had a real bad habit of vanishing." It had happened at least half a dozen times over the years he'd been a patient. *Bam!*—the male nurse gesticulated wildly—and he'd disappear into thin air. Nothing was ever missing aside from Held himself. His books, of which there were plenty—complicated mathematical works with charts and equations and unthinkable symbols—would all still be neatly stacked on their shelf. There would be his pillow and blanket. His toothbrush and toilet paper. A gopher skull, an ugly thing they let him decorate his cell with, his single personal item. The only strange thing, the nurse added, was that there was always a faint smell of something electric whenever he disappeared, something cold and almost…ozonic. What he imagined nerve endings would smell like if they had an odor.

"And that didn't strike you as odd?" Zeiger asked. He had the increasing, incontestable feeling that something was not as it should be. He thought of the punk, how he could feel his own brain happening. He touched the side of his face. It was burning.

"He always showed up again," the nurse said. "Same day. Unchanged. As long as they're around come bedtime, it's above our pay grade to care." Plus, the disappearances had stopped when they moved him into a padded cell. No one knew why, but for whatever it was worth, Held preferred it that way, the nurse claimed.

"Those old cells, the unpadded ones, had loose ceiling tiles," the doctor supplied.

Anyway, the nurse said, he left the girl in the nurses' station and went to see Held, the poor skinny bastard, who looked at the nurse like he was a lunatic when he told him his daughter was there to see him. Didn't say a word, according to the nurse. Just stared at him with those large, childlike eyes until the nurse went back to the girl and told her to beat it. She refused. Instead she started chanting the names *Katja* and *Zeiger,* over and over, like a sick, magic mantra. He felt sorry for the girl, the nurse said. He tried telling her that Held wanted nothing to do with her, but she wouldn't budge, just kept chanting. Then she started rummaging in a bag, going through it like her hair was on fire. He had an inkling she was going to pull out a weapon, a gun. But she emerged with a weird-looking porcelain dog, which she said was for Held. The nurse balked at first but then, feeling pity, took it from her and went back to see Held. When he got to Held's cell, the man was crouching on the floor, scribbling—as he was in the habit of doing—strings of vastly complicated but somehow quite beautiful numbers onto sheets of paper splayed on the floor in front of him.

There had always been something boyish about Held, Zeiger remembered. The way he'd turned his head, this way and that, like a child deeply absorbed by some banal but mystic thought. He would have grown thinner over the years, more fragile. Zeiger pictured a sack of silver-stubbled skin under his chin, and remembered how, when he smiled, which he'd done toothlessly and often, the edges of his face, his cheeks, his eyes, broke into rays of folded skin.

The nurse paused his story. He'd liked the man, he said. Everyone else had too. Some staff, even the nuns, visited him regularly to discuss problems with him. Held had a way...But here the nurse fell silent, examined the floor, smoothed the carpet with a foot, took a deep breath, calming a quiver in his voice. Held had a way, he continued, of making you feel that all was well, that all had been well and would be well, that nothing much mattered, and that if nothing much mattered, everything mattered, including them.

There was hope. That was quite something for some of these people to hear, many of whom had come to rely on Held to make them feel, well, that things weren't quite as shit as they appeared.

A cracking sound, hollow and buoyant, fractured the silence.

Zeiger contracted, shielding his ears. The sound was close, from just beyond the blackened window. *Only fake gunfire sounds real,* Mother had said. Zeiger glanced at the doctor, the nurse, but they were both motionless and unperturbed. It was just firecrackers, no doubt set off by a pack of teens, or perhaps a lone schoolboy making himself known to the world. Zeiger lowered his hands, composing himself.

When he reentered the cell and mentioned the names *Katja* and *Zeiger,* and showed him the porcelain setter, the nurse said, it was the first time he'd seen Held look somehow frightened. Crouching still, on the floor, his papers strewn about him like a blanket of snow, Held raised his head and angled it, and although he seemed to be looking right at the nurse, really he was deciphering, decoding, measuring something, his mobile face evolving, morphing from confusion to dread to joy to bewilderment. Finally, the nurse said, Held told him, in a whisper, to show the girl in, and he went to retrieve her from the nurses' station and brought her to Held.

"And what happened then?" Zeiger asked, his voice barely audible.

"I don't know," the nurse said with a defensive shrug. "They just looked at each other. It was real awkward, the whole scenario. I'm not good with stuff like that, and I had to take care of the situation with the spoons that I mentioned, so I left them together. I locked the door behind me, but when I came back an hour later, they were both gone." The nurse gave a brief but vigorous nod, content, it seemed, with the end of his story.

An elaborate silence unspooled. The doctor, staring into space and pursing her lips, issued a profound sigh.

A hot panic spread through Zeiger. He felt possessed, untethered, spasmodic, near death. He searched the faces of the doctor and nurse, one after the other, incredulously. "What's the matter with you?" he screeched. "What happened to them?"

"I don't know," the nurse repeated.

"What happened in there?" Zeiger screamed, rising from his chair.

The nurse inched backward, away from Zeiger.

"Something must have happened," Zeiger yelled. "What happened in there?" He was desperate now. "Did someone tell you to say this to me? I know how this works. Someone came here, sat you down, told you to tell me this if I came around."

"All I know is they both disappeared," the nurse said, evincing his own agitation and confusion. "I led her inside the room, locked the door, and went back to the nurses' station. To deal with the spoon situation, like I said. You have no idea the shitshow that was."

"Look here, Herr Zeiger," the doctor said, in a soothing, diplomatic tone. "There are a number of explanations. Trades aren't unusual. West Germany pays, patients get to emigrate. It happens often. We're a travel agency rather than a hospital, as far as I'm concerned." These trades, she said, might well be the nation's last source of income. There would be no indication of such a transaction in the file, though, so she couldn't say if that's what had transpired. "Not even I know everything that goes on around here," she conceded. "Other explanations? We just don't know. Perhaps the girl helped him escape? The nurse here assures me he locked the room behind her. What else can I say? They're gone."

Zeiger heard it even before he felt it: a bestial squawk, fierce like animal panic. There was a short lag, one befuddled second, and then another shriek erupted from his mouth, this time more nuanced. His gaze careered around the room, and through watering eyes he spotted the doctor, her apple-round cheeks. She rose from her chair behind the desk, hunched and leathered, like a dinosaur. Laughter like misery ejaculated from his throat. This was happening to him, he couldn't control it, which struck him with equally violent hilarity. What creatures they were, what lonely children.

What had he expected? Lara had known. All through their conversation, she'd known what he'd done. And she had forgiven him. She had taken Father's pin, Mother's gun, and the porcelain setter. She had come to see Held, and now they were gone. Maybe they'd gone to find Katja. Maybe they'd teleported themselves into the ether. He grabbed the back of his little chair and attempted to hold his breath, but snorted out savagely instead.

The doctor appeared by his side, patted the small of his back. "Now, now," she was saying. "This is good. This I can work with. We have room for you. Did you know, Herr Zeiger, during the war, the Sisters were able to save countless souls? Hid them right here in plain sight." She guided him toward the nurse. "Right this way, careful, yes, watch your step."

The nurse jumped into action, cupping Zeiger's elbow. With a gentle weightlessness, like death shepherding the sick, he steered him through the reception room, where a dozen wax-molten faces—some familiar, others as bizarre as a new species—gawked at him with loose-hanging jaws. His arm was transferred to another set of hands, warm and firm, attached to a woman. Words were exchanged; short, nonsensical sentences.

Zeiger squawked, one last desperate grunt, before he was ushered from the room.

3.3

Zeiger was placed on an exam table. Two old nurses with raven-black habits and liver-spotted cheeks swarmed mutely about the halogen-lit room, opening drawers, checking papers, taking his pulse, jotting bold numbers onto a pad. They probed his lymph nodes with their deadly cold fingers. When they drew close, he caught a scent of lavender oil and amaretto liquor. They spread his lids and peered into his eyes, explored the depths of his ears with a tubular device, scraped his tongue, examined his scalp. They knocked his kneecap with a tiny hammer, failed to produce a reflex, took more notes on the pad.

"I'm sorry," Zeiger said.

One Sister lifted his arms while the other palpated his pits. Orifices, cavities, holes, and slits were inspected. They lingered over a mole on his shoulder, contemplated the varicose veins on his shins. A cloth tourniquet was looped around his arm, pulled taut, and left there while both women turned their backs and began slotting equipment back into drawers. They were identical from behind; two mountain peaks, as black and wise as galaxies.

"I've been having episodes," he told them. "Familiar things are unrecognizable. People are disappearing. My nose has been bleeding. I'm dying."

Neither looked interested. One of them turned and sprayed his arm with alcoholic vapors, then tapped her colleague's shoulder and began addressing her in elaborate sign language. Their hands flew and flexed, drew long and ornate shapes, while their thin mouths described the occasional strangled sound. Finally, with sighing eyes, one of them assembled a syringe and tended to Zeiger's arm. She took three vials of blood, suctioning with such force that he heard the liquid splatter into the glass, then dressed the puncture wound with a cotton ball, and with a quick, wide-eyed gesture directed Zeiger to crook his arm. He was handed a piece of wrapped candy, but it had fused into the plastic and could not be extracted.

Then the Sisters left. As soon as the door closed, a shiver rattled his limbs. The room was small and intolerably white; he had the inescapable feeling of being an amphibian specimen clipped under a lens and illuminated by mirrored light. He waited, squeezing against his chest the arm out of which he'd given blood, and avoided peeking at the counter, where the vials stood like flutes of freshly poured wine.

Only one Sister returned, bringing with her a robe and pajamas. With folded arms and steady eyes, she prompted him to undress. He removed his shoes and socks. He handed over his clothes: his belt, his clammy wool trousers, his tie, his creased and oil-stained dress shirt, which she hung from the tip of her finger like a boneless cadaver. He spotted himself in a mirror. Tired, fat, naked, and white, an accumulation of bodily folds and protrusions. The Sister grunted and jerked her chin at his underpants. He turned gracelessly, shielding himself from both her and the mirror, and removed them. From a closet the nun retrieved a pair of flipper-shaped rubber slippers and dropped them at his feet. He began to get dressed. The pajamas were stiff and warm. He wrapped the robe around his waist and tied it with the belt. His toes found the slippers, which were several sizes too large.

The nun walked him back down the corridor, head bowed and hands buried deep in the flaps of her habit. Zeiger padded behind her. The corridor had emptied, but a low, barnlike rumble in the distance suggested some greater upheaval had broken loose toward the end of the hallway. They passed food carts bearing pitchers, brown puddings, and trays of anatomized, uneaten Klöpse in gravy whose mealy smell hung heavy in the air. As they approached the common room, the noise grew feverish. Hysteria reigned—the harrumph of moving chairs, the nasal monotony of television voices, and something less definable, not distinctly human, a high-pitched, feline wail.

Just short of the entrance the nun stopped and turned to face Zeiger, who, teetering slightly, came to a halt centimeters away. She stood firm as a tree, looking up at him with wet, multi-creased eyes. Then she dislodged her hands from the insides of her sleeves, fanned her fingers, interlaced them, and cupped her hands as if sheltering a small animal. She balled her fists and rubbed her knuckles together, all the while jerking her head with eager side-ways motions. The anxious, expectant look on her face told him this was important. She was sending a message, dispensing wisdom or secret instructions or a warning.

"Friends?" he said. "We're friends now?"

Squinting at his mouth, she grimaced, joined her fingertips, and flattened her hands so that they formed a wall between their chests. Then, with a quick, aggressive motion, she let them break apart.

"Night has fallen?" Zeiger said. "We're parting?"

A gargling noise poured from deep within her throat. She

turned her eyes to the ceiling, seemed to find someone there, shook her head vehemently, then waved her hands in capitulation. In confusion, Zeiger glanced up at the ceiling after her. But when he returned his gaze to the nun, she was hurrying back down the hallway.

Once, many years ago, on a silent, morning-dazed tram toward Lichtenberg, Zeiger had observed a grown man—about sixty years of age, strawberry-nosed, with hands as large as paddles—burst out unprovoked and for no apparent reason into enthusiastic song. His voice was baritone and quite fetching, and with every passing note it seemed to swell with confidence. Emerging from their morning stupor, fellow passengers turned stiffly to find the source of the song, which encouraged the man, and led him to rise from his seat and walk a handful of steps down the aisle.

A few stanzas passed before passengers gathered the content of his song. It was an elderly, purple-permed woman who first took the initiative, made her way down the aisle, and began belting the man with the flat of her purse. That turned the mood. Other passengers followed her and rose from their seats to accost the man. A soldier about Zeiger's age dropped his knapsack, lunged at the man, and cupped his hand over the man's mouth. A melee ensued, quick, disorganized, with varied shouts and vicious curses. With growing enthusiasm the man billowed his chest, and extending one arm with operatic zest, he crooned: *Only Germans faithfully joined. The class enemy we despise is not of German kind.*

In the back of the tram, clasping his briefcase to his chest, Zeiger had stared out into the rushing, twilit street, grasping for the very first time that everything was always just one lunatic short of pandemonium. He would witness more chaos in the years that followed. Brawls in line at the bakery, unforeseen scuffles at a cashier's ill-chosen word. Sudden, teenagerly squabbles at Zentralkomitee meetings that produced lacerated fists and broken teeth, gushing nostrils, and the increasing prevalence of torn hair and tears.

But all such commotion now seemed fair and reasonable compared to what Zeiger observed as he looked through the doorway and into the common-room hall. Dispersed throughout the white-tiled, white-lit room were robed men in white slippers, dozens of them. A few steps away from the door two elderly men, dressed in identical pajamas and robes, were engaged in a complicated arm-lock. Their fight seemed to have reached an impasse. They remained frozen in this position, cheek to flabby cheek, the belts of their robes dangling, until they dissolved into an embrace. Another man, with a glistening bald spot, stood bunching and lifting the collar of a different man's robe. Men held other men in headlocks, while groups of four or five had gathered to jab one another's chests with pointed fingers and to issue girlish guffaws. A slender, pint-sized man dashed across the room, looping and leaning with the agility of a slalom skier. It was unclear whether he was being pursued.

The room was dotted with large circular tables and plastic eggshell chairs, populated by more men in robes, some of them cowering in the vicinity of a nearby scuffle, others suckling orange sippy cups in a self-soothing trance. A television set, mounted high up in the far corner, was blaring unintelligible noise. A small crowd of a dozen or so silent, white-robed men had congregated before it, staring up and into the television set like herons into the sun. Those seated in quieter corners looked on apathetically, their stunned, slack faces as gray as papier-mâché. A few of them had snatched a deck chair and lay cocooned in heavy blankets, sleeping or whispering gravely with an equally bundled-up neighbor. As Zeiger ventured inside, two male nurses, distinguishable only by their two-piece attire and naked, brutal arms, shouted haphazard orders into the room and charged forward occasionally to intercept a brawl, but otherwise remained motionless, gaping at the television set in the far corner.

Zeiger kept close to the walls. He was stepping over a man sprawled starfish-like on the floor when a feeble voice called out his name. He squinted into the crowd, checked the row of deck chairs lining the far wall. There was Kummer, his old childhood friend, greeting him with a bland stare. Only his pink, piggish head poked out above his blanket, which was wound tightly around the length of his body, lending him the appearance of a rather plump maggot. Zeiger hadn't seen him since that lunch in the cafeteria a month earlier, the day before the parade. Stillness descended, enveloping their moment. Kummer thrust his head forward, as though beckoning Zeiger, and wiggled side to side, seemingly in an attempt to free his arm from the blanket. He was a capsized beetle, desperate and alone.

Yes, something was happening. Zeiger needed to sit. He retreated farther, suctioned his back against the wall. Through blurry eyes he surveyed the scene; the wild assemblage of men in identical robes. Kummer, having extracted an arm from his blanket, was waving eagerly from across the room. And now, as if he were sighting a lone wasp, then another, then a third, then an entire swarm that has been hovering all along, one after another the faces of recognizable strangers came into view. Comrades Mürbe and Torf, the ones who had ordered him to observe the parade, sat cross-legged on the floor, slippered and robed. There the archival-unit clerk to whom he had submitted the Manual those many years ago was rising from a chair. He had gone bald. There were comrades he'd noticed among cafeteria cliques, men he'd passed in hallways, men seated in front of him at Zentralkomitee meetings, their blindingly pomaded hair now in stringy disarray. Seated in a row, three old men with necks like scavenger birds cupped their chins and pondered the scene. The regulars from the corner café. Klaus he discovered at a nearby table, straight-backed, sober, nearly unrecognizable without his setter and beer. And there was Ledermann, propped in a chair, taking in the scene with a faraway smile.

Zeiger inched sideways, step-by-step, toward the far end of the room. He evaluated his options. Each passage was treacherous or blocked by someone he knew. There was a lull, then a vague turbulence. Someone had turned off the television and was sprinting through the crowd, swinging the remote control like a lasso over his head. A few men followed, lifting the hems of their robes, and attempted to snatch the device from his hand. Avoiding eye contact, nearly losing his oversize slippers, Zeiger weaved through the commotion and hastened into the far corner.

From this vantage, a panoramic perspective with a good view of the television, the tumult seemed distant and comically staged, an ecosystem of strange, exotic animals. Zeiger found an empty chair at a table and let himself fall into it. A man emerged from the tussle with the remote. He smoothed his hair, corrected his robe, and turned on the television. Sporadic applause. Zeiger leaned back. From a pitcher of water on the table he poured himself a sippy cup. On the other side of the table a young man with sunken cheeks was scribbling something into the margins of a newspaper, grunting occasionally, then giggling in fits. Zeiger studied the young man, wondering if he, too, wasn't somehow familiar.

Then the room collapsed, spitting someone else into focus. Right next to him at the table, his head angled up and sideways, one ear cast toward the riotous noise, sat Schreibmüller. He looked calm and removed, sage and vaguely entertained. He was like a sophist on a mountaintop, a hermit freshly emerged from his cave. Zeiger felt awestruck, paralyzed with simple wonder, as if he had made a rare discovery: a specimen of a long-lost species, a double-yolked egg, a spring crocus budding from a blanket of snow. He stared at the athletic cut of Schreibmüller's unshaven jaw, the handsome, somewhat apish slope of his forehead. A yellow bandage with three black dots, signifying the asterism of the blind, had been tied around his arm.

"Give me some of that," Schreibmüller said. He cocked his chin, quick and dovelike, and signaled at the pitcher on the table, nearly toppling it. His vacant eyes quivered, landing just above Zeiger's head.

Saying nothing, Zeiger took hold of Schreibmüller's hand and guided it toward the pitcher.

Schreibmüller unscrewed a sippy cup, placed a finger inside its rim, and filled it to his knuckle with water. "Any women in here?" he asked.

"There are nuns," Zeiger said.

"Really, none?"

"Nuns," Zeiger said.

"I know you," Schreibmüller said.

"There's an old man over there," Zeiger said, motioning point-lessly across the room, "who looks a lot like my recruiter. I'd thought he must've died a long time ago."

Schreibmüller shifted his weight, half-turned, and jerked his head at the young man at their table, who was still scribbling on his newspaper. "Do you know this man too?" he whispered.

"He looks vaguely familiar."

The young man didn't break from his writing.

"I'm assuming he was here before this evening," Schreibmüller said. "But I can't keep the loons apart from the comrades. Maybe that's more irrelevant than ever today, though. You just arrived?"

"An hour or so."

"I came the moment I heard Schabowski on television. Something was off. I sensed it. I was one of the first to get here."

His robe was untied. The collar of his pajama top had split open, revealing a triangle of robust hair on his chest. Just a month earlier, at the porcelain shop in Meissen. Just this morning he'd played that foreign music in his apartment and presided over the steps of their apartment building.

"What's happening?" Schreibmüller said. "Do you know?"

"What did you have to do with any of this? Who's Lara to you? You've been following me."

"Or you me." Schreibmüller casually flicked up his palms. "Or them us, or me them, or you everyone. You know how it works. Neighbor against neighbor, friend against friend, kid against mother. It's not personal. You're nothing to me. Neither is Lara, wherever she is. I lost track of her. All I did was what they asked—kept tabs on you and reported back, checked in with Lara to see if she needed anything. Look, I wasn't about to complain, she's a beautiful girl."

"How would you even know that?" Zeiger asked, and reached out to flap a hand in front of the blind man's eyes. Schreibmüller didn't flinch. He must have touched Lara's face with his indecent fingertips. Zeiger scowled, inflamed at his own impotence.

"What does it matter now?" Schreibmüller continued as if he hadn't heard. "Everybody who's been following anyone seems to be in this room right now."

"A month ago, at the shop in Meissen," Zeiger said. "How did you know I'd be there? You're inside my head, is that it? Telepathy, like with those monkeys a long time ago?"

Schreibmüller was smirking. So Zeiger was an amusement to him? "What we've built here," Schreibmüller said, "is the most comprehensive surveillance state in the history of the world. Right? No, it's a rage against reality, is what it is. It doesn't matter if we have you fluoroscoped down to the color of your pee in the morning, there're some things we simply have no control over. Heartbreak, natural disasters, the metaphysical. That's something Herr Held knew a few things about, isn't it? Our friend Ledermann told me stories. Seems he was obsessed with him. But forget about teleportation. Held was immune to these interventions. That's what they should have studied about him."

"I don't understand what you're saying."

"It was a coincidence, the shop. Not everything's about you, Zeiger."

Zeiger asked what would happen to him now.

A flicker of uncertainty crinkled Schreibmüller's forehead, a swift twitch of the head. He was staring through Zeiger, through the wall behind him, his sightless eyes flitting as if across pages of print. "This," he said, pointing at the television. "This is what's happening to us."

Zeiger peered up at the screen.

"Press conference reruns," Schreibmüller said. "Tell me. I want to know everything. The looks on their faces, the color of their shirts."

Zeiger felt light with exhaustion, all but dismembered. The screen rippled and swished as if filled with murky liquid. "There are people in chairs," he said. "A crowd, cameras. There he is, parting the crowd."

It was Schabowski, from footage earlier in the night, calmly advancing toward the podium. Zeiger squinted at the screen, trying to catch a full glimpse of the room it depicted, the reporters in foreign suits, the black television cameras on insectile tripods. Along the wood-paneled walls, where he should have stood, tiny bloated faces observed the proceedings with funereal calm.

"Schabowski looks fine," Zeiger said. "He's sifting through papers. He's smiling."

There was a cut in the tape and a sudden close-up of Schabowski, mid-sentence, orating. The camera panned, offering a wide-angle view. Sedated silence had descended, the conference in full mind-numbing swing. A reporter's voice echoed metallically from somewhere off-screen, wanting to know just how it was possible that Schabowski's face had been appearing with more frequency than that of their General Secretary. There were muffled chuckles, the crowd stirred.

"It's difficult to say what's happening," Zeiger said. "Schabowski's laughing now."

"See what I mean?" Schreibmüller said. "Something's off."

Zeiger glanced across the room at Ledermann, who hadn't moved from his chair and was observing his surroundings with a vacant smile. He didn't seem to grasp where he was.

The press conference continued, with more questions, more cuts in the tape, a cough in the audience, quick and hollow like a shot in a cave. Schabowksi was stressing each and everyone's personal responsibility in being and remaining a good Communist citizen. A reporter with a beard as white as a cloud got hold of the microphone. Zeiger described him to Schreibmüller, who leaned in close and angled his ear. Identifying himself, upon Schabowski's prompting, as a writer for the *Viennese Standard,* he asked just what the government would do should they fail to quell the current exodus from the GDR.

In a quiet monotone, Schabowski denied any such thing would happen.

Seated right below Schabowski's desk, one leg dangling from

the podium as if off the edge of a cliff, an Italian reporter with a singsong voice asked whether it had been a mistake to announce possible relaxation of travel restrictions to the general public.

It was a process, Schabowski explained as if to a child. There had been suggestions, drafts, possibilities, nothing definitive.

There was a murmur onstage.

Now Schabowksi was glancing sideways, Zeiger told Schreibmüller, and consulting an official off-screen. There was some confusion. Something was happening here.

Schabowksi turned his attention back to the microphone. To the best of his knowledge, he corrected, a decision had been made. It was unfair to force upon their neighbors, upon Hungary, a surge of refugees of such dramatic proportions. Hence at least part of said reforms of permanent emigration regulation would be instated.

There was a slight lag. A weightless, rustling second. A bout of contagious shuffling as reporters shifted in their seats. From the bowels of the room came a question.

As of now? a reporter asked.

Schabowski produced a pair of glasses, slid them onto the short bridge of his nose, and fingered the papers on his desk. Comrade, he said, as far as I've been informed, you all should have received such a press release today.

The video skipped, flickered like images in a zoetrope, reemerged with a tinge of green. Zeiger had the impression that he was watching outer-space transmissions.

Reading from the paper in his hands, Schabowski explained that private travel out of the country would be allowed without prior application processes or familial relations abroad. Passport and visa bureaus of the *Volkspolizei* were ordered to grant papers immediately and without delay. He read in haste, swallowing his words. Permanent emigration from the GDR to West Germany would be allowed at all border posts throughout the nation. As to passports, people would have to apply for one first. Or so he assumed, he said, leaning back and resting, in conclusion, his chin in his hand.

A question floated in from off-screen.

Excuse me? Schabowski said.

As of when? the person repeated.

As to my knowledge, Schabowski said, then paused. He skimmed his notes, lifted them, fanned them out, looking for something, hoping, it seemed, to stop time. As to my knowledge, he said, as of immediately. He didn't lift his eyes. He perused his notes, found a passage, read it aloud.

Another question, from an American now, but it didn't matter. Schabowski's voice was extinguished amid the rumbling from the audience, and after he removed his glasses, the camera switched from his profile to a view of the room.

"What's happening?" Schreibmüller asked.

"They're all leaving," Zeiger said.

"*Verdammter Vollidiot!*" someone yelled there in the common room. The remote control hurtled through the air and struck the screen with a clank. "What has he done? This wasn't supposed to happen. Just like that! Why?"

The group beneath the television swelled with curses and hooligan screams. Cackling erupted, then dropped to a wave of whispers.

Zeiger's head filled with hollow vibrations and he cupped his hands over his ears. Schreibmüller scrunched his face and reddened with hysterical laughter. Then a looming shape, black as an iris, eclipsed Zeiger's vision and hovered there above him. It was a dark contour, electric and warm. From the depth of black a hand appeared, horrifically white, and reached toward him. He had not, until this moment, understood the grim, gangly things that hands were. The voice that spoke to him was Mother, it was Witzbold, it was Lara, it was Held; an angel, all-knowing, infinite. But he could not hear what it said.

He closed his eyes and inclined his face toward this vast, extraterrestrial being. It was happening: another episode, though this was sure to be the last of them. He saw Held, young and kind-eyed, standing, as he'd always imagined him, at the edge of a pockmarked desert, illuminated and invincible in the neon glow of a virulent sunset. He'd done it. He was gone. He'd taken Lara. Zeiger choked, overwhelmed with the unnamable, sorrow and envy, joy and relief.

"What now? Yes or no?" the voice said. "Get on with it." The angel had a dialect, thick and mocking, structurally displeased. It was from Brandenburg.

Zeiger opened his eyes and looked up into the aggravated face of a nurse. She was extending a paper thimble in his direction, rattling it impatiently. Two pills, one white, one red, rolled inside like marbles. A laxative and a sleeping aid, she said, and told him to take the pills now, at the same time. She shoved the thimble into his hand and moved on.

More nurses were at work in the common room, handing out thimbles, drifting through the crowd. A queue had formed by the exit. Having already ingested their pills some time earlier, a few men sprang from their chairs and sprinted with great urgency to join the line at the door.

"To the Party," Schreibmüller said, grinning perversely, and lifted his thimble in Zeiger's direction, as though he were toasting.

By now the television had been turned off, the crowd had dispersed. Across the room Ledermann was drawing himself up.

He pulled his robe taut, straightened his back, saluted, and swigged back his thimble as if it were filled with hard liquor.

At Zeiger's table, the young man who had been scribbling next to him jumped from his chair. He flung up his arms and exclaimed: "We made the skull confess! Tell me that isn't the funniest thing you've ever heard!"

3.4

Those twenty-something years ago, in Held's apartment, the physicist had explained to Zeiger that there were no words to describe the sheer desolation, the all-encompassing, omniscient, and pink corporeality, that was the Arizona desert. It was a vast, cold, and alarming sight. The enormity of it, the lack of confines, the pale sand and cratered rocks, the lunar loneliness. But it was also spectacular, in a terrifying way. Like anything else that is murderous—an alien spaceship, a titanic ice shelf, the galactic vacuum—it is agonizingly, beautifully indifferent to your existence. And so, during those long and languid hours, after delivering his nonsensical calculations, he found himself drifting ever farther, without aim or reason, stupefied by his own unhinged emotions for Katja, into the dunes.

He wandered and climbed. He roamed and zigzagged across expanses of pulverized stone. He trekked through ancient-sea dust and distances of inhospitable, multi-armed flora. Here and there he stopped amid a gathering of bone-dry bushes to behold unlikely objects, the inconceivable evidence of humans. He passed many molten tires, torn magazines, and bottles; once, the southern hemisphere of a globe, a car door riddled with bullet holes, and an unfurled and possibly used condom, which gave him particular pause. He walked daily, losing himself, if not geographically then spiritually, in the monochrome haze, until the sun would dip behind the bloodred layer cake of canyons in the distance, and he would return to the compound.

Except for one time. One evening, Held had told Zeiger, arching his agile eyebrows to punctuate the occasion, when the sun was setting and he had turned back toward the quivering glow of the compound, he spotted something: a glimmer, a tear in the landscape, a quantum mirage, another set of buildings twinkling in the distance. The Americans. How he hadn't noticed it before, he couldn't say. It felt like a trick of the light, as if only this specific hue of dim twilight, and only for these short moments, could break the optical illusion of the desert to reveal what appeared to be a low, white, square complex some kilometers away. A few windows glistened. There was a chain-link fence. Two guard towers, possibly manned. Held hesitated a moment, squinted. Darkness was collapsing with rapid finality. He decided. For months he'd been locked in a compound surrounded by dirt. His feet ached, his heart ached. He felt callous and brave. What did it matter? He deserved to understand. He changed course, first walking, then strutting over crunching pebbles and rocks, toward the far complex. They could shoot him—or capture him, hang him upside down by the skin of his back, and then shoot him. It was worth it.

It was fully dark by the time he reached the perimeter of the complex. He sprinted, rabbit-like, from creosote bush to creosote bush, ducking awkwardly on his long legs as he went, then hid behind a cluster of cacti with an unimpeded view of the complex. It looked modern, freshly landscaped, disinfected.

The buildings resembled a warehouse structure, with white metal paneling that radiated an enamel sheen. The surrounding paved roads were illuminated by tall, long-necked streetlights. There were no people, not a car in sight, not so much as a sound aside from the cicadas, which electrified the night with their habitual, adamant screams. From Held's angle, crouched behind the cacti, the guard towers were clearly visible. Faint lights shone in their high-up cubicles. Someone was up there, guarding the unthinkable. Without a plan, Held dashed forward and found cover directly beneath the nearest tower. The sand was littered with cigarette butts, flung by the guards from their towers. He scanned the fence, made a reckless run toward what looked like a gash in the wire, and slipped inside. This was the desert; this was nowhere. Despite all precautions, it seemed nobody was expecting intruders.

Keeping to the shadows, Held darted into the complex and pressed his backside against the flank of the nearest building, out of sight of either tower. Here he could rest. He was out of breath, he realized, and with a surge of heat and weakness in his chest, he became stupidly aware of what he was doing. This was enemy territory, there was no returning. At the far end of the building, dashes of light emanated from two windows. He would crouch, approach, and look into the windows, he decided. He would find nothing out of the ordinary and would return as swiftly as he could through the hole in the fence and home through the desert. He reached the first window, hooked his fingertips onto its slim sill, and raised his head to spy inside. A hallway with glistening rubber floors and dots of ceiling lights narrowed into eternity like an infinity mirror. Held sank back. This was sheer insanity, what he was doing, irreversible. He hunched and proceeded to the next window, which appeared to be open.

A chorus of voices—rolling, rasping, high-pitched like barking—froze him. Americans, he understood, by the implausible volume and sheer number of *r*'s.

"A really leery Larry rolls readily to the road right as Rory raunchily roars," one of them seemed to be saying.

He'd seen nothing, Held reminded himself. He could circle back toward the fence and sprint home through the desert. Paralysis stiffened his limbs. He tasted his heartbeat, sick and sweet. He'd come this far. If they were going to shoot him, they should.

He prodded the next windowsill for a good grip, lifted himself, and peeked again. The room was brilliantly lit, a clinical environment, with hues of pastel green and matted metal, and two doors, one simple, the other secured with a vault wheel. Huddled around an operating table was a group of four men dressed in reflective white decontamination attire, with sagging posteriors and full-coverage gas masks complete with two circular glass eyes that gave each of them an unblinking, insectile appearance. Their hands were gloved and sealed with elastics. Whatever toxic thing they were doing, they looked absorbed by it, transfixed. The others would watch as one of them bent forward, fiddled with something, then leaned back to give someone else access to the table.

"Goddamn piece of shit," one of them said as he leveraged himself forward to inspect something closer.

"That's not gonna work," said another guy, folding his arms in frustration.

"Got any better ideas, asshole?" the first one said.

Horror, sheer stomach-coagulating disgust, washed over Held. Whatever those Americans were doing, it looked hazardous, noxious. Organic, possibly, one of those Mexican children. Just then, a loud shattering caused him to release his grip and drop from the window. He squatted and waited.

"What'd you do that for, George?" someone said.

"It's dead," was the reply.

There was movement inside, a few muted curses, silence. Held peeked again. The room had emptied. He didn't want to see it. He told himself not to look. Then he looked. On the matte metal table lay parts and pieces, wires and coils, strewn about in grotesque dismemberment. The remnants of a coffee machine, exploded to pieces. Held gaped at it for a very long time, not comprehending. They'd been trying to fix it. He released a sharp burst of air. Then two of the men reentered. Held ducked, cowered for a beat, then gawked over the edge of the sill. Both men were in the process of covering their shoes with white plastic booties.

"They're just not manufactured to last," one of them said with great dismay. "That's capitalism for you."

"Which is why," said the other, "I always try and get my appliances from my buddy over at Caserma Ederle, in Italy. Stuff falls off a Soviet truck once in a while. Let me tell you, their appliances will outlive us all."

In their thick, billowing protective gear, they moved as if through viscous liquid. They grabbed pencils tethered to the wall by strings and bent their heads unnaturally, studying their clipboards through the glass eyes of their gas masks. One of them squatted and with laborious motions rotated the door's vault wheel as far as it would go. The other stored away his clipboard and joined his colleague, who with a practiced crank opened the door wide.

What Held saw through that door he was unable to explain to Zeiger. The face of the physicist had chilled. He shook his head and stared off into the cold, dust-dotted light of his apartment. This interlude, this story of the Americans, was one that Zeiger had never betrayed to anyone—not to Management, not to Lara. He had kept it for himself, entombed and undead.

"What was it?" Zeiger had asked that day, in a hoarse whisper. And he'd clasped the arms of his chair to avoid propelling himself forward.

He couldn't explain it, Held said. It wasn't an object. It was bright. He cocked his head and narrowed his eyes, as if trying to summon it. It was blinding, he said, and loud. Yet it hadn't frightened him. It had a scent that made the tiny hairs in his nose stand at attention. He'd never heard a sound quite like it.

"What did it sound like?" Zeiger said, nearly shouting, desperate now.

"It was visceral," Held insisted. "Not sensual. It can't be described. It was…" And Held paused, searching for the words. "Astral," he said, finally. The radiance had been fantastical, at once cold and perishable, and it seemed to possess self-awareness, like a living thing. "It jittered," Held said. "It was very old and it was breathy—like it had a throat—and it seemed to be afraid." Then the two Americans closed the door and it was gone.

Zeiger listened, his mouth agape. He blinked a few times, trying to comprehend. "What does it mean?" he whispered.

"Nothing whatsoever," Held said, smiling illegibly. "I'm not even sure it was real."

Zeiger awoke with a whimper. Blank darkness and elemental silence enveloped him. The coarse fabric of a pillowcase stuck to the side of his face. His body was damp, mummified, swaddled like a child in the wet wool of his pajamas and a dense knot of sheets. The rubber mattress had captured the heat and released puffs of it now as he fought paralysis and untangled his limbs. He was not alone. Someone stirred in the dark, released an apneic snore, muttered briefly, then subsided. With acclimating vision, Zeiger discerned in the small hospital room the outline of an iron-frame bed and the lumpy silhouette of whoever was in it. He had no memory of having been put to bed, and in fact couldn't remember much at all after the moment when he'd ingested the pills in the thimble. He searched in the gray darkness for his watch, then recalled that it had been taken from him, along with his clothes and the rest of his things. He promptly fell back asleep.

The next time he woke, someone was standing beside him. A gaunt man with thinning hair and badger eyes looked down at him with a benevolent smile. He was dressed in a robe and pajamas. Zeiger stared past him at the neighboring bed, which was now empty. The room had lightened somewhat, but it was still dim.

In what seemed meant as a soothing, fatherly gesture, the man closed his eyes and placed a hand on Zeiger's shoulder. "It's okay," he whispered. "I know who you are."

Zeiger shrank back, pulled up his blanket. "Who am I?" he asked.

The man scoffed, revealing his catastrophic teeth. "You're Bernd Zeiger," he said, and bent forward to mutter in Zeiger's ear. "The Manual? That work of pure genius? Without you this nonsense would've all happened a long time ago. Only a handful of people can say that, you know? That they were responsible. I, for one, have done nothing. Kept my head down, said nothing, did nothing. I'll be forgotten. But not you."

A panicked shiver rattled him and Zeiger inched sideways, closer to the other side of the bed, away from the man.

"All I'm saying is don't be afraid." The man had a crazed look in his eye. "We won't forget about you," he said. "Soon the whole world will know." He squeezed Zeiger's shoulder, closed his eyes again, and offered a conclusive nod, then slid back into his own bed. Within minutes he was snoring.

Zeiger was left to stare into the darkness. He blinked drily, clutching his blanket, and a spasm ran through him. A lightness unfolded, a featheriness along his limbs, his back. A dazzling fracture, apocalyptic colors, fizzed behind his eyes, radiant and warm. Everything that needed to be done had been done. It was happening. Calm descended, a fundamental quiet. He took a deep breath, squeezed his eyes shut, and waited for it.

ACKNOWLEDGMENTS

I would very much like to thank: J&N special agent Chris Clemans; my extraordinary editor, Ben George, along with Ben Allen, Pamela Brown, Lena Little, and the rest of the Little, Brown team; as well as Matthew Thomas, John Freeman, and Aleksandar Hemon, for their support in the early stages. Kathi Hansen, fairy godmother of this novel, and Mindy Kay Bricker for reading and cheerleading. Johanna Schirm and Christine Schellenberger for their support, humor, and friendship. My parents, Katherine Hofmann *(Du rufst mich nie an)* and Karl Hofmann *(Du rufst mich noch weniger an)*, for their inexplicable belief in me. And my oldest friend, my sister, Nicole Hofmann, in spite of whom I managed to complete this novel.

Thank you, also, to the Berlin public libraries and keepers of on- and offline archives. Most importantly, thank you to those Berlin neighborhood plumbers, building maintenance workers, storekeepers, electricians, park-bench drunks, chatty hairdressers who had me trapped in their chairs, and random coffee shop patrons who told me their stories, as well as those Berlin taxi drivers who, during late-night fares through the city, turned their meters off to share with me intimate details of their lives in former East Berlin.

ABOUT THE AUTHOR

Jennifer Hofmann was born in Princeton, New Jersey, to an Austrian father and a Colombian mother, and grew up in Germany. She received her MFA from NYU and currently lives in Berlin. This is her first novel.